PRAISE FOR *HEY SUNSHINE*, BOOK ONE OF THE *HEY SUNSHINE* TRILOGY

Avery Kent knows that life can change in an instant:

One second you're on your way out of small-town life, the next you're left heartbroken and stunned when your thrill-seeking high school boyfriend runs off in pursuit of a potentially dangerous dream.

Four years later, everything is different. When Chase returns, admitting he made a mistake and asking for a second chance, Avery wants to think she can trust him again.

But when the arrival of a handsome, quiet stranger named Fox shifts Avery's focus, she realizes that things are about to get a lot more complicated.

When is a lot of history enough reason for a future? And how do you ignore the way someone makes you feel, especially when they were **the last thing you ever expected?**

"Romance is ON POINT."

— *Brianna's Bookish Confessions*

"Not only is this book one of my favorites of 2015, it's one of my new all time favorites."

— *Taylor Knight at Bibliophile Gathering*

"Hooked from the very first page."

— *Monica @NightReads*

"Incredible romance and the perfect amount of drama to keep you turning every page until the end."

— *Allissa Lemaire @ABookishLoveAffair*

Also by Tia Giacalone

HEY SUNSHINE

Cover design © Sarah Hansen, Okay Creations

Cover photograph © Maximilian Guy McNair MacEwan

ISBN-13: 978-0-9962774-4-0
ISBN-10: 0-9962774-4-7

Tia Giacalone
Visit my website at www.tiawritesbooks.com

NIGHT FOX

Tia Giacalone

This book is dedicated to anyone
who has ever felt caught up in the dark.

PROLOGUE

AVERY

"Avery Fox? Mrs. Avery Fox? This is Officer Jonathan Crick, Washington State Police Department."

For a moment, the only sound I heard was the thud of my heart and then a silence so loud that I wanted to scream. No. Why was this man calling me? *No.*

"Ma'am, I regret to inform you that your husband, Beckett Fox, has been seriously injured in a motorcycle accident earlier today on I-90 by Snoqualmie Pass. He was stabilized on site and airlifted to Harborview Medical Center, but when he arrived the physicians made the decision to send him on to the UW Medical Center, where he's currently being evaluated."

His words cut right through me. I was sure you could see through my chest to the other side, as there was a huge, gaping hole where my heart and lungs used to be. My hands slid helplessly over my midsection, trying to piece together something that wasn't physically broken.

"Mrs. Fox?" he asked, his voice gentler. "Are you still

there?"

"Y— yes," I managed. "I'm here."

"Do you have a pen, ma'am? There's some information you're going to want to write down."

"May I offer you a beverage?"

"No, thank you," I whispered, trying to curl myself into a ball in my assigned plane seat.

Lucas had arranged my travel, somehow managing to book me on the only available flight leaving from Midland the next morning. I was on the second leg of my journey, after an hour layover in Denver, and the minutes passed agonizingly slowly. I just wanted to see Fox, to reassure myself that he was real, that I hadn't imagined it all only to abruptly wake up from what I'd always suspected was a dream but could now be classified as a nightmare.

Our relationship so far had been a whirlwind: the undeniable initial attraction that we hadn't been able to act on, the friendship we'd built long before our first date, Fox's bond with Annabelle, and the way my heart finally felt whole the minute he'd slipped that ring on my finger.

Tears filled my eyes as I remembered the last video Fox had sent me, not even three weeks ago. It was a montage of some of his trademark photojournalism-style footage, a hobby he used to show me what he was thinking with more than just words. This clip was exactly that — scenes from our wedding ceremony, Joy wearing a Santa hat as she waited tables in the diner, Annabelle on the hotel dance floor, the light of the Christmas tree as it sat in our living room, our impromptu snowball fight the morning after Fox and I had said 'I do.'

"I miss you," he'd said in the email. *"My mind is here but my heart is at home."*

I was so glad that my little girl wasn't here to see me fall apart. I'd kept it together at home as I packed and made arrangements, for her and for myself. I was traveling alone to Seattle. Fox's family would meet me there and, until we knew more, Annabelle would stay with my parents.

The flight attendant gazed at me for a moment with concern in her eyes before she walked away, but in a short while she was back with a blanket and a small pillow.

"Here," she said, tucking me in.

I didn't want to be that person, the one who needed special treatment, the one who garnered sympathetic looks and hand pats. I wanted Fox, agile and strong, running the path through the park near my house. I wanted me and Fox, laughing in the diner as he drank one of his endless cups of coffee. I wanted Fox and Annabelle doing puzzles on the floor, taking breaks for hot chocolate and Saturday morning cartoons.

I wanted me, the way I had been just days before. I knew what fear and loss really felt like, what it meant to make hard decisions and never be quite sure about a future for Annabelle and myself. But ever since Fox had come into our lives, I'd allowed myself to relax a little, to let him wrap me in his arms and enjoy what I had, thinking that maybe most of the struggle of an uncertain plan was behind me.

And now, with one terrible sentence, my new life threatened to crumble down as I watched helplessly, trapped on a plane with no idea what to expect when I reached Fox.

They say that it rains when a good man dies. I wasn't sure who 'they' implied or if 'they' were even qualified to make such sweeping generalizations, but the sun shone brightly in Seattle — a place of perpetual cloud cover — when the plane's wheels touched the tarmac at Sea-Tac, and every single part of me wanted to take it as a positive omen.

The gaping wound that had appeared in my chest twenty hours ago when I'd received the phone call hadn't even scabbed and, as I sat there on the plane, it burst open again and I gasped for breath as the realization hit me.

He would live, they assured me.
He would live — if he woke up.

CHAPTER ONE

FOX

When the wind shifted, I knew this would be more than an eighteen-hour day. We all did. I went through the motions I'd been trained for, checking supplies, working the containment line, keeping up communications with air support and the ranger station. Trying not to get burned alive by the furious inferno that seemed intent on taking down all four million acres of the Oka-Wen National Forest… the usual.

No time to think about anything else, no time to dwell on the months-empty condo back in Seattle or the fact that lately everything I did seemed like a prequel to my life actually starting. This fire wanted us, and she wasn't giving up. Mother Nature had it in her to be the worst girlfriend you'd ever had.

"Damn, Foxy," McDaniels panted, jogging up to my side. "Is today over yet or what?"

I cracked a grin at him, feeling the blistering heat from the sun and the fire mix into one and swirl around us as I hefted my chainsaw. "Not by a landslide."

McDaniels gave me the side-eye. "Really? You wanna joke about landslides?"

"Hey now," Sloane popped his head out of the crew buggy where he was listening intently to the handheld radio. "None of that."

"We need to be monitoring this backburn more closely." Landry spoke up from the ground, where he was seated against a tire with a damp rag over his face. "The wind is changing."

If anyone could tell where the weather was going, it was Landry. Even with his face half buried under a towel, he was more in tune with the elements than anyone I'd ever met. If Landry said the breeze was out to get us, we needed to hustle.

Sloane jumped out of the truck, swearing. "Shit!"

"What now?"

"Base camp got a call. Campers they thought were accounted for are actually missing."

My nerve endings thrummed into action. I knew it. Summer time, prime hiking season. Evacuations had gone too smoothly. "Where?"

Sloane was already plugging coordinates into a GPS. "About three miles from here. We'll get as close as we can and hump it the rest. Let's take a split, have five head in from the other side," he said, referring to more members of our twenty-man Hotshot crew.

"Where's Dempsey?"

"Ghosting, as usual. I'll grab him." McDaniels headed around the truck toward the trees.

"He needs to keep his head in the game," Landry muttered from under his towel.

I knew Landry was right about Dempsey but I was too focused on the lost campers to give it much thought. Grabbing the GPS from Sloane, I checked the coordinates and swore softly under my breath. These kids were inside the damn containment line. Our long day had just morphed into a ticking time bomb.

"We have a semi-conscious male, twenty-seven years old,

with blunt force trauma to the left cranial region and superficial flesh wounds consistent with a vehicular accident. B.P. is eighty over sixty and dropping."

"Let's get him into a room, move it, move it!"

"Call Simms, get her down here ASAP!"

"We need a CAT scan!"

My eyes were so heavy. I wanted to open them, to ask who this poor guy was, this unlucky bastard everyone was buzzing about. Did they need a crash cart? What could I do to help?

Fluorescent lights flickered through my half-open eyelids as shadows loomed over me, talking amongst themselves. My stomach churned with the sensation of rapid movement, and I tasted vomit in the back of my throat. I tried to move, to sit up, to turn my head, but my limbs were leaden, immobilized. The voices continued over me, discussing a fate that seemed doomed at best, and as I struggled for breath I felt the darkness that threatened to consume me finally take over, and then everything went black.

"This is like trying to find five needles in a burning haystack. We might have to bring in air support, see if they can spot anything before we head this way."

"We've looked everywhere else, Sloane. This is it. If these kids are out here, this is the last possible place they could be." I wiped my brow and pulled a rope from my pack. "We move now or we lose them for the night."

"He's right," Landry said. "If they were down in this valley, they probably didn't smell the fire until this morning. They've been upwind with a creek between them."

"Until that wind changed and fucked us all," McDaniels muttered.

"Let's do it." Sloane shifted his eyes to Dempsey. "Everyone ready?"

Dempsey nodded, his mouth set in a serious line. "Yeah."

I watched Landry scout the area, taking in our surroundings. "Cut through here and we'll drop down."

"He's stabilized again, for now. Keep the oxygen at ten liters." The doctor wiped her brow. "Where are those CAT scan results?"

"Here, Dr. Simms."

A shuffle of papers and a few clicks of a mouse.

"This can't be accurate."

"I thought the same thing."

"Let's order an MRI. I need to know more."

The bottom of the valley was dark, a thin layer of ash hanging in the air with residual smoke trapped by the thick trees. McDaniels and Sloane led the way, hacking through with their Pulaski axes to make a path where there was none before.

"You got anything?" Dempsey asked me.

"Not yet."

This part of the forest was relatively untouched by the actual fire but it was still. Too still. Nothing moved, nothing hid as we approached. The birds were gone too, long since relocated to better air and clearer skies. No wildlife was never a good sign.

"There!" Landry pointed.

Under a craggy outcropping, huddled and afraid, we saw them.

"Vitals are steady, brain function is high. His GCS is still concerning, however."

"With his MRI results, his GCS is abnormal. He should be at least semi-lucid. I want to call in a consultation from Virginia Mason Hospital."

"I'll arrange for it right away."

"I appreciate you wanting to be a part of this team, Dr. Buchanan. Mr. Fox will enjoy seeing a familiar face when he regains consciousness."

"Thank you for approving my request, Dr. Simms. I know the protocol doesn't always allow for a potential conflict of interest."

"At this point, he needs whatever encouragement he can get. When is the family arriving?"

"His parents and brother are already here. The wife is on her way."

"As soon as she gets here, let's put her in his room, have her touch him and speak to him, if she's able. I want him to know he needs to come back."

They were all here, all accounted for. Five kids, ranging in age from fourteen to eighteen, with sweat-and-dirt-streaked faces, deep scratches, and skinned knees and hands between them.

"We left the campsite for a hike and got lost," one of the older girls told me, tears seeping from her red eyes. "And then we saw the smoke."

"We're going to get you guys out of here," Sloane assured them.

Dempsey passed around canteens while McDaniels and I searched for the best path to lead them out of the valley. The way we had come was steep and too dangerous for these under-dressed, under-experienced hikers. Sloane radioed in to base camp, telling them that we'd secured the group and asking the best way to proceed via information from air support.

"North." Landry came up behind me.

"We can't." The containment line was too far away.

"We have to." He pointed over his shoulder, and I saw the unmistakeable black billowing cloud rising up from a fresh burn.

"Fox?"

My lips twitched when I heard her tearful voice call my name.

"Fox, can you hear me?"

"Good, that's good. Keep talking to him."

"Fox, I—" The girl's voice broke slightly.

I struggled, for what felt like the nine hundredth time, to open my eyes. A small slit of light appeared in my darkness, and I barely glimpsed the outline of a woman silhouetted against the sun, her blond hair shining like a halo.

"You have to keep moving. You can do it."

The boy looked up at me with huge, scared eyes. He was one of the younger ones, barely fourteen, in the beginning of that awkward phase where you haven't grown into your limbs quite yet. I reached for him as he stumbled again, slinging an arm around his shoulders to hold him upright.

"I've got you."

The blow-up was chasing us now, licking flames down the sides of the valley as we headed north and into what we hoped would be easier terrain. We'd lost our chance at climbing out of here before things got heavy.

I signaled to Dempsey, who was leading a girl and two boys with McDaniels and Sloane bringing up the rear. Landry was all but carrying the youngest girl, her feet dragging more with each step. The air was thick with smoke and ash, and all of them were coughing frequently despite the makeshift masks we gave them, their bodies growing slow and lethargic.

Our ticking time bomb was about to explode.

"Any change?"

This new voice sounded like my brother, Lucas. But that couldn't be right. He was half a world away.

"He, um— he moved his fingers a couple times." The girl again. She sounded tired, sad. "The nurses said it was probably just a reflex, but I think it's good."

"He knows you're here."

"I hope so." I felt pressure on my hand, a soft, warm touch.

"It's good, Avery. It's going to be okay." Lucas' voice was far away. I tried to hold onto him, to something familiar, but I felt myself slipping away, back to the darkness.

I could barely see the helicopter overhead through the trees and smoke, which meant they likely couldn't see us either, but the promise of getting these kids to safety made me push even harder to reach the north-side containment line.

The fire was burning steadily behind us, whipping through trees with the aid of that fickle fucking wind. As ash rained down, I saw fire devils come whirling off the burn whenever a gust enabled it.

"Veer off, we have to get to higher ground so they can see us!" I called to Dempsey.

He looked over his shoulder and nodded, taking in the struggling campers and the ever-encroaching flames. Landry was carrying the little girl now, her body limp, one arm encircling his neck. The boy I held to my side was gasping for every breath. They wouldn't last much longer in this heat with the poor air quality.

McDaniels and Sloane quickly cut through brush until they reached the rocky hillside. I propped the boy against a tree and took off my pack, reaching in for rope and rappelling gear.

"What happens now?" one of the older boys asked.

I glanced up, pausing as I pulled on my harness. "Now, we climb."

"She hasn't left his side."

Lucas again, this time his voice was faint and tired.

"What do you expect, dear? Of course she hasn't." My mother's low whisper was unmistakeable. I felt that warm pressure on my other hand and I knew it was her.

"Beckett wouldn't want her to be suffering like this, not taking care of herself." Lucas' tone was frustrated. I imagined his hands raking through his hair in agitation. We both had that habit.

"At least she's resting."

"Yeah, in that awful fucking chair."

"He's going to wake up, Lucas," she said gently.

"I know. I know he is. I just want to know when."

It only took two tries for me to get the grappling hook secured at the top of the ridge. I pulled myself up as quickly as possible, using my hands and feet as well as the rope to help me climb. McDaniels was right behind me and, after we rigged a pulley harness and two more support ropes, I rappelled back down to help get the campers up from the valley floor.

"Sloane, head up to help McDaniels."

When he reached the top, we organized the kids. The two older boys went up first, the older girl following them easily enough. I climbed up halfway behind them, assisting as needed, before I came back down. Landry, Dempsey, and the two youngest waited for me at the bottom.

"Let's send the girl—"

My words were cut off as a tree crashed down in the middle of where we stood, its branches completely consumed by flame, sending sparks into the dry brush all around us.

"I've pushed you, Beckett. There's no denying that."

A heavy sigh followed what could only be my father's

voice. The General? Here?

"Every step of your life, I wanted you to be looking ahead to the next goal. Every milestone you hit, I was already past it and onto the future, without acknowledging what you'd accomplished."

Three heartbeats. Five. Ten.

"If I pushed you to live faster, I'm sorry."

"FOX! Are you okay?" Dempsey picked himself up from where I'd shoved him out of the way of the tree's line and ran over to my side. Dazedly, I looked down at my leg. A gnarled, smoking limb of the fallen tree impaled my thigh at an angle, clear through the rectus femoris muscle. My pants were burned and torn, exposing my skin in many places, and I could see the angry red burn marks starting to form. I waited for the pain, but between the adrenaline and my dulled senses from the acrid, smoke-filled air, I felt nothing.

"Yeah."

Ripping my belt from its loops, I secured it tightly above the wound and then gritted my teeth and pulled the fallen snag out. A stupid move, definitely, but I had little choice. There was no answering gush of blood, which likely meant no major artery had been hit. If this counted as me being lucky today, I'd take it.

"Thanks, man. That branch would've gone straight through my chest." Dempsey's eyes were as wide as they could be with all the smoke in the air. I nodded to him, scanning the area. It was too quiet again.

Where was the kid? I spotted him still where I'd left him, propped up against a tree out of the fallen branches' hot zone. He blanched at the sight of my leg and pointed weakly behind me.

I heard a grunt and a swear, and we looked around quickly for Landry, finding him a couple yards away under a bunch of burning debris. He struggled to straighten and push the tree branches up and off of him, and I heard McDaniels and Sloane yelling from above.

"Landry! Landry!"

It felt like hours before Dempsey and I broke through the smoldering tree limbs to reach him. He'd thrown himself over the girl to protect her from the fire and, when I ripped away the charred wood, his jacket was smoking from the contact, his face scratched and bleeding.

"Are you okay?"

"My ribs… I'm fine." His face was ashen, his breathing labored. Dempsey picked up the girl, unharmed by the tree. I watched Landry attempt to take a breath, the air rattling as he inhaled. He coughed violently, wetly, and I realized how much more smoke was building due to the brush that was now in hot spots all around us. Another gust of wind could make the entire thing flare up again.

"He had another restless night."

"The nurses told me. Interesting," a man's voice — Buchanan? — mused. The rustling of paper followed, and a short tearing sound. "I can see it here, too. His brain activity was all over the place. I'll be sure to show this to Dr. Simms."

"Thank you."

The door shut with a barely audible click.

I felt the familiar warmth whenever she was near, especially now as the bed dipped slightly and she hesitantly, gently pressed her body against mine, wrapping an arm carefully around my torso.

"Anytime you're ready, Fox. I miss you so much."

I sent Dempsey up next, to help with the kids already at the top. Sloane and McDaniels had their hands full with all of our ropes.

"Let's get them out," I said to Landry. I could feel every beat of my heart in my leg, but I pushed that aside and focused on the job.

"Can we do two at once?" I called up to Sloane, and he nodded. "Let's go then."

We strapped the girl into the harness first, noting her rapidly worsening state, then rigged the boy. They would go up, then I'd make Landry go next because I knew he was in pain.

I was about to send them up when a gust of wind blew the embers at my feet into actual fire — not a rager, but too many hot spots for comfort. Reacting automatically, I pulled my arms through the harness and buckled us both in together, with the kid behind me like a backpack, and Landry did the same with the girl. We started to climb in tandem, me ignoring the pain that finally came from my wrecked leg.

"Fox!" Sloane called down to me. "I don't know if these ropes can take this weight!"

I knew that from the time I sent Dempsey up. The ropes were singed in places and worn in others where they'd repeatedly scraped against the rocks. They weren't meant for repetitive climbing. I held onto a jutting stone in the side of the ravine, bracing my bad leg against my good one in an attempt to take some of the stress off the lines.

"Landry? You good?"

I snickered as he pointed his middle finger straight up in the air.

"You good, kid?" I asked the boy, craning my head in his direction. I felt him nod weakly, his breathing shallow and delayed. "We're going to get to the top."

We didn't have a choice. The way we had come was not an option.

I heard her shifting in her chair, the metal legs scraping lightly over the linoleum.

"I can't take it anymore, Heather. I need to have Annabelle here with me. Can you ask my—"

A pause, a sniffle.

"Thank you so much. I love you."

I felt one rope snap and we suddenly dropped six feet, that bitch wind swinging us around like a pendulum, knocking my bad leg repeatedly into the uneven, rocky cliff. I bit my tongue from the pain, tasting blood as I tried to shift so my body took the brunt of the battering, sparing the kid on my back.

"FOX!" Sloane yelled again.

"Throw me another line!"

"Can you climb?"

Blood from my leg smeared all over the side of the ravine's wall, and in a moment of untimely delusion, I felt satisfied that I'd leave a part of myself here, a sign that showed I was still alive, no matter what Mother Nature tried to throw at us. Dead men didn't bleed.

Sloane threw down our last rope, a thin woven cord that could hold weight but bit into my skin when I wrapped it around my hand and wrist. I used my other hand and both legs to leverage up slowly, steadily, while my blood dripped out onto the rocky earth.

Landry and the girl were above us now, making steady progress, when I felt the wind shift again and heard the sound I dreaded most — the snapping of more rope. I turned my head just in time to see both of Landry's lines slip right past me as he and the girl plummeted down to the smoldering ground fifty feet below us.

"Here, if you won't eat anything, at least drink this."

"Thanks." The girl's voice sounded tired as she whispered to Lucas.

"You have to go back to the hotel later. Get some real sleep."

A pause. "I'll leave when he does."

Lucas sighed. "He'd kill me for letting you stay here."

"Good morning, thank you all for coming." Dr. Simms' voice interrupted their whispered conversation. "This is Dr. Buchanan, one of our residents and a member of Beckett's care team. First, I'd like to say that we are pleased with Beckett's progress. His scans are clean, his organs strong. His body is healing and strength is returning. His comatose state, however, is concerning and at this point, unexplainable."

"I'm sorry?" My mother's voice echoed in the silent room.

"Physically, your son is remarkably lucky," Simms said. "The scope of his injuries are minor considering the type of accident."

"But?" Lucas asked.

"Head injuries are tricky," the doctor continued. "Beckett suffered a major blow to his skull, one that probably would've killed him instantly had he not been wearing a helmet."

Dr. Buchanan spoke up. "We expected much more damage when we did the MRI, but aside from a slight bit of swelling, which has already receded, he's doing incredibly well."

"Then why isn't he conscious?" Carter Fox's voice was gruff, impatient.

"I know this has been a nightmare for you and your family. The short answer is that Beckett will likely awaken on his own, on his own time. As I stated, physically he is more than capable of regaining consciousness at any moment."

"And the long answer? The worst case?" Lucas demanded.

"The fact that your brother is still comatose — with full brain activity and no debilitating injuries — makes it impossible for me to predict when or even if he will ever fully awaken. His body is healing itself, but his injuries shouldn't warrant a days-long coma."

"What does that mean?" The girl finally spoke up.

"It means that now Beckett's recovery is entirely up to him."

"So Fox isn't waking up because… he doesn't want to?"

A deafening silence, familiar by this point, was the only reply.

"NO! NO! LANDRY!"

Sloane pulled us up with all his might, and Dempsey barely had a chance to unbuckle the boy from my back before I was rappelling back down to Landry and the little girl. Sloane came down next to me, his harness half on, and as soon as we reached the ground we ran over to where they'd fallen.

My hands shook as I frantically tore at Landry's Nomex jacket, ripping aside the charred fabric to press my palms against his chest and begin compressions.

Oh fuck, oh no, this isn't happening. "LANDRY! CAN YOU HEAR ME?"

Sloane was yelling something undecipherable at me, his hands so big on the girl's small chest, as we tried to bring them back.

"C'MON, LANDRY! BREATHE! BREATHE, DAMN IT! DON'T GIVE UP!"

And then I was climbing again, not of my own volition but at the end of the medevac's cable. This time I had my friend strapped to me, my friend who wouldn't breathe when I asked him to, who wouldn't respond when I pleaded with him, who wouldn't wake up even when I begged him.

The wind blew us back and forth through the air as the medevac helicopter tried to stay steady, throwing us first one way against the trees and then the other against the rocks… and then everything went dark.

Something didn't feel right. Something still nagged at the corner of that day, of that memory, and I tried to push it aside. I didn't want to know any more or feel anything else. Whatever I'd done in that valley, whatever I'd done right or wrong, didn't matter worth a damn anymore because the only thing I knew now was this darkness — the darkness that continually blinded and confused me but always welcomed me back like an old friend. And I was starting to think that I liked it.

CHAPTER TWO

I opened my eyes and looked around groggily. Lucas hovered just to the right of my bed and a pretty blonde stood on the other side, chewing her lip nervously as the nurse checked my vitals.

"Lucas? Why are you here?" I growled, my voice low and raspy from lack of use. "Weren't you in London? Shouldn't you be protecting billionaire teenage rock stars or something?" I searched my memory, trying to piece together a coherent thought. I was in the hospital, my head hurt like hell, but other than that I felt okay. Experimentally, I shifted my legs and tried to stretch my arms. My left shoulder screamed in protest.

"Stop moving, dear," the nurse said gently. "We're all happy that you're back, but I'm trying to get an accurate read."

Happy that I'm back? Where had I been? I closed my eyes briefly and the whooshing sound of helicopter blades beat through my ears, the acrid smell of fire-singed fabric and debris rushed into my nose.

"Landry!" I shouted, my eyes flying open. "Where is he? Is he okay? What about the rest of the crew? The campers? The girl?" I struggled to sit up in the bed, pulling at the wires taped to my chest when they wouldn't give.

"Mr. Fox, I need you to calm down," the nurse said, pushing me back down onto the pillows firmly. She glanced up at Lucas and the blonde before speaking again. "You've been unconscious for close to five days. Can you tell me the last calendar date you remember?"

Lucas' face was a mixture of worry and confusion, but the blonde looked like she was about to pass out. She probably needed to lie down more than I did. If this nurse would let me get up I'd gladly let her have the bed.

"I need to know, Lucas. I need to know what happened." I strained to look around the nurse to see my brother.

"Mr. Fox, the date?"

"It's May," I told her impatiently. "Probably the fifteenth or sixteenth, I guess?"

She looked to Lucas again. "Of what year, Mr. Fox?"

I took a deep breath, trying to curb my irritation. The nurse smiled at me encouragingly.

"2014."

"I see," she said. Turning to Lucas and the blonde, she spoke softly. "I'll send the doctors right in."

"What's going on? Lucas, what happened?" I started to sit up again, jostling the cords, and one of the machines started beeping incessantly. "Where's Landry, McDaniels? What about Sloane? And Dempsey?"

"Just try to calm down, B."

"Not until I know what happened to my crew and those campers." Why wouldn't he tell me? And who was this girl?

"Campers?" Lucas and the blonde now had identical looks of disbelief on their faces.

"I'm coming, Fox! I'm coming!" I heard a little voice coming down the hallway, and suddenly the door burst open and a tiny towheaded whirlwind hurled herself onto the bed directly on top of me. My arms closed around her automatically to prevent her from tumbling down, and she looked up at me and grinned.

I realized then that she looked just like a mini version of

the beautiful girl standing like a statue at the foot of my bed, her huge eyes terrified and sad when she looked at me.

"Did you miss me, Fox? Did you? I missed you a lot!" the little girl cried.

"Sorry, sorry!" A petite brunette slipped through the door a moment later, holding her hands up helplessly. When she saw the little girl perched on my chest, a huge smile spread across her face. "She was so excited to hear you'd woken up, I couldn't hold her in the waiting area any longer!"

When no one spoke, she looked to the pretty blond. "Avery? What's wrong?"

Avery. That name was familiar but I couldn't place it. Now I knew her name, but it still didn't explain what she was doing here, or why her mini-me was trying to burrow her way under my arm to curl up by my side. I looked to Lucas helplessly, hoping for some clarification. Reaching forward, Avery pulled the little girl off my chest and into her arms.

"Annabelle," she said quietly. "Fox is still—" Her voice hitched. "Still not feeling well," she continued. "You can't climb all over him, okay?"

Avery and Annabelle. I searched my memory again, trying to recall where I'd heard those names before. I wouldn't put it past Lucas to bring a date while he visited me in the hospital, but this seemed more complicated than that. My shoulder throbbed and I reached up with my other hand to rub the muscle.

Annabelle sniffled and Avery hugged her tightly.

"Mama—" she protested, but Avery was already walking over to the door.

"Go with Auntie Heather, please. I'll be out in just a minute and we'll go down to the cafeteria to get some frozen yogurt."

Annabelle glanced over her shoulder at me with an imploring look. "Bye, Fox."

"Bye, Annabelle," I said automatically.

Avery jerked her head up and turned at the sound of my

voice, her eyes searching mine. For a brief second, our gazes locked and I couldn't look away. Lucas cleared his throat to get our attention.

"B, what is the last thing you remember?"

"Lucas, don't you think we should wait for the doctor? And your parents?" Avery said timidly, flicking her glance back to me.

Between the worried look on Lucas' face and the scared expression on Avery's, I'd had enough.

"This is bullshit." I sat up and pulled the sensors from my chest, starting a cacophony of beeping from the machines by my bed. I reached over to enter the bypass codes, stopping the noise. "Tell me what happened or I'm getting out of bed right now and finding out for myself."

Lucas scrubbed a hand through his hair and looked from me to Avery. "Do you know who this is?" he said, gesturing to her.

"No, but you've never been big on introductions so don't worry, I'm not offended. Is this your girlfriend?"

It still wouldn't explain why her little girl acted like she knew me, but I was grasping at straws here. I managed a quick smile for Avery, hoping to get the greetings out of the way so Lucas could fill me in on why I was here and, more importantly — when I could get back to my crew.

Avery's face paled and she put a hand on the bed rail to steady herself. Lucas came closer and slid a palm under her elbow, ready to catch her if she fell. He looked at me over the top of her head.

"No, B. Avery isn't my girlfriend. She's your wife."

Time hiccuped.

"My… what?" I asked incredulously. Not the time to fuck with me, Lucas. Seriously, not the time.

Lucas glanced at Avery, her face growing paler by the second, before he spoke. "Your wife, Beckett. You and Avery are married."

"That's impossible. I've never even met her before today."

The door to my room swung open again and two doctors came in with the nurse from earlier.

"Mr. Fox! Thank you for deciding to join us," the woman doctor said to me warmly. She looked to the monitors and frowned. "What happened?"

The male doctor stepped forward, picking up the discarded cords and sensors. "He took them off," he said shortly. "Really, Fox?"

I looked up at him, actually seeing him for the first time. "Buchanan?"

"You can't just remove the equipment," Buchanan said in exasperation.

"Dr. Buchanan and Mr. Fox were acquainted in early medic training," the female doctor explained to Lucas and Avery. "He made a special request to be a part of the care team when he realized who our patient was."

She turned to me. "You already know Dr. Buchanan, so allow me to introduce myself. I'm Dr. Gretchen Simms, chief neurologist."

I shook the hand she offered automatically. This was getting stranger by the minute, and I could feel my anger building.

Dr. Simms had her stethoscope on my chest, and I breathed deeply for her when she requested it, trying to calm down. After submitting to the rest of her quick examination, I pulled myself up farther in the bed and crossed my arms over my chest, wincing slightly when my shoulder strained and the bandages on my forearms rubbed together.

"Can you tell me the last thing you remember, Mr. Fox?"

I paused, hoping that if I answered correctly, she'd answer a few questions of mine. "A helicopter."

"Yes, good," she said, nodding. "You were airlifted to the

hospital after your motorcycle accident."

"What? No," I protested. "In the Oka-Wen." Blank looks all around. "The Okanogan-Wenatchee National Forest."

Out of the corner of my eye I saw Avery sit down heavily in a chair. Lucas remained standing, his arms crossed as well, likely unaware that he was mirroring my own actions.

"The forest?" Dr. Simms repeated.

"We were out for days, it was a big one, had a lot of re-burn." I ran my fingers through my hair agitatedly. "There were lost campers, I had to double back, we got caught up… Landry had the other girl. Landry was hurt. They fell. Is Landry here? Where is everyone else?"

I needed someone else in this room with me, someone who could corroborate my story, someone who wouldn't make me feel like I was delusional. I wished in vain for McDaniels or Sloane to come walking through the door, even Dempsey, though lately all he did was mope about that girl, what's her name… Avery.

Avery.

My eyes flew back to her, catching the way she watched me with an expression that was one part fear, one part hope.

"You're Chase's Avery," I said.

Before she could respond, the door to my room opened quickly and my mother rushed in, directly over to my bed, the General at her heels. "Oh, Beckett," she exclaimed, hugging me with tears gathering in the corners of her eyes. "It's so nice to see you awake."

"Don't cry, Mom," I said in a low voice, taking her hand in my slightly busted one. "I'm okay."

The General stood close behind her, his usually stoic expression visibly relieved. I felt immediately guilty for what they'd been through. The nurse said I'd been out for five days? My mother must've been panicked. And the General was probably wondering why I wasn't already out of bed and back to work.

Savannah looked to Avery, noting her distance and the frightened expression on her face. She then looked to Dr. Simms and Buchanan, whose composure remained neutral.

"What's happening?" my mother asked warily.

Dr. Simms cleared her throat. "Beckett, can you tell me what month it is? What year?"

This again? "May 2014." The edge in my voice was even sharper now.

The room was too silent.

"Are you sure about the date, Mr. Fox? I want you to think very carefully," Dr. Simms said.

I felt the anger, the frustration bubble into my chest again. "Of course I'm sure!" I shouted, no longer willing to cooperate.

My head started to pound, and all I could hear was the roar of blood rushing to my ears. I took three deep breaths, trying to steady myself so I could think, and closed my eyes. I suddenly realized that something seemed off. My body was banged up, but that was to be expected. My shoulder was killing me but my thigh felt pretty good, considering the trauma to the muscle…

The blood drained from my face as I whipped the blanket back, frantically pushing the hospital gown aside to get a good look at my leg.

The thick wounds covering my thigh were healed, the marks faded to a pinkish white. I stared at my scars, my brain scrambling frantically to keep up.

"Fox?" a gentle voice called.

Avery got up, crossed the room to me, and placed a hand on my arm. "What is it?"

I flinched at her touch, looking up at a room full of people staring at me with concern.

"WHAT… THE HELL… IS GOING… ON?" The timbre of my voice reverberated through the walls, and I dropped my head into my hands, lost and defeated.

CHAPTER THREE

"Look, Lucas, it wasn't my idea to sedate him, okay?"

"I'm just not sure WHY you would VOLUNTARILY put a man TO SLEEP who just woke up from a COMA!" I heard Lucas shout.

"He was going to hurt himself!" Buchanan sounded just as frustrated. "He already broke about ten thousand dollars worth of equipment and who knows what else he would've done. You're lucky he's not in the hospital wing of the county jail."

"He's scared, Charlie," Lucas' voice was pleading now. "He has no idea what's happening or why. When he wakes up, just let me talk to him. No more sedation."

"It's not my call."

"You can make it your call. Or I can break some more stuff, including your nose, and I give zero fucks about any consequences or whatever half-assed security protocol bullshit you want to threaten me with."

"You're still an asshole, aren't you, Lucas?"

"No, I'm a guy who's trying to help his brother. You have a brother, don't you, Buchanan? If it were him lying here, tell me you wouldn't feel the same way."

Buchanan sighed. "I'll make a note in his file, a strong suggestion, but that's all I can do. When he wakes up, you need to keep him as calm as possible. That's why they want to sedate him, to prevent him from doing more damage to himself. And to this hospital."

I heard the door open and close, and then Lucas slumped into a chair next to my bed. Cracking open an eye, I surveyed him.

"Buchanan was always a rule follower."

Lucas' head snapped up at the sound of my voice.

"Hey," he said, scanning my face quickly.

I struggled to push myself up with my elbows, wincing when my body weight hit my shoulder. "Hey."

"How do you feel?"

"More tired than when I was in a coma," I tried to joke. "What the hell did they give me?"

"I don't know, probably some horse tranquilizers or something. You were out of control, B."

I sagged back into my pillows. "I broke stuff?"

Lucas nodded. "A bedside table, two chairs, the TV monitor, an IV stand, that vitals machine thing—"

"I get the picture," I groaned. A thought occurred to me, and my body tensed. "Did I— was anyone in the room?"

"No," Lucas said immediately. "No, B. We'd all stepped outside to speak with the doctors."

I relaxed slightly, thinking of my mom… and of Avery.

"She's just down the hall," Lucas said, as if he were reading my thoughts. "She wanted to stay, but she was afraid if you woke up and saw her it might upset you again, given your, um, confused state."

My shoulders immediately tensed again, the pain spiraling through my body as my mind raced. Avery. *My wife.* My wife that I didn't remember, except in context with Chase.

"How did I end up married to Dempsey's girl?"

Lucas grinned at me for a second before answering. "The Fox men have a certain charm that is irresistible, as you well know."

I groaned. "Cut the shit, Lucas." *Again, not the time to fuck with me.*

"Sorry, sorry," he said, sitting forward with his hands on his knees. "You met her in Texas, when you went along with Chase after he decided to go home. You were still hurt, still trying to rehab your leg. From what you told me, and what it seemed like when I first met her, you and Avery had an immediate connection, one that way overshadowed whatever was going on with her and Chase."

An immediate connection. I could see that. She was certainly beautiful, with those bright blue eyes and all of that hair. And there was something about the way she looked at me that made me think she really knew me. It was unnerving as shit.

"Love at first sight doesn't sound like me," I told Lucas.

"Yeah, well. I think you've kind of broken all your rules for this girl."

The fact that I'd decided to go to Texas with Dempsey seemed like an odd choice, too. I hadn't been back to Texas in years, not since I'd trained there early in my career.

I considered that for a second while I weighed the options for wiping that damn smirk off Lucas' face. I was faster than him but slightly incapacitated at the moment.

Playing back the scenes from earlier, when I regained consciousness to see Lucas and a very concerned Avery, another thought occurred to me, one that made me sit straight up in the bed.

"Is Annabelle… she's not mine, right?" My logic was jumbled, I felt like I was reaching through cobwebs every time I tried to use my brain. "She couldn't possibly be. Is she Chase's?"

"No, she's not yours, and she's not Chase's either. She's… well, that's a whole different story, B. One that I'm not sure I should tell you right now, but you'll need to know eventually. And probably sooner rather than later."

Curiosity made me wonder why he was being so hedgy, but I pushed that aside for now and asked the question that I needed answered right this moment, the one they'd all avoided since the second I woke up.

"What happened to my crew, Lucas? How is everyone?"

Lucas looked at me steadily, his eyes focused on mine. "Before I answer that, because this will make no sense otherwise, I need to tell you something else."

I waited, and the silence between us stretched a mile.

"Somehow… somehow you've lost some time. The events you're remembering, the fire in the Oka-Wen, the campers… all of that was more than a year ago. And a lot has happened since then. You might not want to believe me, but when you saw your leg, the healed scars, you knew something was off. That's why you flipped out."

My head spun and I tried to focus on the sound of Lucas' voice, distant but anchoring.

"That night, you guys were all airlifted out of the Oka-Wen and taken to the hospital. Sloane, Dempsey, and McDaniels were fine, banged up, but whole. Your leg was in bad shape, you'd tied a tourniquet on it, which was probably the only thing that saved you after you climbed up the ravine with that kid on your back."

One flash after another hit me, coming in waves that I couldn't stop. Landry stumbling, trying to stand after we got him out from underneath the burning tree. Dempsey and Sloane, their faces streaked with smoke and sweat, helping to haul me over the crest of a brush-covered slope, the barely conscious and barely breathing teenager on my back. The ropes snapping, the hush in the air while Landry and that little girl fell down the side of the mountain. Sloane cursing, our voices commingling as we pleaded and prayed for them to take a breath, just one breath. Landry strapped to me, our bodies bearing the brunt of the wind's wrath while the medevac's blades churned through the air, creating a storm within a storm.

I pressed the heels of my hands against my temples, trying to hold together a mind that felt like it was being torn apart.

"He's dead, isn't he? Landry is dead. And the girl too." My voice was hollow, empty… I hated that I recognized it. It was the voice of someone who was reliving a nightmare they'd barely made it out of in the first place.

"I'm sorry, B. I'm so sorry." Lucas looked at me with eyes so like my own, except… they weren't. His had never watched a friend — and someone they were supposed to protect — die in their arms. It was an experience I wouldn't wish on anyone.

There was still much more to discuss, but I couldn't take anything else tonight. Lucas sensed my withdrawal and left me alone, promising he'd be around if I needed anything.

For two hours, I sat in the dark, piecing together everything I thought I knew. Landry was dead and my leg was healed. I'd failed to protect one of the civilians I'd promised to save.

I had a wife I couldn't remember, who I might've stolen from a member of my crew. And there was a little girl with huge blue eyes who wanted to know if I'd missed her.

"Where are they staying?" I'd asked Lucas before he left.

"I set them up in a hotel with Heather."

"Heather? Oh, right."

"I suppose they could've stayed at the condo, but I didn't know how much you'd been there since…" Lucas had trailed off, avoiding completing his sentence.

"Since Leigh moved out? You can say it, Lucas. It was a long time ago." *Even longer than I'd thought*, I wanted to say. "Yeah, that was probably a good call. All her stuff is gone, but still."

We'd exchanged a look, and I shrugged.

"The hotel is nice? Safe?" I didn't think Lucas would put a single woman and a child alone in some seedy motel, but I asked anyway.

Lucas rolled his eyes. "Of course it is. We're all staying there."

I pushed myself up to a sitting position and swung my legs over the side. My head spun, and I reached out a hand to steady myself on the bed railing. Apparently I hadn't been out of bed for almost a week, other than when I'd trashed my last room, and I had a feeling that had been mainly fueled by adrenaline.

My body felt weak, achy, and my shoulder throbbed in time with my heartbeats. I moved the blanket aside and stretched, inspecting the scabbed and puffy road rash that dotted my arms and legs. Aside from a finger monitor and an IV, I was free of most of the cords and wires I'd had previously, and I decided to take a chance and shuffle over to the en suite bathroom, using my replacement IV stand for balance.

I put one shaky foot on the floor, then the other, pulling myself to my feet with the help of the metal pole. Out of the corner of my eye I glimpsed my bruised and busted knuckles, and my brain swam out of focus for a moment.

"C'MON, LANDRY! BREATHE! BREATHE, DAMN IT! DON'T GIVE UP!"

I felt my knees weaken and my body give out as the memory overtook me, and I slid to the ground, one hand still holding the metal pole.

Avery crept into the room, probably thinking I was asleep as I sat there in the dark. I'd woken up this morning with the remnants of my memory of Landry's death still lingering in the air, which hadn't exactly inspired me to throw open the curtains and let the sunshine in.

"Hi." My voice was rougher, more gruff than I intended.

I startled her so much that she jumped, banging her elbow on the bedside table hard enough to bring tears to her eyes that I could just barely make out in the dim light.

"Are you okay?" Shit. I hadn't meant to scare her.

She nodded, her hand straying to the blinds questioningly and when I shrugged, she opened them enough for a reasonable amount of twilight to filter through and crack the depressed mood that filled the room. She looked over at me, trailing her gaze over my body like she was reassuring herself that I was actually there. I knew she wanted to come closer, but something stopped her and she sat down in the chair by the bed instead.

"Can I ask you a question?" I tried to smooth the words a little more this time.

Avery nodded again. "Of course. Anything."

My brow knit as I studied her open, honest face."Where is Chase?"

"He's— he's in Lubbock," she stuttered.

"Does he know?" I gestured to the two of us with one scab-knuckled hand.

"Yes."

"And he's fine with it?" I was so confused. I only knew this girl in context with Chase. They'd had a high school thing that he'd ditched out on, and he'd never made things right. I was pretty sure that was the scenario, but Dempsey talked a lot and I didn't spend my time recording his love life. And now, apparently, Avery and I were together. Married. I couldn't wrap my mind around it.

"He is. He… his family even sent us a wedding gift. It was potentially the fanciest-slash-ugliest set of glassware I've ever seen, but Janice — his mom — meant well." I couldn't quite read her smile but it bordered on amused, and a remote part of me wondered about the rest of the story.

"We're still friends?" I definitely couldn't understand that, how Dempsey could possibly be okay with me marrying his girl, especially if he'd come all the way back to Texas to be with her again.

"More like friends *again*."

When I didn't respond, she continued. "Things were

awkward for a while, and he did some very—" Avery stopped short, like she was reconsidering her words. "He was having a hard time," she said finally. "With… everything that happened."

My heart thudded in my chest, two low beats. Of course Avery didn't know what to say. How could you describe the feeling that came with losing a friend and a child that had counted on you?

"You helped him out a lot," Avery said, trying to read my face. "He's doing better now."

I nodded. "I'm glad."

If my influence had helped Dempsey reconcile a few of his demons, or had pointed him in the direction of someone who would, then I'd done what I could, probably more than I was willing to do for myself. I was glad that Chase was doing well, that he'd apparently moved on and tried to continue his life out of the forest, without that day hanging over his head with every step. I wondered briefly about McDaniels and Sloane. They were lifers — I couldn't imagine them anywhere else but out on the fire line.

I didn't say anything else, and our uncomfortable silence grew as I picked at the thin, scratchy blanket covering my legs. I couldn't wait to get out of here, put on actual clothes, and get away from all of this hospital shit. Before, I'd always viewed medicine as a safe-haven practice, something that allowed me to help others and improve people's lives. Now it seemed like a bunch of bullshit. People died all the time, regardless of anyone's best intentions.

"Would you like me to bring you some clothes?" Avery asked softly, breaking through my thoughts.

"Clothes?"

"Maybe some… sweatpants? Something to change into? I could go to the store." Her voice was hesitant, her expression uncertain as she looked at me.

I really just wanted to leave, to go back to the condo or maybe home to Los Angeles, but that wasn't happening today. "Um… I probably have some stuff back at the condo but yeah, a change of clothes would be nice. Thank you."

"The condo?" she repeated.

Shit. Lucas hadn't told me that she wasn't even aware I owned property in Seattle. "I have a place here. You didn't know?"

"Nope. Or maybe I just forgot," Avery said, trying to diffuse the ever-present awkwardness.

I didn't know what to say to that. I knew it was a cop-out but I kept silent.

"Okay, well, I'm going to go see about heading to the mall then."

Now she was the one who couldn't get out of here fast enough, and I didn't blame her. "Good night, Avery."

She jerked her head up and stared at me like she was looking for something, searching my eyes with hers, a slightly hopeful expression on her face for just a moment until she shook her head slightly and looked away.

"Night, Fox."

And I just let her walk out the door, because not caring was getting easier every day.

CHAPTER FOUR

"Beckett, this is Dr. Simon Woods."

I shook the man's hand when he offered it, wondering which kind of specialist they were introducing me to now. I'd met a plethora of them already, from visiting neurologists who couldn't believe my high levels of cognition following a five-day coma, to physical therapists and kinesiologists who marveled at my muscle tone and reflexes.

"Dr. Woods is a neuropsychologist here at UW. He'd like to schedule some sessions with you to try and work through your memory blockage."

The way she said 'memory blockage' was irritating to me, like it was a minor hurdle that I needed to skip over instead of a severe case of amnesia and therefore a completely life-altering mind fuck.

"Hello, Mr. Fox. I look forward to meeting with you."

"Beckett or just Fox is fine." The formalities of hospital protocol were starting to wear on my nerves. Dr. Simms and her associates were nice and tried to keep things fairly informal, but I still couldn't shake the feeling that I was one big experiment to them.

"Fox." Woods eyed me with a calm gaze. "Tomorrow? My office at three?"

I thought about it for a moment. When a member of our crew died or we lost a civilian, department therapy was highly recommended. I'd probably done the required grief and trauma hours already, but I obviously didn't remember. I didn't want to talk — but this was about my memory, not about Landry.

"Tomorrow."

After the doctors left, I fell asleep for a while out of boredom and, when I woke up, Avery was curled up in the chair next to my bed, her knees drawn up to her chin.

"Avery." My rough, raspy voice broke the silence, and she turned her blue eyes toward me.

"Hi," she said shyly.

We stared at each other for a beat, and then two, until I looked away. *Coward,* I told myself. *You're hurting this girl every time you pull back.*

But I couldn't help it. I didn't want to be close to anyone right now, because I knew what loss felt like. Another would be debilitating.

"I— I bought you some things," she said, reaching down next to her chair and pulling up a large shopping bag. "Sweats, some shirts, boxers…" She trailed off, a faint blush rising to her cheeks when she mentioned my underwear.

For a second, for just one second, I imagined what it would be like if I held out my arms to her, drew her in the way I knew she wanted. I could rest my chin on the top of her head, cradle her in my arms, maybe even find a little peace. The empty hole of my loss was growing exponentially every minute I drew breath, and I couldn't fill it. Maybe she was part of what was missing. Or maybe letting myself care for her would only break me further.

"I'm going to take a shower." I wasn't supposed to get up without calling the nurse, but I'd done five or six laps around the room earlier without incident so I felt fairly confident I could manage a three-minute shower.

"Let me help you." She rushed around to my side and put a hand under my elbow.

"I'm fine," I said curtly, avoiding her gesture.

I saw the hurt in her eyes when I refused her, but she wasn't easily deterred.

"What about your IV? Can it get wet?"

Shit. I hadn't thought about that. Technically, the answer was no, but that would take some maneuvering on my part. *Let her help you,* a tiny voice admonished me.

"It's okay. But… thanks."

I could be standoffish, but I couldn't be downright mean to her. She hadn't done anything. The entire problem was me.

Me, my messed-up head, and the fact that I hadn't done enough.

I knocked at the door of Dr. Woods' office on the bottom floor of the hospital at exactly two fifty-five the next afternoon. My nurse this morning had sprung me from my IV and, after I put on a pair of the shorts and a shirt that Avery had brought me, I felt less like a lab rat and almost like a normal human, albeit a fairly banged-up one.

The physical therapist who had visited me the night before had given me a sling for my separated shoulder, but I left it in my room. The pain was a good reminder of what had happened, in case I tried to move on. There was no way I was letting the nurse escort me downstairs in a wheelchair either, but I bit back my frustrated words and tried to rationally assure her I'd be fine and take it slow in case I got dizzy. Pretty sure it was breaking protocol for her to let me go alone but the look on my face must've changed her mind, because now I was completely ambulatory.

Woods opened the door after my one knock. He surveyed

me for a second, a quick evaluation, before he spoke.

"Fox. Come in. You're right on time."

I nodded to him, suddenly feeling very exposed.

"Please, have a seat."

After we'd taken our respective places in the two chairs around the coffee table in his office, Woods gestured to a mini fridge. "Would you like a bottle of water?"

I shook my head no, tugging at a string hanging off of my new shirt as if it were the most interesting thing in the world. He reached over and grabbed a drink for himself before picking up a notebook and a pen.

"I'm going to take a few notes, with your permission."

Another nod from me, which did not go unnoticed by Woods. He balanced the pad of paper and pen on his lap and crossed his arms, his gaze intent. "This isn't mandatory, you know. If you want to leave, it's up to you. I'm not going to make you talk."

I hadn't expected him to say that, and irrationally it pissed me off. My tendency to be purposely detached with the doctors and other hospital staff wouldn't work with this guy. That made me even more angry, because I didn't want to sit around and play kumbaya on a ukulele with anyone. Woods didn't strike me as the campfire-singing type, but I still wasn't buying whatever he was selling, this reverse psychology 'it's up to you' crap. It was easier to internalize. I was a pro at it already.

"I'm here, aren't I?" I was surprised by the bitterness in my voice. It wasn't my intent to be deliberately disrespectful, which is why I found it easier to be silent. Once I let some of the anger out, it was hard to rein it back in.

"Yes, you are. Involuntarily, it seems, but nonetheless." He paused. "I want to help you, Fox. If it's at all possible, I want you to get your life back. You've been through enough this year." He reached over to his desk and pulled out a file.

"Is that mine?" I wanted to snatch it away, to see if it even skimmed the surface of what was underneath. I'd read enough medical files to know that they were mostly cold observation, but maybe seeing everything spelled out in black and white would make it easier to process.

"Would you like to read it? You can take it back to your room." Woods offered me the thick folder and I took it with a slightly shaking hand.

"Thanks." I meant it. Holding a tangible piece of my life felt better somehow. It was all right here.

"So. What now?"

I looked up from the cover of the file where I'd been absentmindedly tracing the letters of my last name. For a second I'd forgotten where I was, and why. "You tell me. You're the shrink."

"Are you always this personable?" Woods' comment was sarcastic, but from the tone of his voice I knew he wanted to know.

"I'm—" *I'm different now*, I wanted to say. *I'm afraid to care too much, to lose anything else. I've already lost so much.* "I'm not sure," I finally answered.

Woods leaned back in his chair, his face serious. "Do you want to change that?"

I thought of Avery, her face sad and cautious when she looked at me. I thought of the moment earlier when I'd debated taking her in my arms, considered holding her pressed against me to feel her warmth and let her try to fix me like I knew she would attempt to do. And then I thought of the crushing blow that would be losing another person I loved, that I was supposed to keep safe.

"No." I stood up, tucking the folder under my arm as I began to pace in the small space in front of the door. "Fuck. I'm sorry. I don't know."

Woods regarded me calmly. "Okay. I think we're done for today."

I nodded, and before I could stop myself I was out the door and into the hall, taking a deep breath of undiagnosed air as I walked quickly to the elevator, trying to put as much distance as I could between me and the idea that remembering Avery would be the best thing that could ever happen to me.

"What are you doing?"

Avery's voice almost stopped me in my tracks, but I kept shoving clothes into the shopping bag she'd brought me the day before.

"I'm leaving." Curt, again. Too curt. I wasn't even trying. The guilt of my callousness penetrated through the angry, indifferent skin I'd grown over the last few days.

"You're… you're leaving? What do you mean? Where are you going?"

I turned to look at her, and the look in her eyes almost brought me to my knees. I saw disbelief there, and fear, but most of all love. Even after this week, when I'd rebuffed her, ignored her, and essentially rejected her, the love was still there, so strong that it almost broke my resolve.

"I can't stay here anymore," I said a little more gently.

"But they didn't release you, did they? I spoke with Dr. Simms this morning, she didn't say anything about—"

"No," I said, cutting her off. "I'm checking myself out."

Dr. Buchanan walked through the open door, a stack of papers in his hands.

"It's called leaving AMA, or against medical advice." The irritation in Buchanan's voice was clear, but I ignored it. "We don't advise or condone it, obviously, but seeing as Fox has done whatever he wanted to since he regained consciousness, it probably makes no difference at this point."

I winced a little at his words. A dig at the trashed hospital equipment, I deserved that. I'd asked Lucas to tap into one of my accounts and pay the damage without involving our insurance company in anything but my actual medical expenses. It was my fault, and inexcusable — just more chaos I left in my wake.

"Is that the paperwork?" I wished Buchanan would give me the AMA form and leave because I could tell he was upsetting Avery further with his disapproval, but he seemed determined to make his point.

"Yes. By signing this you acknowledge the fact that you are sound of mind, fully aware of your current condition, and have been informed of a list of potential consequences of your early departure from the hospital, including brain damage and death."

Just had to tack that on there didn't you, asshole? I speared Buchanan with a dirty look as Avery's face paled. After scribbling my signature, I shoved the paper back at him. "Are we done here?"

"Not yet. I might not be able to keep you from leaving, but I can limit your risky activity. The DMV has medically suspended your driver's license until we do a follow-up MRI in three weeks." Buchanan looked almost smug as he handed me a separate, official-looking letter.

"What? I've never even heard of that," I said incredulously. "What will three weeks prove?"

"Hopefully, nothing," he said, and I saw a glimpse of the conscientious, dedicated doctor underneath his annoyance. "If in three weeks — a month after your injury — your scans are as good as they are today, you'll be considered a medical marvel.

"You've suffered a major blow to the head during a vehicular accident, you had a Glasgow Coma Scale score of six to seven, which should indicate severe brain injury, and yet you regained consciousness with full brain functionality and muscle control. The odds of this type of recovery are unprecedented, as are the odds of your one apparent side affect — retrograde amnesia."

Dr. Simms had mentioned the lapse in my timeline of memory and the high improbability that this would occur in any condition where the patient was fully functional in every other area, so I wasn't surprised by Buchanan's words. I'd also sifted through extensive notes about this very subject in my file I'd taken from Woods' office, which I'd been reading in small doses since yesterday afternoon. I told myself that starting with the most recent reports and working backward wasn't avoidance, but it felt like it.

"What is your prediction?" Avery asked Buchanan, her tone betraying her nerves.

"Officially?" He looked at me intently, and I steadily stared right back at him. I wanted to hear this as much as Avery did.

She nodded, moving slightly closer to me. Again, I resisted the impulse to put my arm around her, brush the hair away from her nape, run my fingers along her smooth skin. Her warmth was calling to me, my body responding to her as she stood there, close enough to touch but so off limits for my current frame of mind.

"Officially, all signs point to a complete physical recovery and we have no reason to think otherwise. I expect Fox's scans to be even better in three weeks time — his fitness level is extremely high and his blood tests are impeccable. His body is incredibly good at healing itself."

Avery nodded, seeming pacified, but I read between the lines of what Buchanan wasn't saying.

"And unofficially?" As my friend, physician, former friend, colleague, or whatever, I hoped he'd give it to me straight.

He stared me right in the eye as he spoke. "You're an extremely lucky jackass who would be six feet under right now in any typical manifestation of this situation. I don't like your dismissive, cavalier approach to your recovery. And if you break anything else, I'm calling the police."

My lips curved into a wry smile as he turned and abruptly walked out of the room, muttering something that sounded like *dickhead* as he passed me. Avery stared after him, shock plainly written on her face, but then she giggled once before smacking a hand over her mouth.

"I'm sorry, that wasn't funny—" she turned to me and stopped talking suddenly, her eyes wide.

"What?" I asked, uncomfortable under her gaze.

"Your dimple," she said simply, her voice soft.

"My… what?"

"Your dimple. I missed it."

She reached a hand up like she wanted to touch my face but stopped when I took a step back involuntarily. Her face fell and my guilt surfaced. Every time she reached for me, I hurt her. Every time she tried, I rejected her. *I can't do this,* I wanted to say. *Please don't ask me to. You'd be better off without me.*

I opened my mouth to tell her something to that effect but closed it again when she carefully composed her features and squared her shoulders.

"I can drive you somewhere, if you want." She gestured to my bag.

As my brain struggled to process her unexpected response, I still managed to admire her resiliency. She wasn't giving up on me, even though she probably should.

I'd made promises to this girl, whether I remembered them or not. I knew myself enough to know I hadn't made those decisions lightly — altered state of my brain notwithstanding. But being someone's husband… I still couldn't wrap my mind around it.

Regardless, at every interaction, I was breaking my word. Just like I'd promised those kids I'd get them all out of that valley safely, and I'd failed. Just like I was supposed to have my crew's back, and I'd lost Landry.

And the worst part — Lucas had told me I'd been in a wheelchair for the funeral. I couldn't even be a pallbearer because I couldn't fucking walk. I hadn't been able to do that last thing for him, and it killed me now like I'm sure it had killed me then. I would've traded anything for a strong leg that day, to have been able to carry Landry like I was supposed to and say goodbye.

"No."

She nodded, seeming unsurprised.

"I'm sorry, Avery. I really am." The words rushed out of my mouth before I could stop them. "I need some time by myself. We'll… we'll talk soon, okay?"

She nodded again, her eyes brimming with disappointed tears. I couldn't help myself, I reached out and pulled her to me briefly. She felt good in my arms, natural, but I let her go after her shaky sigh brought me back to reality. I moved away quickly, turning my back to her as she watched me pick up my bag and walk out the door.

CHAPTER FIVE

Three days went by as I holed up in my condo, ordering pizza and mindlessly watching reruns of 90s sitcoms on the old TV in the living room. Turns out that a hefty bribe to the cable company can get your service restored in a matter of hours, and I was now a fully functioning member of society with every channel imaginable and a high-speed internet connection that would let me stream, browse, or chat on every social media platform all at once, if I'd felt like being social with anyone.

Every time Avery entered my thoughts I pushed her right out, preferring to feel numb over feeling guilty. On the evening of the third day, after calling me multiple times during my hibernation, Lucas showed up.

"You look like shit."

"Nice to see you too, Luke."

Lucas gave me an annoyed glare. "Of course I'm glad to see you, B. I came over, didn't I? You weren't a great conversationalist on the phone and I wanted to see your ugly face. I was hoping that you'd want to go grab some dinner, get out of the house for a while."

I shrugged. "I'm good here."

He gestured to the stack of pizza boxes littering the breakfast bar. "I see that. Glad you're taking care of yourself. When was the last time you showered?"

"Did you come by just to break my balls, or what?" It was my turn to be annoyed.

Lucas sat down heavily on the couch. "I'm sorry. I just—this isn't like you."

"I love pizza." *I don't want to get deep, Luke.*

"You know what I mean." He looked around the dim apartment. "I get it, B, I do. I know that shit is all messed up right now and you're having a hard time. But sitting here like this, all alone in the dark, this isn't like you."

He was right and I knew it. But… what was the damn point? No matter what I did, I kept getting kicked back down. I'd apparently rehabbed my body, moved on with my life and found happiness, and then an oil tanker hits a jackknifed semi-truck, I lay my bike down and eat asphalt for half a mile, and it all goes to hell. And then I'm back to the beginning like time rewound itself, except this time I'm disoriented and angry, and I can't help it.

"Give me a break, Lucas."

"That's the thing, I've already given you a ton of breaks. When you trashed the hospital room, I gave you a break. When Avery came to me crying every day after being rejected by you, I gave you a break. When you ditched your physical therapy sessions and copped out of the neuropsychology, I gave you a break. When you LEFT THE FUCKING HOSPITAL five days after a five-day coma, I gave you a break. I don't have any breaks left for you."

Avery came to you crying? Every day? "What do you want me to say?"

"Say you're going to try." Lucas' eyes were hard, unrelenting. "I know that this is real, that it doesn't all go away with a pep talk or a goddamn magic wand. But that doesn't mean you throw in the towel and sit on this couch for the rest of your life. Say you're going to man up and fucking try to crawl your way out of this. Say you're going to call your wife and figure out where the hell to go from here. *That's* what I want you to say."

The truth was, I'd picked up my replacement cell phone to call Avery about fifty times. Every time I thought about her, I found myself scrolling to her number, my finger hovering over the talk button until I realized I had no idea what to say.

Then the guilt came and mingled with the uncertainty until I was robotically flipping channels in an effort to distract myself with something, *anything*, so I wouldn't have to think of her and the hurt I saw in her eyes before I turned my back and left the hospital without her.

"I don't know what to say to her." The truth was always best with Lucas. He'd ferret out lies too quickly, that's why he made such a good security expert — he always knew when someone was full of shit.

He nodded. "She's nothing like Leigh, if that helps."

Leigh. When I'd first returned to the condo, I thought it would remind me of her because the last time I'd stayed here regularly was three years ago when we were trying to play house. But she'd taken all of her weird, uncomfortable modern furniture and fake houseplants when she left, so it felt safe and uncomplicated to be here alone. And I needed uncomplicated more than anything.

"I know. Leigh was—" I searched for the right words.

"Not for you."

I laughed once. "No, I guess not."

Leigh had never liked that I didn't keep regular hours, that I couldn't accompany her to all the social functions thrown by her PR agency. She'd hated that I was gone for months at a time, that we couldn't plan vacations over the summer, or that I often came home dirty and smelling of fire.

"You knew what I did when you met me," I reminded her.

"And I thought it was sexy, I still do," she assured me. "It's just lonely being by myself all the time."

Both of us were so career driven, there had been no question of a compromise or a change in plans. We had tried moving in together to see if it would help but it had only made things worse, and eventually she'd packed her stuff and moved back into her downtown high-rise that she'd sublet as a contingency plan. That right there should've been enough for us to know that it would never work out. Love couldn't operate on contingency.

"I'm sorry, Fox. But you know this isn't working."

"I know. I'm sorry, too."

"Maybe someday, if things were different…" The look in her eyes didn't match her words.

I took her bag from her, placing it in the cab myself, along with the two other large suitcases, while the driver held her door open. "Take care of yourself, Leigh."

"Avery really loves you." Lucas brought me back to the present. "She wants to be there for you. Why won't you let her?"

Because I don't know what to say to her. I just keep hurting her and I don't know how to fix it, how to let her in again. "She doesn't even know me."

"Bullshit. C'mon, B. I've seen you look at her. There's something there, even with your memory loss, and you know it."

Of course I did. I'd be more of an idiot than I'd already demonstrated if I couldn't admit that. Every time I pushed Avery away I felt like I was denying myself something that I desperately wanted. If I could get back to my stoic self, the self that pushed and worked and kept going no matter what, maybe things would feel normal. Maybe they'd feel less out of control.

But until then, I was stuck in my downward spiral with little to no motivation to pull myself out. Maybe I'd left it on the road that day, with a bit of my blood and skin and the memories of loving Avery. Or maybe I just wasn't as strong as I thought.

Lucas was waiting for a response but I had nothing more to say on the subject. "Let's go eat."

"I'll have another, please." I gestured at the bartender.

"Hey! Hey, you!" The guy a few seats down shook his empty glass, his inebriated voice carrying across the room. "What about me?"

The bartender ignored his rude finger snapping until he'd set my drink in front of me. I saw Lucas eyeing me from his stool as I took a healthy sip of my third double scotch, but he said nothing.

I never drank like this, just like I never lost my shit, just like I never sat around feeling sorry for myself, just like I never married girls and then forgot them.

My brother clearly wasn't a fan of all of my new firsts and honestly neither was I. Every time I looked at him, though, I saw the disapproval of the General staring back at me, and that called for a good part of a fifth of Johnnie Walker and maybe even an instigated confrontation between me and that loudmouth jackass at the end of the bar if I tried to finish the bottle.

"What, Lucas? I can't have a drink now, either?"

"Shut up, B. I'm not your babysitter, I don't give a shit if you want to get hammered."

"Good."

"Eat some of this, will you?" He pushed the greasy appetizer plate we'd ordered toward me.

I chose a limp mozzarella stick and inspected it closely. "Pass."

"You picked the bar," he reminded me.

"They have good wings and lots of liquor bottles. I can't vouch for anything else."

I was halfway through my third drink and Lucas was still nursing his first, but I signaled for another round anyway. The scotch was just beginning to take effect; I could feel it running through my veins, easing some of the tension in my body. Numb was good. Numb was better.

"Turn the fucking volume up!" The drunk guy waved his hand at the television mounted to the wall. "I can't hear the game! I got money on this game!"

The bartender rolled his eyes as he set down our drinks then turned to reach for the remote. "Calm down, man. I'm doing it now."

"Was that so hard?" the man sneered, his bloodshot eyes half closed. "I got money on this game," he repeated.

Lucas looked up at the TV. "That's impossible. Or you're even drunker than you look, because you're watching a highlight reel from last season."

I snorted and the guy turned his attention to me, his unfocused eyes landing somewhere along my clavicle.

"Mind your own business," he slurred.

"I can't," I told him truthfully. "You're a real shit show." I tossed back the rest of my glass and picked up the fresh one.

He mumbled something unintelligible and went back to watching the television, so I turned back to Lucas. "Drink up."

"I think I'm good," he said, still eyeing the would-be gambler.

"Whatever." I sipped my drink in semi-companionable silence for a few minutes, but the sound of glass breaking at the end of the bar made me turn on my stool again.

"No, thanks." A girl's voice.

Lucas was already standing, arms at his sides, fists clenched.

"Don't be like that, sweetheart. I just wanna buy you a drink." The slur was unmistakable.

"You spilled the one I already had. Please stop." A clear refusal, and I felt my blood heat up from more than just the scotch.

I looked around Lucas and saw the man leaning in close to a young woman's face, her eyes huge and scared as one of his hands gripped the top of her arm hard enough to indent her bare skin. He shook her slightly, eliciting a small whimper from her lips, and the numbness I'd welcomed before vanished, leaving me plenty of room for rage. Out of the corner of my eye I saw the bartender poised to interfere, but I'd dodged past Lucas and was already there.

"Let her go."

When he didn't respond immediately, I closed one hand over the fingers on her arm, quickly prying them away and using my other hand to gently guide her behind me to where Lucas was standing.

"Are you okay?" he asked her.

I didn't hear her answer because I was focused on slowly tightening my grip on the man's fingers, watching his face pale as I ground bone against bone. "Do you make a habit of forcing unwanted advances on women?"

"Whaaa—?" he gasped.

I squeezed a little tighter. "I could break your hand right now, and I'd like to, but see… I'm not sure if I could stop there. Just like you couldn't stop when that girl asked you to."

"P— please—"

"That word obviously means nothing to you." For a split second I imagined it had been Avery's arm under his hand, her blue eyes panicked.

Tighter still.

"Beckett," Lucas said from over my shoulder. "That's enough."

I waited a beat, two, three, then released his fingers, dropping his hand onto the bar.

"You're crazy, man," he cried, pulling his hand to his chest and cradling it there.

I felt the numbness seep back in. "You should've seen me last week."

"Go home and sleep it off, asshole." Lucas hauled the guy up from his stool by the collar of his shirt. "You're gonna want to ice that hand, too. I hope you don't do a lot of needlepoint. Call him a cab, make sure he gets in it," Lucas told the door security as he came up to help. The guard pushed him forward, herding him out to the front of the bar.

I turned to the girl, who had been sitting calmly in my

vacated seat. "Are you here alone?"

The fear was mostly gone from her expression when she nodded. "My friends flaked on me." She paused. "Thank you, by the way."

"Did he hurt you?" I gestured to her arm.

"No. Scared me, though." She shivered. "I hate feeling that way."

"You told him no, loud and clear. I should've broken his hand."

She looked at me closely, a small, curious smile on her pretty face. "You're a little intense, but I appreciate it. Next time I'm going to pepper spray first, ask questions later."

"I hope there isn't a next time," I told her seriously, "but that's a good plan."

Lucas called Savannah's car service to take the girl home, despite her protests that she would be fine in a regular cab. When she was safely on her way, we settled our tab and headed out into the crisp night air to walk the few blocks back to my condo.

The cask of scotch I'd consumed was surging through every limb of my body, commingling with the leftover rage and irritation over what had happened at the bar. It would've only taken that girl another split second and then she would've raised hell to get that drunk idiot off of her, I was confident of that. But it still didn't mean it was okay.

My fingers tensed again, my fists clenching as I imagined a man putting his hands on Avery, causing her pain and fear. I felt the beginnings of a migraine thump through my head, a very real side effect that Dr. Simms had warned me about. My own pain fueled my anger and, when we got upstairs to the condo, I grabbed my file that I'd left on the counter, intending to toss it into the garbage.

"What's that?"

"A lot of shit I'd like to forget." *But I can't.* I weighed the file in my hands, remembering its contents.

"Is that your file? Did you read it?" Lucas made a grab for

it but I pulled it away.

"I lived it. I don't need a recap."

"You haven't even *tried.* You want to sit in the dark for the rest of your life, alone, feeling sorry for yourself? You want Avery to move on, forget about you? Keep doing what you're doing. You're on your way."

"This tells me *nothing.* It's just words." The lighter in my hand sparked to life, and I watched the flame consume the edge of the paper, curling, smoking, searching for more.

"That's your solution? Burn it down?" Lucas shook his head. "Good plan."

I held the flaming papers until the last possible second before I dropped them into the sink and turned my back on the fire. "It's the only one I have right now."

"Fuck off, Beckett. This isn't you. Pull it together."

The pain behind my eyes spun out of control. I heard my own voice in my head, in between the throbbing. *"BREATHE, LANDRY! PLEASE!"*

I dropped my head into my hands. "I can't." *I let Landry die. I couldn't save everyone. I can't be responsible for Avery, for Annabelle. I can't, I can't, I can't.*

"You can!" Lucas was yelling now.

"Just leave me alone."

"Fine." I heard him walk to the front door. "Careful what you wish for."

CHAPTER SIX

Lucas was true to his word, so a couple days later when my phone buzzed, I was surprised to see his name at the top of the screen.

AVERY'S COMING TO SEE YOU. TRY NOT TO BE A DICK.

I stared at Lucas' text message for a solid minute before dropping the phone back to the floor next to the couch and pulling a pillow over my face. I hadn't seen Avery in a week, not since I'd walked out on her at the hospital. Every time I thought of calling, I decided it was too soon. I didn't know what to say to her. Maybe I never would.

TRY NOT TO BE A DICK.

I could do that. I could try, anyway. The pillow flew through the air as I heaved myself off the couch and crossed to the huge windows on the other side of the room. The curtains were drawn as they'd been for days, but I parted them now and looked outside, taking in the way the wind swept across the water. This is why I'd bought the place — the turn of the century brick juxtaposed with the fully restored architecture and wide expanse of windows looking out over a blue horizon encompassed everything

I was looking for. A solid foundation with something new, something unexpected. I wasn't sure why that was important to me, I just knew that it was.

What would I say to Avery? What would she want to know? The questions swam through my mind while I kept my eyes on the gray sky outside. I could avoid everything forever or I could try not to be a dick and face today. The options were equally appealing and unlikely.

When the intercom buzzed it startled me even though I expected it. Walking toward the door felt like moving forward, like I was headed in the right direction both literally and metaphorically, but it was slow going. The box buzzed again and I imagined her downstairs, wondering if I'd be an ass, wondering if I would respond at all. If I didn't, it probably wouldn't surprise her.

"Yes?" That word sounded like I didn't know it was her, but even if Lucas hadn't given me the heads up, who else could it be? He was pissed at me and on his way back to California anyway, and I didn't get any other visitors.

Her voice crackled through the speaker timidly. "Fox? It's Avery. Can I come up?"

I rested my head against the intercom for a minute. I wanted to see her… and I also dreaded it. How could the same person make me want to run away from her and toward her at the same time? Before I could change my mind, I slapped the button with my hand, allowing her entry.

Shoving back away from the wall, I glanced down at my clothes. I'd showered… yesterday? That seemed right. Not that it mattered. Suddenly, the idea of Avery in my space made me feel vulnerable, exposed. Maybe this wasn't such a good idea. I grabbed my keys and stepped into the hallway, intending to wait for her there.

The elevator dinged, signaling her arrival, and I took a deep breath as I leaned against the doorway of the condo.

Avery stepped out of the elevator, and in this setting, without the hospital and the machines and the constant, unrelenting pressure of life and death and decisions and everything I couldn't control, I realized how beautiful she was. Too beautiful for me.

Her blond hair hung halfway down her back, loose and wild as she pushed it over her shoulder. I took her in from head to toe — long, pretty legs, clad in those tight black pants that girls were always wearing, her shirt oversized, soft, and colorful. Converse sneakers on her feet, glossy pink lips, big blue eyes. She looked young, optimistic, and happy to see me.

"Hi," I said slowly. "I wasn't expecting you." That was a lie only because it was unfathomable that she'd still look at me like that, like I held her heart in my hands. Didn't she know I didn't deserve it?

"I know. I'm sorry for just dropping by. I— I wanted to see you. I missed you." Her words socked me right in the stomach. Always honest, this girl. Always open.

I wavered on the edge of my resolution to push her away. *TRY NOT TO BE A DICK.* "Do you want to come in?"

She nodded, and I opened the door and stepped back so she could enter. The condo was dark, the only light coming from the large balcony off to the side of the living room — I'd closed the other curtains again. I tried to see the room through her eyes, a typical bachelor pad mess that was not my usual style. Blankets on the sofa, clothes and shoes on the floor, and dishes in the sink. Lucas was right — this wasn't typical of me. But maybe it was now. How many repeats until something became a pattern?

I walked past her and cleared a space on the old brown couch. She sat and at the last minute I decided not to join her, instead walking over to the balcony and staring out, crossing my arms over my chest to ward off the uncomfortable feeling I had knowing that her eyes were following me.

"I know why you're here." My words reverberated through the silence. "I'm sorry I haven't called."

"It's okay," she said quickly. "You need space, like you said."

"I don't know what I need, Avery." Saying her name was almost a guilty pleasure, and it felt familiar.

"Can I help you? Can I do anything for you?"

I shook my head, feeling the frustration of keeping her at arm's length radiate off of me. I looked over and saw that she was looking down at her hands, her wedding ring glinting even in the dim, depressed light of the living room.

"Where do we go from here?" Her voice was soft, but it carried easily in the silence.

"I don't know." It was the only answer I had.

"You could talk to me. I'd listen to whatever you wanted to say."

"I— I don't think I can." I wanted to. Fuck, I wanted to so badly.

"You don't?" Her surprise was palpable, laced with disappointment. "Ever? Never?"

The idea of never, or always, was foreign to me at this point. Every day I felt like I was starting over, like I was learning new hard truths that I was forced to accept and then sit back and watch as those truths wreaked havoc over everything. I didn't want to hurt her, but I couldn't do what she asked. I couldn't be who she wanted.

"Not right now."

I heard her intake of breath, sharp, painful. "Okay."

"You have to understand, Avery, I can't—"

"No, Fox," she interrupted me. "I don't have to understand." She got to her feet, brushing tears away with a slightly shaking hand. "I don't have to understand why this happened, why you almost died, why you can't remember me, and most of all why you don't even fucking want to."

"Avery—"

"I love you. I promised to love you forever and I don't plan on breaking that promise any time soon." She picked up her purse and clutched it to her chest. "But I can't help you if you don't let me. And I can't keep feeling like this, like you're crushing my heart every time you push me away."

The sight of her standing there, proud, terrified, but so strong, burned into my brain and seeped into my heart, stirring something I hadn't felt since I woke up in the hospital… something like hope. But as quickly as I felt it, it was gone again, replaced by the ever-present numbness.

"I don't know what to say." I never knew what to say to her, because everything sounded wrong.

Avery pushed her hair out of her face. "Tell me something true."

"I don't know who I am anymore." The words were out of my mouth before I could stop them, not just true but alarmingly so, because that was something I only admitted to myself, alone at night when I thought about the things that scared me the most.

Her eyes softened and she bit her lip, pulling the soft pink skin between her teeth. "I do."

It would be so easy to open my arms to her right now, to draw her in like I had wanted to a thousand times, to pull her vitality to me and try to use it to jumpstart my body into living again. But I couldn't do that when I didn't know where it would lead and what it would mean for her and Annabelle. "You *did*," I corrected her gently.

Avery shook her head firmly, like she could erase my words. "No. You're still in there, I know you are. I just wish you believed it. Things might never change, Fox. I know that. You might never love me again, and that's the hardest reality I've ever had to face. So instead of putting myself out there for you over and over while you reject me, I'm going to take a step back. I will be here if you need me, but you have to reach for me."

Tears welled up in her eyes again, but this time she let them spill over her cheeks. "You have to reach for me, Fox. I can't do it alone."

After Avery left, I took a long shower, letting the hot water practically scald me until it chilled down to ice. I couldn't shake the feeling I'd had since she turned and walked out, the one that told me I was making the biggest mistake of my life by letting her go.

It wasn't until I walked into the kitchen to scrounge up something to eat that I saw the simple white envelope propped against an empty pizza box on the breakfast bar. Something jumped in my chest at the sight of my name scrawled in her even, pretty handwriting. She must've left it for me before she exited with tears in her eyes — just seconds after she'd told me that if I wanted her, I'd have to make the effort.

I knew that, of course, even without her saying it. Everything that was currently wrong with our relationship came from me. She'd done nothing but support me, whereas I'd just done nothing.

Uncertainty about the potential contents of the envelope made me attempt to ignore it for several long minutes as I stood in front of the refrigerator, staring blankly at the meager offerings inside. Cold pizza was an obvious choice, but along with it I made the conscious decision to grab a bottle of water instead of killing the rest of the six-pack of beer I'd bought yesterday.

I'd thought the final cold minutes of my shower would help me go back to the numbness that I'd started to lose when Avery's eyes pierced straight through me and awakened something in my chest. It was a sensation I was trying to ignore but it wasn't working now, and I had a feeling the beer wouldn't do the job either.

For once, being numb wasn't all that appealing. It was lonely. And although I'd once craved it, I was so fucking tired of feeling alone.

Dear Fox, the letter started. I pulled it out and read that opening line, the sheet of hotel stationery weighty in my hands. Her handwriting reminded me of her — simple, effortlessly beautiful.

If you're reading this, it probably means that things didn't go the way

I wanted them to when I saw you today.

That would be the understatement of the year. My mind flashed to Avery's hurt, tear-filled eyes.

Honestly, I didn't expect it to go well, and that's why I wrote you this letter, just in case I wasn't able to say everything I wanted to. There's so much I want to tell you, Fox. I don't even know where to start, and every time I see you there's a hundred more things that I think you should know — things that I would tell you if our lives were still the way they used to be, and things I think you should know about us as we are now.

I felt that. Every time we were together, she was holding back a little, no matter how open she seemed. Because now I was a stranger. Or at least, that's how I treated her.

I've rewritten this so many times, trying to find a balance between unbelievably fucking sappy and objectively factual, but I can't. It's always been all-in with us, and any other way seems false. So I can only tell you about me, about how I feel, and hope that it's enough.

My brow furrowed at the idea of Avery not being enough. She was more than I'd ever expected. It was terrifying and exciting at the same time.

I can be strong for you because of all the times you were strong for me. I understand that now. You showed me a determination that I didn't know I had, far beyond what it takes to get out of bed every morning and plod toward a future that I couldn't define. I knew unconditional love because of Annabelle — she's always been the driving force behind everything I am, but I was so tired. You woke me up, Fox. You made every possibility real. I'll never be able to thank you enough for that.

I sat down heavily on a barstool. It felt like she was still here in the room with me. I could hear her voice in my head as my eyes scanned the paper.

I don't think I'm qualified to tell our whole love story, not by myself, because you're such a huge, vibrant part of everything I am that most days I don't know where you end and I begin. You are in my heart because you are *my heart — you and Annabelle. It beats for you both but it's yours for the breaking. Please be careful with it. It's the only one I have.*

All the air rushed out of my lungs like she'd punched me

right in the gut. She was killing me with every line.

And if this is all we ever are, if it never goes any farther than today — I'll always be grateful for you. I love you. Don't doubt that for a minute.

It was impossible for me to wrap my mind around this. The love I'd shared with Avery seemed beyond my comprehension, capable of enduring and lasting and inspiring her to write me letters like this one. How could I make her feel this strongly when I felt so empty? Did she really mean it?

So I sent one text, throwing it out there like a lifeline.

ALL TRUE?

Her response was almost immediate.

EVERY WORD.

I believed her, but it almost felt like she was saying goodbye. And I wasn't ready for that.

CHAPTER SEVEN

"I burned it."

"You burned your file." Woods' voice had no inflection, gave no clue to his reaction.

"I was drunk," I said uneasily, rubbing the back of my neck. "It felt like… a metaphor."

"Very deep, Fox." Now I heard a hint of sarcasm and I looked up to find Woods smirking at me.

"Okay, it was stupid. But definitely not the stupidest thing I've done in the last few weeks." *Or the most out of character.*

"No argument there." Woods got up and walked over to his desk, pulling a folder out of the top drawer. "Did you finish reading it before you lit it on fire? Or would you like another copy?"

"Why are you being so nice to me?" I blurted. "I've been a dick to you, to almost everyone in this hospital. Why waste your time on me?"

Woods leaned against the desk, his face serious. "You know why. You're a paramedic, Fox. We all took an oath of some kind, didn't we? To help people? You might consider yourself beyond saving, but I believe the exact opposite. It's time to realize that."

"So what you're saying is that struggling is struggling, whether it's from a blocked artery or a blocked memory?" I meant it to be sarcastic because that was my default lately when it came to uncomfortable situations, but the words didn't come out that way.

"Obviously there's a scientific and sometimes hormonal difference between circumstantial injury-related brain interference and the trajectory of mental health disorders, thus they would require unique treatment based on their origin, but I don't think that's what you were asking. So to answer, yes, I believe that *anything* that causes mental or physical trauma to a human is important. Don't you?"

"Yes." I did. I'd lived both, and experienced both with the guys on my crew.

"Then let's move forward." Woods sat back down in the chair facing me. "It's not your fault, Fox. You did everything you could that night."

I wanted to scream at the world *I'M TRYING, OKAY? I'M DOING PENANCE IN EVERY WAY POSSIBLE FOR ALL OF OUR LOSSES* but nothing like that came out. Instead, I just grew more silent and more sullen. I felt myself slipping so easily into that, and I wasn't even grasping at threads to pull me out — I was just letting it happen. I had no control over anything, and now Woods wanted me to move forward, simple as that?

"I can't."

"You keep saying that but history proves that you can."

"What do you want from me, Woods?"

The doctor's expression was unreadable when he looked at me. "What makes you think I want anything?"

Because everyone did. I looked away. My parents and Lucas wanted me to be my old, steady self again, Avery wanted me to remember that I loved her, and Woods… I wasn't sure what Woods wanted. "Don't you?"

"You're right, Fox. I do want something."

I raised my head to look him in the eye. "Join the club."

Woods ignored my tone. "Today I want you to take one step toward your old life. Anything you want." He leaned forward in his chair. "Ideas?"

"What makes you think I want my old life back?" He was starting to piss me off, acting like he knew exactly what I was thinking all the time.

"Don't you?" Woods echoed my earlier words. "What's it going to be?" He picked up my phone from where it lay on the coffee table. "How about you start with Avery?"

I didn't start with Avery, because it was too soon, and because I could still see the rejection and mirrored sadness on her face when I closed my eyes at night, and hear the words from her letter whenever the room was silent. But I knew too much alone time was bad for me right now, and I needed something to tell Woods at our next visit, so on my way home that afternoon I picked up a new tablet to try and reconnect with a couple familiar faces via Skype.

"Man, Foxy, you sure do have some shit luck." McDaniels sat back in his chair, scrubbing a hand over his freshly shaved head. "Thanks for finally calling me back, dickhead."

I felt a grin spread over my face almost involuntarily. This was a good idea. "Sorry about that."

"You're not sorry about anything," McDaniels huffed. "If I didn't hear from Lucas, I'd think you were roadkill. What the fuck, man?"

"It's been weird. I didn't know what to say." That was my favorite phrase lately, so I figured I'd try it out on McDaniels.

"Bullshit."

I felt my grin widen. That went about as well as expected. "Where's Sloane?"

"Don't try to change the subject. We're not done. But if

you must know, Sloane's got a girl in the city so he took off for the weekend."

I couldn't hold back my surprise. "He actually took time off?"

"I know, I know. I couldn't believe that a girl gave him the time of day either, but I guess wonders never fucking cease. Next thing we know he'll be getting married and buying a ranch next to yours out in cow country."

I laughed uncomfortably when McDaniels mentioned marriage. And I was pretty sure I didn't have a ranch, but who knew?

"Fucking quitters, is what you guys are. But that's not the point. What's going on with you, Foxy?"

I shrugged. "You know."

"I do know." McDaniels' expression turned serious. "And it doesn't sound good. What do you remember?"

"Not much. When I— when I came out of the coma, I thought it was that night in the Oka-Wen."

"Shit." McDaniels blew out a breath.

"And so I've been trying to— with Landry—" I stumbled over my words and looked at my hands. This wasn't how this Skype call should be going, heading into things I didn't want to discuss and memories I couldn't get away from. But here we were.

"Look, we were all fucked up after that. There's no question. Sloane overworked himself practically into the grave, I hit the bottle harder than I should've, and Dempsey decided he was out. But you… you were focused. You knew that you wanted to get back out there, heal yourself so you could do the job again."

"But I went to Texas?"

"Change of scenery turned out to be the best thing you ever did. We were skeptical at first, and I'm sorry about that."

"It's okay, I don't remember." I cracked a wry grin at him.

"You came back for this season with a vengeance, Fox. I knew it would be your last hurrah, and you killed it. The superintendent wanted you to stay, but you couldn't wait to get home. After seeing you with Avery, I understood."

My mind went completely blank when he mentioned Avery. Everyone was so sure about us — why wouldn't I try harder to let her in?

"How's she doing with all of this, anyway? Gotta be hard for her."

"She's—" The look on my face must've given everything away, because McDaniels swore softly and shook his head.

"Don't do this, Fox. Don't you dare let her be another casualty of that night."

"I'm trying, McD." I wasn't, not really, but maybe it was time to start, and I was the last one to realize it.

"Are you?" He raised an eyebrow at me. "Let me put it to you this way. Landry doesn't get to have a love of his life. Don't throw yours away in some fucking misguided attempt to do penance. We all did enough of that already."

Avery and I hadn't spoken since the day she'd left my condo with her eyes full of frustrated tears, leaving the letter that made me start to reevaluate everything. Our only communication had been that one text exchange, so it was a complete leap of faith I took when I called her and asked if she'd meet me for lunch.

Her formerly open and sweet voice was guarded as she agreed, and I couldn't blame her. Our last few conversations hadn't gone very well, and this one could easily head the same way.

I got to the restaurant early, using Savannah's car service as I still couldn't drive. It was a nice place, not too fancy, with comfortable, high-backed booths that would give us some privacy and a wait staff that didn't hover. I'd been here before, years ago, on a first date. Seeing as today felt like our first date to me, I thought it was appropriate.

My seat faced the front door, so I had a perfect view when

Avery arrived. She inquired with the host, who led her back to the booth where I waited for her. As she approached our table, I stood up nervously.

"Hi."

She smiled hesitantly at me. "Hi."

We stood there staring at each other for a few seconds until the host cleared his throat. "Would you like to sit, miss?"

Avery slid into the booth and I took my seat again on the other side. Drinks were ordered and once the host left us, I lowered my menu.

"Thanks for coming."

"I don't know what I'm doing here, Fox. I haven't heard from you in a week, other than your text. This afternoon I was planning to book our flights back to Texas." Her voice was resigned, sad.

"What?" She was leaving? I was right, that letter was a goodbye.

Avery put her menu down as well. "I don't want to go. The only thing I wanted was for us to all walk out of that hospital together, but we didn't get to do that. Things are so unbelievably messed up right now. And if you need more time… well… we don't live here. I have to go home eventually, if not for me, then for Annabelle."

Panic gripped me, closing my throat. Everything she wasn't saying sounded like it was being shouted at me from every corner. If Avery left, I didn't know what would happen. I needed more time, yes, but not to avoid her. I needed time to show us both that we could find a common ground. My life had pretty much fucking sucked the past few weeks, and the only bright spot I had was her. I didn't know what to do about it, how to navigate it, but suddenly I wasn't willing to just let go. Not like this.

It didn't matter if Woods and McDaniels and Lucas were all telling me the same thing. I needed to feel it. And I wasn't ready to even consider opening myself up to her until now — and now she wanted to leave.

"Please don't go." The words were out of my mouth and into the air before I knew it, and her lips formed themselves into an 'oh' of surprise.

"Why not?" It wasn't a challenge, just an honest question.

"Because— because I need to know more." That was the tip of it.

"About what?"

"About us."

Avery shook her head. "You can't decide you want me just because you're afraid to lose me, Fox. It doesn't work that way."

"I know. I know that."

She cocked her head to one side, surveying me. "What do you want to know?"

"How's Annabelle?" I'd start there.

Avery smiled. "She's great. Thank you for asking. She's with Heather right now — that's another reason I was planning to head home. Heather has to be back in Texas for a wedding."

"Oh." That made sense. "Would you be able to stay without Heather?"

She paused for a long moment. "I think so. For a little while."

"Great. That's great."

Two hours later, we wrapped up lunch. I asked Avery everything I could think of about our lives in Texas, nothing too personal, but enough to try and piece together what was missing. I learned about her parents' diner, where I'd moonlighted as a cook, and her small town of Brancher and what I liked to do there. It wasn't everything but I felt like we'd made a solid start, and I hoped she thought the same.

"I'll call you," I said after we were on the sidewalk.

Avery regarded me dubiously. "Sure."

"I will, Avery, I promise."

She glanced up at me and her skeptical look cleared slightly. "Okay."

We stood there for another few seconds, awkwardly

dancing around the decision to hug or just part ways, and eventually Avery backed up a few steps, gesturing down the street. "I'm going to go."

My eyes followed her as she walked down the block to her rental car, and when she climbed in she gave me a little wave. I lifted my hand in response and watched as her car disappeared down the road.

When the intercom buzzer woke me at six the next morning, I stumbled to the front door and slapped the button without even asking who it was. I'd find out in a matter of minutes, so I chose to just lean against the wall and shake the fog of sleep from my head while I waited for my visitor to come up in the elevator.

Momentarily, there was a brisk knock on my door and I opened it to reveal the General standing there.

"What— what are you doing here?" I spoke the first words that came into my brain.

He fixed me with his serious stare. "The day has started already, Beckett. Go get some clothes on."

In two sentences, the man could reduce me to a nine-year-old boy. I walked quickly into my bedroom and threw on a pair of jeans and a shirt, then headed into the bathroom to splash some water on my face.

When I came out, he was standing exactly where I'd left him, glancing distastefully around the condo with an annoyed look on his face. I'd seen that look my entire life so I kept walking into the kitchen. "Want to sit down? I'm going to make some coffee."

"What are you doing here?"

That's what I asked you. "I'm sorry?"

"I said, what are you doing here? If you need me to elaborate, I'd be happy to. What are you doing in Seattle, without your wife and your career, spending your days sitting around this apartment in the dark? What are you doing here?"

The General came to stand next to the breakfast bar, adjacent to where I remained frozen in the kitchen, holding the bag of ground coffee while I tried to process the abruptness of his words. After all this time, it shouldn't surprise me.

Whatever bullshit I'd tried to give Woods, or Lucas, I knew it wouldn't work with him. "I don't know."

He nodded. "That's what I thought. Can I tell you a story?"

I watched in disbelief as he settled himself into a stool at the breakfast bar. As far as I could remember, my father had never asked me for permission to do anything in my life. He was staring pointedly at me so I nodded.

"There was a time when, much like you, I felt a little lost."

His first sentence was enough to make me drop the coffee bag onto the counter and focus all of my attention on him. Never, and I mean not EVER, had the General admitted any weakness. I didn't think he knew the meaning of the word in relation to himself.

"I'd lost a couple friends, started questioning if this path was where I wanted to go with my life. I'd set my sights straight for the top, and suddenly I realized that it could be lonely. I already felt alone, both because of decisions I'd made and opportunities I'd passed up."

I nodded. I'd had that feeling, lying alone at night in a smoldering forest, thinking that there had to be something missing here, otherwise I'd be happier.

"And then I met your mother. I'd been promoted, invited to a few fancy bullshit parties, and she was the guest of honor at one of them. A young, up-and-coming artist making waves in East Coast society. She had me in the palm of her hand from that first night."

This was a surreal conversation, talking to the General, or listening to him talk, about emotions. About meeting my mother.

"Things happen that way and I've often wondered, what if I hadn't gone to that party? Where would I be now? I'd convinced myself that being strong meant being stoic, and I almost lost the most important thing in my life because I tried to push her away when things got too real."

I looked down at my hands. "And she didn't let you."

The General laughed, and I jerked my head up in surprise. "No, quite the opposite. She told me to take a hike if I couldn't get it together and admit my feelings for her. That's when I realized, whatever I faced, I could do it as long as I had this woman next to me. Her strength would carry us if mine ever failed."

I can be strong for you because of all the times you were strong for me.

Avery's words from her letter echoed in my head. "You've never failed at anything in your life." Not the General.

"I've failed at plenty — including being a supportive father. I know I pushed you boys, Beckett. I did it out of love, but it was a misguided attempt to help you avoid this very feeling — lost and out of control."

My fingers found the coffee bag again and I fumbled to set the pot to brew. Lost and out of control essentially summed up how I'd felt over the past few weeks.

"I wanted you both to be like me, focused, career-oriented, driven as all hell — but I didn't take into account that you have your mother in you too, so you'd be better. You wouldn't be as unforgiving or as detached. Your mother would nurture that necessary side of you and let it grow. Everything you've done, and everything you'll still do — that's not my influence, Beckett. That's you."

I let that sink in. "And now what?" *Where do I go from here?*

"Find your focus again. Let Avery in — and let her strength carry you both for a little while."

CHAPTER EIGHT

After the General left, I sat around with my third cup of coffee, wondering what my next move should be.

"Let her strength carry you both for a little while."

There was something I'd been wanting to do but I kept putting it off — shoved it out of my head every time it entered, thinking I'd do it another day. Maybe today was that day.

Before I could change my mind, I grabbed my phone and dialed Avery's number.

"Hello?" Surprise and, if I wasn't mistaken, pleasure filled her voice.

"Hey, it's Fox. Um, Heather leaves the day after tomorrow, right?"

"Yes. Why?"

"Do you think— do you think that you could go somewhere with me today? Take me somewhere, actually? And Heather could watch Annabelle?" I paused. "Please?"

"Okay," she said slowly. "Where am I taking you?"

I took a deep breath. "To Landry's grave."

When Avery arrived, I was already waiting for her in front of the condo building, my hands shoved into my pockets and the hood of my sweatshirt pulled over my head to thwart the sudden gray drizzle coming from the sky.

"Sorry," she said as I slid into the car. "Hope you weren't standing out there too long."

I pushed my hood back and looked over at her. "No problem. Thank you for coming with me today, for driving me." I was so fucking tired of not being able to drive, of depending on cabs and public transportation to get around the city. Just a few more days until my scan, and then hopefully that part of my life would go back to normal. It was a start.

Avery gestured to the car's navigation system. "I put the cemetery's address in the GPS but I'm not sure if it's correct. Heather says the key is to tell the narrator lady not to give you any shit, but so far it hasn't worked for me."

I tapped the screen a couple times. "We're good to go."

We drove to the outskirts of the city, the window wipers methodically clearing the rain from the windshield as a low blues station came over the radio.

After Avery pulled through the cemetery gates, I directed her as best I could based on the information McDaniels had given me.

"You sure you want to do that, Fox? Go out there, I mean? You could wait awhile."

"I have to, McD. I don't remember saying goodbye."

We parked in the shelter of a maple tree, and Avery shut off the engine slowly and turned in her seat. "Do you want me to wait here or—"

"Will you come with me?" I asked suddenly. Then I remembered the rain. "Never mind, I don't want you to get wet. I'll, um, I'll be right back."

"Fox." Avery put her hand on my arm, her eyes bright with understanding. "I'll come." She grabbed a rain slicker out of the backseat and opened her door.

I could still feel the heat of her hand even though she'd let me go. I led the way up the small, grassy hill dotted with plaques and stones until I found Landry's resting place. Fourth row from the top, seventh stone, just where McDaniels said it would be.

Seeing his name carved there was so formal, so final. Slowly, I sank to my knees, reaching out to touch the wet marble.

"Hey, Landry."

I felt Avery's presence behind me — she'd moved off to the side slightly to give me some privacy, but it was still a sort of comfort knowing she was there. I needed to do this, to say what I came to say, and at this point it didn't matter who heard it. If Avery really wanted to know me, to understand what was happening in my head, she needed to hear it more than anyone.

"I haven't been out here in a while, man, and I'm sorry about that." The truth was, I had no idea when I'd been here last, but I thought Landry somehow knew that. Somehow, Landry always knew everything.

"I think about you a lot, about that night when everything went all to hell. Sometimes I can't get it out of my head." It probably wasn't especially appropriate, talking about hell in a graveyard, I realized. Too late.

"I'm sorry, Landry. I'm so fucking sorry that I couldn't be there for you when you needed me, that I couldn't catch that rope when you started to fall. I tried, man. I tried so hard." I swiped at my eyes with the back of my hand, suddenly glad for the rain.

"And after— after you hit the ground, we got to you as quickly as we could. But it wasn't soon enough, and I'll never forgive myself for it. You died that day and you took a piece of all of us with you — you and that little girl." My head bowed, and I took a deep breath as I tried to collect my thoughts.

A hand on my shoulder had me looking up into Avery's eyes, where tears of her own shone through the gray mist. I put my hand over hers, holding her warmth there, while I finished what I had to say to Landry.

"I've taken these last few weeks for granted, like they were punishments instead of opportunities, and I'm sorry about that, too. It won't happen again."

Avery's hand slipped away from my shoulder as I rose to my feet. We walked to the car in silence, and it wasn't until we were driving out of the cemetery and back on the main roads that I spoke again.

"Thank you for coming with me today, Avery. You didn't have to, and it means a lot."

"You're welcome." Her eyes darted over to mine as she drove, still filled with the warmth of her understanding. What I saw there emboldened me to say what came next.

"Do you want to get some coffee? Maybe… talk a little more?"

I caught a hint of a smile, her face in profile as she watched the road. "Sure."

"Great." A small weight slid silently but significantly off of my chest. This was a start — or it could be. I could make it that way. I pointed to the intersection up ahead. "Turn here. I know a good place."

Because today was the first day of the rest of my life, or something to that effect, I got an early start. I'd been up late the night before, planning and figuring out exactly what I needed to change to get my shit together. Spending the day with Avery, even when she held me at arm's length, was the best few hours I'd had since this all started. I wanted more of that. More of her.

The General hadn't told me anything I didn't already know. He'd just flipped a switch in my brain, gave me a push that I'd needed after dragging my feet and being annoyingly stubborn. Hearing from him that he'd struggled too, that he hadn't always known exactly what to do in every step of his life, was the kick in the ass that I needed. The man with all the answers didn't always have the right one, and that meant I could be human too and take a gigantic step out of his shadow.

"I never saw you happier than the day you married her, Beckett. She calmed you, helped you find your center the same way your mother did for me."

I inherently knew that was true because every time we were together, I felt her pulling at me like a compass to true north. If meeting Avery had shocked me out of my self-punishing and brutal cycle, she was a huge part of my recovery after Landry had died. I wondered if I'd ever told her so.

"Whatever you do from here will be the right choice because you've made it with a clear head. Trust your gut, son. It doesn't lie."

As soon as the clock struck nine a.m., I started making phone calls. The first one was to a cleaning service I'd used in the past. I made an appointment for them to come within the hour, achievable with a hefty fee. I didn't care. I needed to get the condo in order if I was going to have Avery and Annabelle come over, and hopefully even consider staying here with me instead of at the hotel.

I'd been hemorrhaging money lately to fix my mistakes, but it was only money — a small price to pay for getting my life back on track, and the investments I'd made with my trust fund were finally coming in handy. Wealth had never mattered much to me as I usually spent half my year in a burning forest, cat-napping on the dirt in a sleeping bag, but now I was glad I had it.

The look on Avery's face when she saw the inside of the condo that day was a cross between uncomfortable and disbelieving, and I realized then that I'd never taken the time to update the place after Leigh moved out. She had taken most of the furniture because it had been hers, and I'd acquired an unwanted couch from one of my neighbors and called it a day on the decorating. When I was active in the Hotshots, I spent the occasional weekend and sporadic months in the winter in the city, but largely the condo sat empty. I didn't want it to be that way any more. I wanted Avery and Annabelle here, filling the place with life and light and chasing away the ghosts of the last time I'd stayed here.

My second phone call was to a local home-furnishings

store. Being unable to drive was incredibly frustrating, but I spoke with a woman on the phone who assured me that she'd get all of the furniture I'd picked out on the website delivered as soon as possible today.

"You've made some excellent choices, sir. Relaxed and comfortable but extremely high quality. Your family will enjoy this furniture for years to come."

My family. I had no idea how long Avery would stay in Seattle, or what our future held, but I was going to try my hardest to show her that I was now making decisions with her and Annabelle in mind.

"Do you need anything else? Art for the walls? Kitchenware?"

I knew I was skyrocketing her whole month with this commission, but the truth was that she was saving my ass by helping me, and I told her so.

"I can't thank you enough for making this happen on such short notice. Send whatever else you think I'll need, but I have the art taken care of."

That led me to my third phone call, one that I should've made a long time ago. I was severely behind when it came to apologies.

"Hi, Mom."

"Beckett! How nice to hear from you." She meant it. My mother never saw the point in lying.

I wanted to punch myself for taking so long to pull my head out of my ass. My parents had been in Seattle for weeks, ever since they got the phone call about my accident. I knew what it had taken for my mother and the General to uproot their lives and come here, and I'd been largely ungrateful and oblivious. It stopped now.

"Can I take you to lunch? Just the two of us?" I needed to tell her I was sorry in person.

"I'd love that, sweetheart. I'll send the car for you."

I took a deep breath. "I need your help with something

also, if you have time. Do you still have your prints featured in that gallery downtown?"

I could almost hear her smile through the phone. "I do. There's a lot of other wonderful art there as well. I'll ring the manager, let him know to expect us after lunch. Anything specific you're looking for?"

"I'm doing a little redecorating, but the walls… that's where you come in."

"It's about time you cleaned up that bachelor pad," she teased. "Beckett?"

"Yeah?" I was surprised by the amount of gruff emotion in my voice.

"I'm very proud of you. We both are," she said, referring to my father — and to way more than the redecorating of my condo.

"I haven't done anything yet," I protested, but I knew what she meant.

"You will."

"Here it is." Buchanan handed me a piece of paper. "Your letter of reinstatement from the DMV."

I took it, glancing over the document. "Is this your way of telling me that my scans came back clear?"

"I'm not going to sugarcoat this for you, Fox. You did a stupid and reckless thing by leaving this hospital early, and you are alive today merely because of a combination of luck and physics. Those two things don't often go together, which makes the entire thing even more unbelievable. I know you're struggling with the residual amnesia, and I feel for you in that aspect. But as far as your overall physical health, I think you're an asshole for putting your family through the uncertainty of an AMA recovery. You got lucky. Period. Now unless there's something else, I have to go."

I moved aside to let him exit. Buchanan's irritation stung a bit but he was right. I'd been selfish, and it almost cost me the people I cared about the most.

Glancing at my watch, I strode down the hospital hallways and out of the automatic double doors. My cab sat idling in the non-emergency loading zone, and I climbed in quickly. "Nearest car rental, please."

An hour later, I approached Avery's hotel room door with trepidation. We'd had such a great day when I'd last seen her, graveyards aside, but I was taking a huge gamble. I'd spent the last day and a half getting the condo in perfect, comfortable order, and now I was about to see if it was all for nothing.

I knocked, and a few seconds later the door opened just a crack until Avery poked her head out and recognized me.

"Fox?"

"Hi. I'm sorry to just come by like this."

"Is everything all right?" She opened the door wider, gesturing for me to come in. I walked into the spacious suite and looked around, feeling somewhat better that at least she and Annabelle had been staying in a nice place, even though they should've been staying with me. I would fix that today — or try to.

"Did Heather get to the airport okay?"

Avery nodded. "She left last night."

"That's good." I decided to just jump right in. "I want you to move in with me. You and Annabelle."

Avery stared at me, her mouth slightly open in shock. "What?"

"Come and stay with me at the condo. Please, Avery. I should've asked you a long time ago — hell, you should've been there from the beginning of all of this — but I can't go back, so I'm asking you now. Please, let's pack up your stuff so you can come home with me."

"Wh— why?"

"Why?" I'd really fucked everything up if my wife didn't know why I wanted her with me, if she still didn't think I wanted us to move forward. I shook my head. "Shit. I'm so sorry, Avery. You're right, it's too soon. I don't know what I was thinking." I turned to leave.

"Wait, Fox."

I stopped mid-stride and turned to her. "Yes?"

"You don't— I mean, the condo isn't set up for all of us to live there. You hardly have any furniture. I can't bring Annabelle there. Where will she sleep?"

A slow smile spread over my face. "Maybe you should just come over to look. Then you can decide."

"Okay," she agreed.

"You will?" I was halfway there.

Avery nodded.

"You won't regret it, Avery. I promise."

The look on Avery's face when she walked into the newly redecorated, newly cleaned condo was everything I'd hoped for — it erased that first day completely. She turned around in the living room, taking in the new couches, the art on the walls, the tub of books and toys my mother had helped me pick out with Annabelle in mind.

"When did you do all of this?" She laughed, a real laugh, as Annabelle ran into the hallway to check out the bedrooms.

I'd left them simple, left them for Avery to decide. A huge bed in the master — that one was already there — a queen bed in another, and two twins in the third. That room was Annabelle's, and it had the most decor — all princess themed and age appropriate. The lady at the furniture place really helped me, and it had turned out great. I put two beds in there on purpose, thinking of Avery's comfort. I was so happy that they were here, I didn't give a shit if I had to sleep on the kitchen floor. Whatever worked could be our new normal.

"After the cemetery." *After you heard everything I hated about myself and still stood next to me.* "Do you like it?"

"It's wonderful."

"Does this mean you'll move in? Or think about it, anyway?"

"Mama, can we stay here? There's a princess room just for me!"

Annabelle came running back to the living room and into Avery's arms. She looked at me over Annabelle's head and nodded.

"Yes."

"Hi, Fox!" Annabelle's little voice greeted me cheerfully as she bounded into the living room.

"Hey, Annabelle." I looked around. "Where's your mama?"

I heard the front door close and then slow footsteps as Avery approached. They'd moved in only yesterday, and we were all still adjusting. Avery and Annabelle had been out picking up a few things they'd need to stay a bit longer in Seattle, and I wasn't expecting them back until later that afternoon.

"Hi."

Avery's voice sounded strange, and I put down my tablet, rising to my feet as she came into the room. Her face was pale and she looked tired, I realized.

"Are you okay?"

She nodded. "We're going to take a nap."

"Let me know if you need anything."

She gave me a small smile as they headed back to the bedrooms. "Thanks."

I was dozing on the couch a couple hours later when I heard Avery coughing in the kitchen. Getting to my feet, I poked my head into the hallway, registering the sound of cartoons coming from the room we'd designated as Annabelle's.

"Avery?"

Her back was to me, but when she turned around, I immediately started toward her in concern. Avery's skin was still pale, a thin sheen of sweat visible under the kitchen lights. She coughed again, her body hunching over a bit as she did so.

"You're sick. Did you catch cold from the other day in the rain?"

I was a selfish bastard. I'd asked her to get out of the car with me at the cemetery and now she was sick.

Avery shook her head. "I'm fine."

She turned to open the refrigerator, and I put out a hand to keep it closed. "What are you doing?"

"Annabelle wants grilled cheese." She coughed again.

"I'll make it."

"No, it's okay. I can do it." She propped herself weakly against the counter and reached for the wrapped loaf of bread.

It was hard to realize she didn't want my help or, more likely, didn't totally trust me to give it to her. "Avery, go back to bed. Let me help."

She looked up at me quickly, and for a split second I felt like I recognized her expression, like we'd been here before. Another conversation? Another time I'd wanted to help her and she resisted?

"We've had a similar conversation before, haven't we?" I studied her face intently.

She managed a small laugh, her skin so pale. "Maybe. A few."

I lifted a hand to brush her hair away from her face almost involuntarily, but at the last moment I hesitated. Maybe it was too much, to think I could touch her so familiarly. This had to be on her terms. "So is that a yes?"

Avery hesitated, and I could see her chest rise and fall as she took a breath. "Every time I feel like I want to believe you, I keep remembering how you pulled away from me. I can't forget that, Fox. I want to. I want to so badly but it hurt too much. It still hurts."

"I'm sorry." It was all I had. I had no other excuse.

"We don't do that, you and me. We don't push each other

away. You never allowed it before, and then suddenly it was the only thing you wanted. How am I supposed to take that?"

She looked up at me with tired eyes, and I felt a stab in my chest. "I don't know. I just— I'm trying."

"I want to think you've made this big dramatic one-eighty, Fox, I do. You're telling me that you want us and I want to believe you. I've never wanted anything more."

I took a deep breath. When she said it like that, it sounded unbelievable even to me. The events that led to me pulling my head out of my ass were part of a solitary timeline that almost no one had experienced with me. She hadn't known when I'd started to think differently because I hadn't told her. I hadn't let her in, not until it was almost too late.

"You asked me to try, to reach for you. This is me reaching. Everything I've done since you walked out the door and left me that letter, that's been me reaching. Please don't pull away now."

She nodded slowly, her face even more pale than before. "I'll try, too."

"Thank you." I wanted to kiss her, to open my arms and see if she'd let me hold her, but between the exhausted look on her face and the conversation we'd just had, I knew this wasn't the time. "Go back to bed." The tip of my index finger whispered over her cheek. "I've got this."

CHAPTER NINE

"This was delivered to the precinct, sir. It's your personal effects from the accident site. My beat is right around here, so I thought I'd drop it off. Sorry it took so long." The young uniform cop shrugged. "You know how it goes."

I nodded as I took the box from him. "Thank you."

"Have a nice day." He turned to walk back down the hallway but hesitated. "We don't usually make house calls for backpacks, sir. You were in paramedic training with my brother at UCLA, and I think you ran into each other again recently? Charlie Buchanan."

I glanced at the name tag on his uniform. *N. Buchanan.* I knew this kid had looked familiar. He was a younger, more wiry version of his brother.

"Nick, right? You here to arrest me? Because if so, you're going the wrong way." I raised an eyebrow at him.

He smirked. "We don't make a habit of arresting decorated firefighters for exercising their right to leave a hospital AMA, sir. Or any, um, accidental property damage. My brother's ego rivals the size of his student loans these days, but his heart's in the right place."

I cracked a grin in spite of myself. "Noted."

After the younger Buchanan left, I went back inside to the kitchen counter and sat on a stool while I started to dig through the box. According to the police report, which I'd read the other day courtesy of Lucas and his sources, the crash site spanned over half a mile. No casualties but a few other injuries and a shit ton of damage. Mine was the only motorcycle involved, and that was probably why everyone else walked away.

Pulling my helmet from the box, I grimaced. The entire left side was scraped to hell, dented, cracked, and the strap severed where they cut it off of me on the side of the road. I turned it in my hand, examining it thoroughly.

"I must have nine lives," I muttered to myself. *Well, maybe only seven now. Or six. Five, at least.*

The sound of Avery's key in the lock made me jump to my feet, the helmet still in my hand. I didn't want her to see this. The dent in the side of that helmet would do nothing to reassure her that someday her husband might remember what life was like when they were in love. I shoved the helmet in a cabinet above the refrigerator and came out of the kitchen just as she and Annabelle walked in.

"Hey," I greeted them, taking the pizza box and to-go bag from Avery's hands. Her cheeks flushed when I smiled at her, but when I leaned forward to kiss her cheek, she stiffened.

"Hi," she replied hesitantly.

Damn. I really thought we'd made progress the other day when she was ill.

"Fox!" Annabelle threw herself at me and I just barely got the food on the counter in time to catch her. "You're home!"

Avery stepped forward like she wanted to take Annabelle from me, but I turned quickly with the little girl still in my arms. If I could make things somewhat normal for Annabelle, I would.

"Hey, Bells," I said, remembering the nickname I'd heard Avery use.

She wrapped her arms around my neck and squeezed, and I flinched a little. My left shoulder separation was still healing, but at least the pain was mostly manageable now.

"Careful of my bionic shoulder, okay?" I shifted her to the other side and tickled her ribs.

"Annabelle, don't climb all over Fox, please." Avery's voice was still tired, worried. I'd rarely heard it any other way. At least, not that I could remember, and I hated that.

Avery went over to where I'd set the food and started to open the bag, pulling out packets of parmesan cheese and plastic utensils. "Are you hungry?" she asked me.

"Sure." I set Annabelle down and she ran into the living room. "Smells good."

"It's just pizza," Avery said softly.

I'd eaten enough pizza in my self-imposed solitude to make me never want to taste another slice, but I'd binge the whole pie if it'd make her happy. I used to make this girl smile. I knew I had. I also knew I'd been a dick since I woke up in the hospital, and that my previous radio silence hadn't gone a long way to convince her that I wanted her and Annabelle here with me.

And I did.

My mind might not have remembered her, but the rest of me never forgot. Every time we were within three feet of each other, I felt like her body was actually touching mine. I was aware of every breath she took, of the erratic beat of her heart, of her pupils widening when she looked at me. She was as engrained in my skin as the angry marks left by the road — a part of me now forever.

I touched her bare shoulder lightly, felt her shiver. "I got my things. From the accident," I elaborated when she looked up at me. "My backpack, some other stuff."

She nodded, waiting for me to continue.

"I was thinking, after Annabelle is in bed, we could go through the box? Maybe help me figure out what I'm looking at?" I waited for her response. It would serve me right if she said no.

"Sure." It wasn't enthusiastic, but it was affirmative.

I blew out a breath. "Thanks."

I poured coffee for myself and set a teabag to steep in a cup of steaming hot water for Avery. Carrying both mugs in one hand, I hefted the cardboard box with the other and headed out into the living room, ignoring my weak-ass shoulder. *Can't expect things to right themselves on their own*, I heard the General say in my head. *Takes hard work.*

I was willing to put it in, the hard work. Avery was worth it. Annabelle was worth it. I just needed Avery to believe me, and to somehow take that look out of her eyes, the one that said that everything she thought was true had just disappeared.

"Tea?" I set the mug on the low table in front of the couch where she was reading.

"Thanks," she said, her eyebrows raised slightly in surprise. I watched as she slid a bookmark into her novel and turned to me. A small smile played on her pretty lips as she watched me take a long pull of my coffee. "It always amazes me that you can drink caffeine all day and still sleep at night."

I half-shrugged with a grin. "Just habit."

This was good. It felt comfortable, sitting here with her, an easy conversation, like I'd done it a million times. In reality, I probably had. I studied her over my mug, watching the way her graceful fingers reached for her cup, the curve of her shoulder slipping out from the wide-necked shirt she wore, the way her eyes closed and her eyelashes rested against her cheek for just a moment as she took her first sip.

She looked up, caught me watching her, and I couldn't bring myself to look away as a slow, steady blush crawled its way up her throat and curled itself into her cheeks. If there was a girl more beautiful in this world, I'd never seen her. It's no wonder I thought she was an angel in my comatose haze.

"Did— did you want to look through that box?" she asked.

"Right, yes." My voice sounded husky and distracted, which perfectly mirrored my brain.

I set my coffee aside and reached into the carton, pulling out a leather jacket. I heard Avery's sharp intake of breath and instantly wished I had hidden the jacket along with the helmet. One entire side of the dark leather was scraped almost white from where I must've skidded along the asphalt, worn through in a few places, and covered with dirt, debris and, if I wasn't mistaken, a little dried blood.

Shoving the jacket back down into the box, I turned to Avery and started to apologize. "I'm sorry, you shouldn't have had to see—"

My words were interrupted as she threw her arms around me and started to cry. "I almost lost you," she sobbed softly into my neck. "It took me so long to find you and then I almost lost you again."

Even though I was taken aback by her sudden, forward, and lately uncharacteristic gesture, I reacted immediately to her touch. My shoulder screamed as I tightened my grip on her and shifted so she was sitting in my lap. Her sobs continued as I smoothed a hand from the top of her head down her back over and over again, letting her cry it out.

Waves of regret and shame washed over me as I listened to her heartbreak. What an ass I'd been to her, trying to push away the one person who'd stood by me unequivocally these past few weeks. I was the one who bled, but she was the one who felt all the pain.

"You promised me," she whispered after what seemed like ages. She lifted her head and her blue eyes pierced right through me. "You promised."

I slipped my hands up and cupped her face, using my thumbs to wipe away the streak of her tears. "Don't give up on me now," I told her. "We're not over yet."

Avery was still sleeping every night in the room we'd set up for Annabelle. After seeing what was left of my jacket, she excused herself and went to bed. I couldn't say I blamed her. Whatever else I might've pulled out of that box would only hurt more at that point.

I finished my coffee and rinsed the rest of the pot down the drain. My body already felt jittery, wired, like I needed a run or a swim to get my head together. But it was late, and I didn't want to worry Avery in case she woke up and I was gone, so I settled for the next best thing.

"Hi, Mom." I let myself out onto the balcony, where my voice wouldn't disturb anyone and instead let it carry off into the distance over the bay.

"Beckett? Is everything all right?" Even through the phone, Savannah Miller was one of the most perceptive people I knew.

"Sorry, I know it's late," I said by way of response, even though I was familiar with her night owl tendencies.

She laughed, a sound that always reminded me of music, of crystal glasses clinking together at one of her late-night dinner parties, of the wind sweeping over the ocean near the house in Malibu, of the quiet melody she hummed while she worked on a painting.

I had all of those memories, and so many more, but none of the past months. None of my wife in the other room, or the little girl who didn't understand that I couldn't remember her. Cradling the phone between my ear and my shoulder, I scrubbed my hands over my face in agitation.

"Beckett?"

"I'm here."

"What's going on?" she asked again. "She liked the condo, right? The new furniture?"

I pictured Avery's face the first time she saw the newly redecorated space. Hopeful, that's how I'd describe it. Hopeful because I was making an effort after weeks of nothing. Hopeful, but still guarded, because I'd hurt her more than I'd reached for her.

"I'm afraid she'll never trust me again," I admitted. Saying it out loud had the exact opposite effect I was hoping for, as I realized it was true.

"Oh honey," Savannah sighed. "What happened?"

"In the hospital, and after, I was so angry and confused. I pushed her away, ignored reality. You were there. You saw me."

Saw me being a fool, is what I should've said. But she knew. Mom always did.

"Avery loves you. I've never seen someone so scared, so deathly terrified as she was when you wouldn't wake up." Savannah's voice was strained but still strong. "We were all so worried, but she knew you were coming back. Even through her fear, she told me the same thing every day. 'He wouldn't leave me, not now,' she said. She believes in you."

My heart thudded slowly in my chest. "And now I've let her down. She thinks I don't want her anymore, that I regret our life together, when really it's just that I can't imagine it — and I'm not sure I deserve it."

"Deserve it? Why—"

"What if I can't do it?" I interrupted. "What if I can't come back, be the man she needs? Be the man she remembers?" The words burst out of me, out of the tightness.

"The man she knows would never give up. You do whatever you need to do so that girl believes you want to fight for her, to remember her."

"And if it's not enough?"

"It's love, Beckett. It's messy and unpredictable, but if you give it your whole heart, it's always enough."

CHAPTER TEN

Did you think at all about what we discussed yesterday?"

This was a twofold test. One, how was my short-term memory? And two, are you truly finished being an obstinate dickwad and thus ready to commit to your recovery by continuing your forward momentum? Woods had a right to doubt me, given my initial behavior, but I'd been coming to see him consistently over the past few weeks. And despite my original misgivings… things were looking up. But after seeing Avery's tears last night, I knew I had to work even harder.

"Yes."

"Good." A couple seconds ticked by. "And?"

"I don't see the point in going back to Los Angeles. I remember everything from my life there." LA wasn't what was missing from this puzzle. "I'm going to Texas." As soon as the words left my mouth, I realized I must've decided last night. Of course I needed to go to Texas — it was the key.

"Interesting." Woods spun his pencil as he studied me. "You're sure?"

"I want my life back, Woods. I know it took me a while to

realize it, but I'm there."

"Very good. Keep going with our cognitive exercises, and I'll give you the contact information for a specialist in Odessa. Do me a favor, check in with him once in a while." The doctor scribbled on a slip of paper and stood up, offering it to me. After I took it, he put out his hand and I shook it firmly.

"Thank you for everything." I meant it. "I'll be in touch."

Woods cocked his head, a wry but pleased smile on his face. "You're welcome, Fox. Good luck to you."

I made it home before Avery and Annabelle, who'd gone to a morning matinee at the nearby movie theatre. When I walked into the living room, I saw the cardboard box still sitting where I'd shoved it under the coffee table last night.

No time like the present. Another one of the General's favorite sayings.

Curiosity had me pulling the box out before I could second guess my actions. I shoved aside the trashed jacket and reached for my backpack. It was made of a heavy canvas and neoprene webbing, padded along the back and sides, making it perfect for motorcycle riding — comfortable and protective of its contents. I was surprised that it had held up so well, considering the state of my jacket, but aside from a little dirt and a few scuff marks, it was fairly intact.

Inside I found a small laptop, headphones, an iPad, and a GoPro camera, all wrapped in a towel, along with a change of clothes, a toothbrush, and deodorant. Made sense, considering I was planning on taking the bike all the way back to Texas with minimal stops. I usually traveled light.

I turned my attention to the electronics. The iPad's battery was drained, but the screen unharmed thanks to its heavy-duty case. I set it aside for later and examined the laptop. The towel and the thin padded sleeve probably saved it, I decided, because it didn't have a mark on it. In the front pocket of the backpack I found a couple charging cords, and I nervously waited for a disastrous start-up, but the machine instantly came to life and presented me with a desktop picture of myself, Avery, and Annabelle at what had to be our wedding.

Our wedding.

To see yourself in a photograph at an event you don't remember, on a day that you weren't aware existed — surreal doesn't even come close.

My eyes immediately zoned in on Avery. She looked beautiful, radiant, *happy*. We held Annabelle between us, both of our faces turned toward her as she laughed. Before I realized what I was doing, I'd reached a hand out to touch the computer screen. This Avery was so alive. She looked at me and Annabelle with love and something close to adoration, and the image of me staring back at them emoted volumes of the same.

I had to find this Avery again.

And this version of me, because they looked like they couldn't live without each other.

I tore my eyes away from the photo long enough to flip through some of the documents on the hard drive — nothing interesting: some bill receipts, a few saved articles on wildlife activity, a couple lists of what looked like materials and ideas for home-improvement projects.

Closing those windows, I debated about where to look next. Typically I had lots of raw video footage stored on my laptops for later editing, and there was no reason that this computer wouldn't have the same. But when I clicked through to my favored application, I was floored at the amount. I must've upgraded this computer's memory to the very max to be able to store all of this. Almost nothing was fully labeled, but I mostly recognized my usual system of cryptic numbers and abbreviations.

I clicked on one that said "12/25 A A" and watched as Annabelle's happy, giggling face filled the screen.

"What did you get from Santa, Annabelle?" I heard Avery ask in the background.

Annabelle's smile beamed out at me before she turned and ran over to a Christmas tree in a room I didn't recognize. The floor was strewn with wrapping paper and bows that fluttered in the breeze she created as she whirled past.

"I got a castle! For the princesses! Lots of them!" she cried, pointing at a plastic doll house that was almost as tall as she was. "I love it!"

Avery's laugh filled the background again and the camera slowly panned until I could see her in profile, sitting on a couch in her pajamas with her legs tucked underneath her. She turned her head to look directly into the lens, and the love and joy in her eyes hit me squarely in the stomach.

"What did you get for Christmas, Avery?" I recognized my own voice coming from behind the camera.

She reached up to push a strand of her wavy blond hair behind her ear, and I saw her engagement ring sparkle in the low morning light.

"The best present ever," she said, her eyes twinkling almost as brightly as the diamond on her finger.

"And what was that?" my voice persisted.

"You."

I snapped the lid of the laptop closed and roughly scrubbed both hands over my face and through my hair. This was killing me. I took a deep breath and slowly opened the computer again. I wanted to see more, but at the same time I wasn't sure if I could handle this voyeuristic look into my own life.

Scrolling through the list of the videos, I took in the pattern of dates, initials, and sometimes a partial location or event. I'd filmed almost every day, sometimes for just a few seconds at a time, often longer.

I clicked on another video that said "KK TG" and watched nervously.

The screen started out black, then abruptly shot into color.

At first all I could see was a crowd of heads, and then the camera spun around from a bird's eye vantage point and settled into a panorama of what looked to be the inside of a restaurant. Maybe Avery's parents' diner? My suspicions were confirmed when I saw myself on the screen, wearing an apron and gesturing up to the lens, which must've been my GoPro on a stick. Avery was next to me, on her other side was a woman I presumed to be her mother, and an older man — her father? — also wearing an apron, who held Annabelle in his arms.

"Today was such a success!" Avery cried, grinning into the camera. "We fed more families than ever before, and Kent's Kitchen wants to thank our local community of Brancher for helping us with food from their own tables every year. We couldn't do it without you. Happy Thanksgiving!"

The crowd whooped and cheered, and I saw all kinds of people, young and old, farmers, cowboys, mothers with babies in their arms, teenagers, those plainly dressed and those in their holiday best, as the GoPro I held panned over the faces.

"That was from last Thanksgiving," a voice said behind me, and I spun around to see Avery watching me, her eyes bright with unshed tears. "We— we always cook a big meal and offer it to anyone who has nowhere else to go. Your footage was on the local news, celebrating our biggest turnout ever."

I couldn't form words or thoughts when I looked at her. I just stared.

"I'm sorry I startled you," she continued, her voice strained. "I came in quietly and laid Annabelle down in her bed — she fell asleep in the car."

I had to look away so I wouldn't see the sadness in her eyes, and I turned back to the computer. "Did you know I had all of this?" I asked, gesturing to the screen and the hundreds of unwatched clips.

She didn't respond aloud immediately, but when I looked her way she was nodding. "Yes."

On a hunch, I closed the video app and opened the photo

album. If I had a few hundred video clips, I must've had a thousand photographs. In thirty seconds I'd scrolled through an entire relationship, from just after the meet-cute to the tearful goodbye when I left for Washington. I'd captured it all and taken it with me.

I could hear Avery breathing shallowly, but I couldn't look at her.

"It's like I knew, like I was afraid I'd forget us."

She made a noise that was somewhere between a thin scream and a stifled sob, and seconds later I heard the bathroom door open and close.

I waited for her to come back, clicking slowly through pictures of my forgotten life: Avery leading Annabelle around a small outdoor ring as she proudly rode on the back of a dappled grey pony; me sitting on the porch swing of a sprawling ranch house, Avery in my lap, laughing as she ruffled the ears of an old black dog; Annabelle running through a field, the colors bright and full of sunshine with Avery's profile just visible in the foreground off to one side; the three of us in a rowboat on a lake, Annabelle bundled in a neon life jacket that clashed horribly with the serene nature surrounding us.

And one that especially caught my eye — a time lapse of three lit sparklers, swirling through a twilight sky with only the outlines of our bodies visible against the fading sunset.

When I heard the shower water turn on in the bathroom, I realized that Avery wasn't going to rejoin me for my trip down unremembered lane. *Why was she hiding from me? Why now, just when I'd started to realize everything I was missing?*

My feet carried me to the bathroom door of their own accord, and I knocked softly, hoping that she could hear me over the sound of falling water. When I got no response, I put my face close to the door.

"Avery?" Still nothing. I called again, only slightly louder because I didn't want to awaken Annabelle. "Avery?"

I turned the knob and the door opened silently. She hadn't

locked it. Stepping into the steam, I saw Avery through the clear glass shower door, standing directly under the spray with her face buried in her hands. A silent sob shook her body, rolling through her until I was afraid she'd break.

I didn't think, I didn't hesitate. Kicking off my boots, I slid the glass door back, stepped into the shower fully clothed, and gathered her into my arms.

She jumped when she heard the shower door scrape, but before she could completely register what was happening and pull away, my body was wrapped around hers, her wet skin soaking my shirt, dampening my jeans. I held her until she stopped shaking, pressing her closer to me while the water pounded us both.

"I'm coming with you to Texas," I whispered into her ear as she clung to me. "That's what I'm missing. That's what I want to remember more than anything. I want to, Avery. I want to remember you, remember us."

She squirmed in my arms, trying to get even closer. That feeling I got whenever she was nearby was magnified times ten thousand with her naked body pressed against mine. I was aware of her breasts, her hardened nipples against my chest through my wet shirt. I felt the gentle sway of her bare back, her hips as I spanned her curves with my hands to pull her against me.

I leaned back to look at her, her beautiful blue eyes red-rimmed and uncertain. Suddenly, she must have realized she was naked in front of a man who was her husband turned into a stranger, and I saw her body try to close in on itself, to hide and protect.

"Don't do that with me, please." I pulled her arms up from where they attempted to cover and instead wound them around my neck. "Never hide from me. You're so beautiful, Avery, I—"

It was then I noticed the necklace she wore. I'd seen the chain, but never what was attached. Water poured over her shoulders, slicking her long hair to her skin, pooling down between her full breasts and swirling around the thick, platinum ring that hung between them. A man's wedding ring. *My* ring. I'd never considered what happened to it, and she'd had it all along.

"I want this back," I said roughly, surprising myself with the amount of emotion in my voice. "It's mine."

I reached behind her neck and with one quick tug, broke the slender chain in half. She gasped as the necklace slid from her body into my hand. I slipped the ring on immediately, feeling a million things in my life simultaneously click into place when I settled it onto my finger.

"*You* are mine." I spoke the only truth I could remember.

The rest of my world righted itself when she rose up on her toes and pressed her hot, open mouth to my lips. In seconds I had her up against the tiled shower wall, her legs around my waist as her hands struggled to pull my wet shirt up over my head. Her breath came raggedly, sweeping over my lips between kisses while her fingers traced every muscle in my abdomen, trailing a fire over my skin that was even hotter than the water.

I broke away, using my hips to keep her steady against the wall as I ripped my shirt off and flung it behind me. Her eyes were already heavy and hooded with lust, and all the blood in my body felt like it was pooling directly into my groin, where her wet, naked heat pushed against me.

Once I rid myself of the shirt, she reached for me again, taking my face in both of her hands while I fumbled with the button on my jeans. I kissed her slowly, unhurriedly, completely out of sync with the rest of my body that was in a mad dash to be skin to warm, slick skin. I sucked her bottom lip into my mouth, biting down softly, loving the way she shuddered and gasped for me.

"Fox," she murmured low in her throat. "Fox, I—"

"I know," I told her. "Me too."

Now, I needed her now. I couldn't get my fucking jeans off fast enough, the wet denim all but glued to my legs as I peeled them down and away from me, supporting all of her weight with my bad arm.

"Your shoulder!" she cried when my face betrayed the strain of how I held her.

"Forget my shoulder," I growled as I finally freed myself from the jeans, kicking them away and reveling in the feeling of all of her against all of me. "Forget everything except you and me."

And then I was inside her and all around her and consumed by her, the water swallowing the sound of her moans as I pushed deeper, straight into our past and out of my head and into my heart, where we'd always been but I couldn't seem to find until now.

I put my hands on her everywhere, making sure she understood what my body inherently knew. Over her breasts, teasing her nipples while I sucked on her neck and she panted into my ear, the sound of her losing control and surrendering to the unknown only spurning me to move faster, to give more, to fight through this to the real us, the one that was buried underneath it all.

CHAPTER ELEVEN

"Are you okay?"

Our morning was busy, and between the early flight and the unexpected traffic, a little more chaotic than expected. Avery smiled, turning her body toward me after she finished getting Annabelle settled in her window seat on the plane.

When she looked at me now, I felt like she liked what she saw. I knew our bond had strengthened these past few days, bridging a gap from the distant and angry first weeks after my accident to a common ground that would lead us back to normal — whatever that was.

"Yes." She slid her hand into mine and squeezed. "Are you?"

I nodded, smoothing my thumb over the knuckle on her first finger. "Getting better every day."

While that wasn't entirely true, I knew she appreciated the sentiment. In the three days since I'd found the laptop full of my life with Avery, things had shifted. It started in the shower, but it hadn't ended there. I was in this, I wanted it, and she knew it. She finally believed it.

Her cheeks flushed, no doubt thinking of the water running over our bodies as we began to find our way back to each other. She looked up at me, and I felt a slow grin spread across my face as I took in her expression. I *hoped* she was thinking about the shower. I'd been unable to think of anything else.

She poked me in the ribs with her free hand.

"Stop that."

"I can't," I said seriously. "Don't make me."

She rolled her eyes and I grinned. These moments when it seemed like nothing had changed were coming more frequently, and I welcomed them. What neither of us were admitting was the desperate, unrealistic hope that somehow I would step off the plane in Texas and suddenly remember everything.

It was fucking unlikely, but I wanted it. Badly.

"Are we going up in the air, Mama?" Annabelle's little voice brought me out of my deep-thought bubble.

"Soon," Avery told her. "And as soon as the pilot says it's okay, we'll turn on one of your movies."

"Okay," she said, seeming satisfied, but then her brow furrowed and she looked at Avery worriedly. "We're going home, right?"

"Yes, baby," Avery reassured her.

This hadn't been easy on her, the traveling, Avery's overwhelming sadness that she'd tried so hard to hide. I was doing my best to smooth the disconnect, but little kids were perceptive. Annabelle was no fool and I never underestimated her.

"All of us together?" Her eyes were huge when she looked at Avery.

"All of us together," I confirmed with a wink, squeezing Avery's fingers lightly.

"Yay!" She switched her baby doll from one arm to the other, bouncing slightly in her seat. "I can't wait to tell Grandma and Grandpa all about my trip!"

Meeting the parents took on a whole new meaning when you were re-meeting your wife's parents that you were actually well acquainted with in your non-amnesiac life. According to Avery, her father and I got along so well that we were friends outside of just a superficial in-law situation. But now… I was certain they knew that things weren't all hearts and flowers immediately post-coma, otherwise we would've been back in Texas weeks ago. I would add them to the list of people whose trust I needed to rebuild.

The plane taxied down the runway and into the air, and after the seatbelt sign clicked off Avery turned on Annabelle's movie. I watched as she sat back in her seat, a cloud of emotions moving across her face. Despite her outward calm, I knew Avery had to feel overwhelmed about everything that still lay before us. There were only so many ways I could reassure her, but I'd keep trying until she understood.

The idea of taking her into my arms was still a luxury, one that I took advantage of every time I could, and so I pushed the armrest between us out of the way and pulled her closer, enjoying the feeling of her against my body.

"Avery." I tipped her face up to meet my eyes, searching for everything she was feeling but wouldn't say.

"Yes?" Her voice was soft, tired, as she gazed at me.

"Telling you not to worry is pointless, so I'm going to to amend it to please try not to worry *so much*, okay? I know we didn't get to all walk out of the hospital together the way you wanted," I paused and brushed my thumb over her cheekbone, trying to keep the regret from overtaking my words. "But this flight — us going home to Texas — is the next-best scenario. Thank you for letting me come."

She smiled. "You're doing that Fox thing again, the one where you look at me all seriously and speak a lot of words and then my head spins a bit." Her voice was light, but her eyes welled up with tears and she blinked rapidly.

I laughed once, pulling her into me a little tighter. "Sorry?"

"Don't be sorry. I missed it. I was afraid for a while that we'd end up leaving without you." She put her arm around my torso, resting her cheek on my chest. "I'm so glad you're here."

I slid down in my seat a bit to make us more comfortable, taking a quick second to check on Annabelle before I kissed the top of Avery's head. "Nowhere I'd rather be," I said, my lips still against her hair.

I felt her body relax slightly in my arms, the combination of her nearness and her willingness to trust me filling my heart and soothing my always-scrambling mind. I rested my chin lightly on the top of her head, smoothing a few errant blond waves back from her forehead with my free hand.

"Close your eyes if you want, Avery. I'll make sure Annabelle has everything she needs."

It didn't matter if I lost my memories from the past year or the past ten years, because I was here now and the woman in my arms and the little girl next to her were my top priority until I took my last breath. Losing people I loved was a fucking terrible part of life that I was in no hurry to repeat, but closing myself off from the ones that loved me was almost worse. I would never do that again. Not ever.

The rest of the flight was uneventful and we actually arrived early, deplaning and heading into the hot sun as we trekked across the airport parking lot.

Avery explained that she'd asked everyone to give us time to settle, and I was glad it was just the three of us, holding hands with Annabelle in between as I took my first steps toward re-acclimating to Texas. I swept my gaze over the flat, dusty landscape as we approached the big truck Avery indicated. There was a familiarity about all of this that was comforting. My episodes of not-quite-deja-vu but *something* were increasing as the days went on, and I took that as a positive sign.

"This is my truck, isn't it?" I asked as I loaded our luggage into the bed.

Avery looked up from securing Annabelle's seatbelt. "Yes. Do you— do you remember it?"

"Not really," I admitted. "But I like it."

Her face registered a split second of disappointment before her expression cleared. "No," she corrected me with a smile. "You *love* it."

I grinned at her as I stood outside the vehicle, admiring the custom wheels and tow package before I hopped into the passenger seat. "Yeah, you're right."

On our scenic route home, I tried to take everything in without pushing myself to identify it. Avery snuck glances over at me as she drove, gauging my reactions, but my overall feeling was relaxed. This felt right, this truck, this highway. I rolled down my window, letting the wind blow through the cab and swirl through the girls' hair, making Annabelle giggle. There was sunlight and open space here that I didn't even know I wanted until I felt it all around me.

When we got to the more central streets of Brancher, Avery started casually pointing out landmarks. Annabelle thought that this was an especially fun game and joined in, keeping a running commentary going while we passed some of her favorite places.

"Look, Fox! There's my school!" she cried.

I looked where she pointed, to the tiny elementary campus and its little preschool bungalow just outside, painted in cheerful colors. "Where is your classroom?" I asked her, turning in my seat.

"Right there!" She pointed. "And there's our park!"

I took a good look at the park. Avery told me I'd spent a lot of time there, especially during my first weeks in Brancher. I could see that — the old pull-up bars and climbing structure would be useful as a makeshift gym. Between that and the jogging path that wound around the trees, I probably did a lot of my rehab right here.

"Coffee, BBQ, laundromat," Avery said as we drove into town a little further.

I knew Brancher was small, but I hadn't comprehended exactly how small until I realized that these streets made up the entirety of downtown. There were no chain stores, no plethora of restaurants or boutiques. Everything was efficient and well-maintained, but simple. Only the necessities, no fuss, no frills.

"Kent's Kitchen." The sign above a diner made me pause. "That's it, right? Your family's place where we worked together."

Avery followed my gaze to the front of the diner, where we could just see an older woman through the window, taking an order at one of the booths.

"Yes."

"It's nice. Looks exactly like I pictured it from the video."

Her face fell slightly, and I knew she was hoping that I'd remembered it. I knew she didn't want to keep asking the same question, but we were all wondering. What would being back in Brancher mean for my memory?

"Do you want to go back to my— I mean, our house?" Avery stumbled over her words a bit. "Or I could take you upstairs at the Kitchen to see your old flat, but most of your stuff is at the house. But we could pick it up, or you could just, um…" she trailed off, her voice unsure.

Her hands twisted nervously as she waited for my response, and for the millionth time since that day I'd asked her to move into the condo I wished that I'd never put her though the hell that was the weeks after my coma. There was nothing I could do to erase it, that time of distance and uncertainty, and I hated it. She was trying so fucking hard to make everything okay for me, when all I wanted was for things to be okay for her.

I shoved my sunglasses to the top of my head so I could really look at her. "I want to go wherever you are. Please keep believing that."

She took a deep breath and nodded. "I'm sorry."

I shook my head, feeling that shame creep up on me again. "No, Avery. No apologies. If anyone owes one, it's me."

She looked away from me for just a second to check on

Annabelle in the back seat, and I followed her eyes. Annabelle was seemingly oblivious, cradling her baby doll and talking softly to it. All was right in her world now — we were home, together, and things could return to normal as far as she was concerned. I hoped like hell that she was right.

"I don't want an apology, either," she told me.

I opened my mouth to argue but she silenced me with a gentle finger over my lips.

"I just want you, here, with us."

I slid my hand up and intertwined my fingers through hers, kissing her knuckles. "Let's go home then."

A few minutes later, we pulled into an old driveway connected to a tiny house, and Avery unlocked the front door with a flourish. Annabelle ran down the little hallway immediately, and I followed Avery inside, trying to take everything in.

The rooms were small but well cared-for. I scanned the kitchen and the living room, noting the clean and colorful decor, and slowly made my way down the hallway. Avery followed behind me, observing silently. I'd kept my expectations of our home carefully blank, not making any assumptions or asking too many questions. I knew that Avery and Annabelle lived simply, that my presence in their lives somewhat eased a financial burden, but all I saw in this house was the hard work and meticulous care that Avery put into everything she did.

She wanted me. She didn't need me, not for money or for security. She'd made a life for herself and Annabelle and very kindly invited me into it. It made me itch to give her the entire world just to watch her laugh and tell me it was too much.

I ducked my head quickly into Annabelle's room, then turned to the last room in the house — what I assumed was our bedroom. Hesitating by the door, I looked to Avery.

"Can I?" It didn't feel right to just go in.

She nodded, and I stepped into the room, turning in a meandering three-sixty. The first thing that caught my eye was a collection of silver picture frames on the nightstand, and I walked over to get a closer look.

I traced my fingers slowly over the photograph of the two of us on our wedding day, me in my formal tuxedo and Avery so breathtakingly beautiful in her dress. There was one of me holding Annabelle, her arms around my neck with her little face pressed against mine, kissing my cheek. The third picture was of Lucas, Heather, Avery, and me, laughing as we toasted our marriage.

"I like these," I said. I liked that she had them here, close by even when I was gone, to look at whenever she wanted.

She smiled. "Me too."

I turned to the closet, skimming a hand along my shirts hanging there, before going to the dresser in the corner of the room. I hesitated again, and Avery walked over to stand next to me.

"Your side is on the left."

I nodded, giving her a quick half-smile before opening the top left drawer. She watched as I methodically worked my way down, scanning the contents of each one briefly. I wasn't sure what I was looking for, but every piece of me in this room made me feel a little more like this was actually my life.

"You have more things in the living room," Avery said. "Books, some computer stuff."

Even better. More of me here with her, no matter where I actually was. I stepped closer, resting a hand on either side of her waist gently. "I know this is weird for you. I appreciate your patience, Avery."

"I— I want you to feel at home," she said into my shoulder.

I pulled her closer, my lips at her temple. "When I'm close to you, it feels more like home to me than any room ever could." It was corny as shit but I'd never meant anything more.

She raised her face to look at me, and I bent my head slightly, touching my lips to hers hesitantly at first, waiting for her reaction.

I didn't have to wait long before she slid her arms around my neck, pulling me closer and deepening the intensity of our kiss.

Trusting me, still, or more accurately, again. I responded immediately, opening my mouth and softly tracing the outline of her lips with my tongue. A slow moan came from the back of Avery's throat when our tongues finally touched, and I sucked her bottom lip into my mouth, smoothing my hands up from her waist to cup her face so I could kiss her more thoroughly. With one hand on her cheek I slid the other around to wind my fingers through the hair at the nape of her neck, massaging her scalp lightly as I scraped my lips from her jawline to under her ear.

She gasped when I drew her earlobe between my teeth and bit down softly, pulling her closer still so she could feel exactly how much I wanted her right now. I held her against me tightly, kissing my way down the side of her neck, her soft skin a welcome contrast against my unshaven jaw. I hadn't forgotten how to touch her — her body was a map I'd memorized for good.

"How did I ever get anything done?" I mused, bringing my mouth back to hers for another long, slow kiss. "I must've spent all my time wanting you."

Avery kissed me again, laughing quietly against my lips. "You did say I was distracting."

"Understatement."

"Mama! Fox!" Annabelle's voice beckoned from across the hall.

I pulled her tightly against me again for another split second, then released her quickly. "And that's our version of a cold shower, then?" I grinned, amusement clear in my voice.

I'd never anticipated feeling so close to Annabelle so quickly. Avery, yes, but her little girl? She'd worked her way into my heart that first day, even though I hadn't wanted to recognize it, when she'd thrown herself into my arms without hesitation as I'd lain in the hospital bed, confused and scared. If it were at all possible, I thought that we were closer now than before my memory loss, because she was the only person in my life that didn't treat me like I had amnesia. Annabelle had never fully understood that I didn't remember her so she hadn't given me time to relearn anything about our relationship — she just picked up right where we left off and expected me to keep up. In some ways, it was exactly what I needed.

"I'm coming, Bells," I called to her, and kissed Avery's cheek before I slipped out of the room.

CHAPTER TWELVE

I wasn't sure how I'd react, but being back in Brancher felt good. The first day we lay low, spending time just the three of us at Avery's house. *Our* house. It was going to take me a minute to get used to that, even if my clothes were hanging in the closet and my books dominated one entire side of her wall-to-wall library in the living room. When she informed me that I'd built those shelves, replacing the old ones to house our expanded collection, I inspected them thoroughly, feeling a slight swell of pride at my work.

I'd told Avery the truth when I'd said that anywhere she was felt like home to me; she and Annabelle were all I needed to feel like I was exactly where I was supposed to be. We could be anywhere for that, and Brancher was as good a place as I could imagine. I honestly didn't give a shit — months at a time of fighting wildfires meant that I obviously didn't need fancy accommodations. I'd live in a mud hut in the middle of a swamp as long as Avery would let me hold her at night.

The second day was more of the same, plus a few errands for Avery to get the house back in order after her absence. We had a quick, only slightly awkward lunch with Avery's parents, who graciously didn't treat me like anything other than a son-in-law they hadn't seen in a while. I knew that was largely because Avery had coached them on exactly what to say and not to say so I wouldn't get spooked, and while I appreciated her effort, I wanted to reassure them that I was done being a dipshit and that I wasn't going anywhere. As soon as I got my bearings, I'd pay them a visit out at their ranch by myself.

On the third day, I went for a run, pocketing my new iPhone and making sure I had the address noted in case I got lost. Avery mentioned that I used to like running through the park, so I headed that way and found the path. It was hot but not too humid, and once I'd gone half of my usual five miles, I stopped second-guessing my location and just ran.

There was something about this place that felt right to me, it was eerily familiar without being obviously remembered. I knew that Avery was really hoping that I'd have a huge memory surge, but so far all I felt was a weird sense of quasi-deja-vu combined with a few moments of awkward second-guessing when I had to ask Avery questions about basic things. Her patience was infinite, and if I wasn't sure I loved her before, I knew it now. I just had to find the right time to tell her.

I jogged up the driveway to the house after I finished my cool-down, damp with sweat and hoping to make a beeline for the shower. The inconvenience of only having one bathroom in the little house was something I planned to tackle as soon as possible. My recovered laptop held ideas for adding an expansion and an en suite to the tiny master bedroom, a project I must've had in mind before I left for the Hotshots. If Avery would let me, I'd start right away.

"Fox! You're home!" Annabelle ran out from her room as soon as I came through the door.

"Stay back, Bells! I'm all sweaty." I made a funny face at her, stopping her in her tracks before she could jump on me.

"Ew!" she cried, then laughed and skipped away. "Mama,

Fox is wet and yucky," I heard her say to Avery down the hall.

I smiled, picturing Avery's reaction. I wouldn't mind taking her into the shower with me and lathering us both up, but that would have to wait for a time that Annabelle was either not home or sound asleep. Remembering the last time I was in a shower with Avery, her soft skin wet and smooth, water running down her body, over those perfect curves, her breasts in my hands… I had to reach down and quickly adjust my shorts before Avery came into the living room.

"How was your run?" she asked me, then saw the look on my face. "What?"

I leaned forward, holding my sweaty body away from her as I kissed her lips gently. "Hi."

"Hi, yourself," she murmured, her low, sexy voice doing nothing to help the situation in my shorts. I wanted her all the damn time.

I pulled away reluctantly, but then I had an idea. "I want to take you out to dinner," I told her. "Could we do that tonight? Is there somewhere we like to go?"

"I'd love it," she said. "Maybe I can call Heather to babysit? She's been missing Annabelle since she had to leave Seattle."

"Great."

Even though we were together now, in our home, every hour she agreed to spend with me seemed like I was getting away with something. I'd come so close to screwing this all up, I took nothing for granted.

"I'll take a quick shower, then you can take your time getting ready. I promised Annabelle we'd make airplanes with that special paper I bought her at the airport."

"Airplanes?"

"It's the only thing I know how to make," I said sheepishly. "I'll have to distract her with them until I can YouTube the origami dinosaurs and flowers she asked for."

Avery's face was impossible to read until I saw her shining

eyes. "I missed you, Fox."

Instead of guilt crashing through me, I felt something more like relief, and certainty, as though I was finally exactly where I was supposed to be. I wanted to reach for her, to pull her up against me, but remembering my post-run status, I settled for taking her hand, bringing it to my lips. "I'm here now, Avery. I promise."

She nodded, smiling. "I know."

I gently released her fingers, wishing that I could wipe that uncertainty from our history altogether. My foul, sweat-drenched shirt was sticking to me, making my skin itch. The faster I got clean, the faster I could have her close to me. "I'm going to grab that shower."

When Heather rang the doorbell, I was sitting with Annabelle at the kitchen table, painstakingly folding tiny bits of paper while she colored with her crayons on the finished planes.

"Is that going to be a really fast airplane, Fox?" she asked, bouncing in her chair.

"Fastest one yet," I told her. "I'm going to answer the door, okay? Heather is here to see you."

"Auntie Heather? I hope she brought us cookies!"

"Me too." I ruffled her blond curls as I passed by, careful not to disturb the ever-present tiara.

I was no longer surprised about how easy it was to be with Annabelle, how much I liked listening to her endless chatter, letting her mess with my hair and pour me millions of cups of pretend tea. If my original connection to Avery was instant and undeniable, like Lucas said, it only made sense for me to feel just as attached to a smaller, louder part of her. That feeling was reinforced every day we spent as a family.

"Nice to see you, Fox," Heather smiled at me when I

opened the front door, taking the bakery box and shopping bag she carried as I let her in.

"Glad to be here."

"I'll bet you are."

She raised her eyebrows at me, and I gave her a half-shrug, feeling a little self conscious. When I said I was glad to be here, I meant it twofold — alive and also standing in this room. There were moments after I'd achieved the first that I wasn't sure I'd ever get to the second.

"Thank you for coming tonight. I really want to spend a little time with Avery, try to normalize things a bit if I can." I studied her, searching for signs of disapproval on her face.

"I'm happy to help, plus I missed my little sweet potato."

Nodding, I turned to head into the kitchen with the bag and box when Heather put her hand on my arm. "Fox."

I waited, wondering what she'd have to say. I hadn't spent much time with Heather, at least not that I could recall, but from what I knew of her, she typically spoke her mind, and often.

"I want you and Avery together. I'm rooting for you. Please know that." She smiled softly at me. "And don't mess it up."

"I'm trying my hardest not to," I told her honestly.

She surveyed me for a second before she spoke again. "I told Avery the same thing once upon a time when y'all were first sniffing around each other. She was afraid to love you too much, and here it turned out to be one of the best decisions she's ever made. Not like she had a choice, I mean, look at you." Heather grinned.

I stared at her for a beat, and then shook my head, laughing. "Thank you. I think."

"You're welcome."

"By the way, Lucas told me to say hello."

Heather stopped in her tracks on our way to the kitchen. "He did, did he?"

I raised an eyebrow, intrigued by her reaction.

"Well, you can tell him that he can get his ass out to Texas and say hello to me in person, otherwise I don't want to hear it." She patted my arm and continued into the room, calling out a greeting to Annabelle.

I set her bag and the bakery box on the counter, my lips curling up in amusement. I had no idea what was going on with Heather and Lucas, but it was going to be so satisfying to relay that message to Lucas after his superior attitude when it came to lecturing me on relationships. It sounded like he was entirely too far in the doghouse with Heather to be giving advice to anyone.

I headed down the hall, still sort of thinking about Heather and Lucas when I knocked softly on our bedroom door. "Avery? Are you almost ready?"

"Yes," I heard her say from inside. "Can you come in and help me?"

I opened the door slowly, revealing Avery standing in front of the tabletop mirror, sweeping some sort of powder over her cheeks. Her hair was down in gentle waves, and she was wearing a loosely fitted, short, silky blue dress with her favorite cowboy boots, showing enough tanned leg to make me wish we were staying home.

"You look beautiful."

She turned around, and when I got the full effect of my wife standing in front of me, I had to shove my hands in my pockets to keep from kicking the door shut and reaching for her. Beautiful was an understatement, like all adjectives were when it came to describing her. My girl was unreal.

Avery smiled and took a few steps toward me, closing our gap. "Thank you." She swept her hair up from her neck, twisting to offer me her back, and I saw that her dress was slightly undone. "Can you finish this for me? I couldn't reach it."

I skimmed my fingertips along the nape of her neck, quickly fastening the buttons. I couldn't help but press my lips to her skin briefly, feeling her shudder under my mouth and hands. I pulled away, spinning her by the waist so she was facing me again.

"If we don't leave now, I'm not sure we'll be able to."

She nodded, her eyes huge and happy, and we walked down the hall to say our goodbyes to Heather and Annabelle.

Once outside, I tucked her hand into my arm as we walked to my truck, making the last-minute decision that I would drive tonight. Avery glanced at me questioningly when I helped her into the passenger seat.

"I'd like to drive us, if you'll tell me how to get there."

It felt right to be sitting in the driver's seat of the big truck. I'd had one similar to this in Seattle, before I bought the motorcycle. Seattle wasn't great for bikes because of the rain, but I spent a lot of time in the northeastern part of the state where it wasn't an issue. I wasn't sure if I'd ever ride a motorcycle again, especially because I couldn't imagine broaching that subject with Avery.

"There's not a lot to choose from, honestly," Avery said, bringing me back to our dinner destination. "We— we usually went into Midland or Odessa, but I'm not sure I want to be that far away tonight, for Annabelle. I was hoping we could keep it kind of casual." She bit her lip uncertainly.

I put my hand on her leg, rubbing a thumb over her smooth skin. "Avery, we could go to McDonald's for all I care. I just want to be with you." I leaned forward to kiss her lips, and when I pulled away I saw amusement dancing in her eyes. "What?"

"The nearest McDonald's is twenty-five minutes away," she said.

"Really?" I sat back. "Um, Whataburger?"

She shook her head. "Pretty much the same distance."

"So if you want to eat in Brancher, where do you go?"

"Well, if you want to get a *good* burger, you go to Kent's Kitchen and order the special. But then you lament the whole time about how that handsome blond firefighter doesn't work there anymore, and wasn't he such a nice boy and didn't he cook such a tasty burger?" Avery grinned at me.

I was speechless for a second then started to laugh. "Glad to know I've been missed. Okay, if you want to get a sub-par burger in Brancher, where do you go?"

"Lucky's," she replied immediately.

"Point the way."

Lucky's was almost exactly as I'd imagined it — dark booths, an acre of gleaming wood bar, and two pool tables that were currently occupied by a group of ranchers in cowboy hats. They nodded to us when we walked in, but largely our entrance was unnoticed, and after we slipped into one of the booths I picked up a menu.

"What's good here? Besides the burgers."

Avery looked at me from across the table, wide-eyed alarm on her face. "Oh, I wouldn't order anything but a burger or maybe the hot wings."

"Noted." I put the menu down quickly.

Our waitress came over and stood at the table, an order pad in her hand. "Hey, Avery." She turned to me with a big smile. "Hi, Fox! Long time no see. We missed you around here."

There was a long pause, and the waitress looked from me to Avery expectantly.

"Fox, this is Janie," Avery introduced us awkwardly.

"He knows me, Avery. Duh."

Avery cleared her throat. "Janie, you know… Fox is having a hard time with his memory lately."

"What?" Janie looked annoyed. "That was for real? I thought your mom was just being weird."

"Hello, Janie," I said, feeling uncomfortable at the way she gaped at me.

"You don't remember me? Like, seriously?" Janie huffed.

"*Janie!*" Avery hissed. "Stop it. Just take our order. We'll have cheeseburgers and rings."

"I can't believe it," Janie continued, unfazed by Avery's

irritation. "You just forgot, like, everything? How is that even possible?"

Avery was staring daggers at oblivious Janie, who was still looking at me like I was completely insane.

"Sorry," I told her. "No offense."

Part of me almost wished I was lying, because Janie was so annoyed at me for something I couldn't control that at least if I were doing it purposely, I'd have the satisfaction of knowing that my hard work was paying off.

"That's really fucked up, just so you know," Janie sniffed. "Like, rude."

"JANIE!" Avery all but yelled. "Just go put our order in, will you?"

"I don't know," Janie said sarcastically. "Maybe I'll *forget.*"

She flounced away, and I looked at Avery in confusion.

"She's really mad. I never… dated her or anything, right?"

Avery tried to hold back a smile and failed. "No. Janie is just egotistical enough to think that every guy she meets should remember her forever, regardless of a brain injury."

Her grin abruptly faded when she looked over my shoulder.

"What? What's wrong?" I said, glancing behind me. I saw Janie talking to a tall brunette as they both looked over at us, not even attempting to conceal their stares.

Avery sighed. "Maybe it was a bad idea to come here."

I didn't know who the brunette was, but if Avery didn't want to see her it was fine with me. I wanted a nice, uneventful night out with my wife, and Lucky's was quickly losing its appeal between the limited menu and the offended waitress.

"We can go," I told her. "I'll have you eating a Whataburger in twenty minutes. Or anywhere else you'd like, somewhere nicer."

"Too late," she said under her breath. "I'm sorry about this in advance."

I watched curiously as Avery summoned a smile to her

face just as the brunette approached our table. "Hi, Elise."

"Avery, Fox! Imagine running in to you two! You know I never eat here, but Daddy is working late at the car lot and just *had* to have one of Lucky's greasy ol' burgers. He much prefers them over the ones at Kent's Kitchen, sorry Avery."

"Not offended," Avery muttered. "Fox, this is Elise... Chase's sister."

The resemblance was there, and now that I got a good look at her, I knew I'd seen this girl somewhere before, probably in a picture shown to me by Chase. My worlds were colliding in the strangest way, merging the past I remembered with a present I was learning more about every day.

Elise turned to me, fake concern brimming in her eyes. "Oh Fox, I can't tell you how glad I am that you're okay. We were all so worried."

"Thank you. But I'm fine."

"But you— you don't remember anything still, right? How is that going to work, with all of the family issues you have coming up? And grad school, Avery? What did you decide to do about that?"

I swear I saw a look of satisfaction in Elise's eyes when Avery's face paled slightly. *Family issues? Grad school?* What was Elise talking about?

"We're handling it, Elise. Thank you for your concern." Avery's voice was tight, clipped.

"My mother heard that you'd decided not to go though! Is that true? You aren't going to grad school? Is it because of Fox's amnesia?"

The fact that Avery had never mentioned grad school to me didn't bode well in this situation. *What else wasn't she telling me?* I tried to search her face for a clue as to what she was thinking, but her emotions were carefully closed off when she answered Elise.

"Nothing has been decided yet," she said icily. "Not that it's any of your business anyway."

"What do you think, Fox?" Elise asked me, ignoring

Avery's not-so-subtle remark.

I looked right at Avery before I spoke, hoping that aside from the fact that she knew I was in the dark about all of this, she'd realize I was speaking the truth. "I'll support Avery in whatever she decides to do."

"That is so sweet. That is just *so* sweet. You are so lucky, Avery, to have a man who is willing to deal with, um, all the *things* you bring to the table." She paused for a beat, and I could almost feel her going in for the kill. "Especially now that J.D. is back in the picture."

There it was. Avery's face went from pale to immediately flushed, and Elise watched her with the satisfaction of a cat who'd finally caught its mouse. The only J.D. I knew of was Annabelle's biological father, a fact that Lucas had divulged to me in a conversation shortly after he confirmed that Annabelle was not Chase's child, and Avery mentioned it again as well during that lunch full of questions. But now Elise was insinuating that J.D. was somehow back in Avery's life? How? And why?

Avery took a deep breath. "That's reaching a bit, Elise. J.D. is not 'back in the picture,' but yes, there's been some contact."

"Oh, really?" Elise blinked innocently. "That's not what I heard. I heard that J.D. got himself a lawyer to gear up for a big ol' custody battle now that Fox wants to adopt Annabelle."

My head spun with all of this new information, especially the part about me wanting to adopt Annabelle. Considering that I'd just wrapped my mind around having a child in my life, I hadn't thought of something like adoption yet, but it made complete sense to me that the non-amnesiac Fox would take steps to make that happen. Regular Fox would want to make it official, to take care of Annabelle and make sure she knew that she could count on me.

I looked at Avery, who was staring at me, waiting for my reaction. I gave her what I hoped was a small, reassuring smile. If all of this was true, then there was a reason that Avery hadn't told me yet. Probably something to do with the fact that until very recently, I wasn't my usual steady self. No wonder she'd been so stressed. I hated that she had been dealing with all of this alone.

"Elise, I'm pretty sure you've done what you came over here to do, and that's try to stir up a bunch of shit between me and Avery that, like she said, is really none of your business." My words were blunt, intentional.

Elise smirked, unaffected by my tone. "Sorry. Just relaying what everyone's been saying."

Avery was silent, so I continued. "Somehow I doubt that. This town might be small, but it seems like everyone kind of sticks up for each other."

She shrugged, starting to look slightly uncertain.

"Even Janie, who's pissed at me right now — at least she came out and said it. This instigating crap you just pulled was below the belt. We're going to go," I said, standing and tossing a few bills on the table, even though we never even got our drinks. "Let me cover your dad's burger. He's working late, and I get to eat with my beautiful wife. It's the least I can do."

I stepped around Elise and offered my hand to Avery, helping her out of the booth. "Let's get out of here."

"Okay."

The amount of love in her eyes justified my brusqueness toward Elise. Avery stuck up for me even when I didn't deserve it, and I would always stick up for her.

Janie approached the table, and as we walked away, she whispered to Elise. "That's the most I've ever heard him talk. He has a point, you know. You were being totally bitchy."

"Shut *up*, Janie," Elise hissed.

"You were! And he didn't remember me either, but I'm not even mad about it anymore."

CHAPTER THIRTEEN

I waited until we were sitting in the truck before I turned to Avery. "I need you to tell me what's going on."

She glanced up at me quickly and then looked away. "I know."

Catching the embarrassment in her expression was all it took for me to reach over and haul her into my lap. My shoulder was mostly healed, but I felt a small twinge that I ignored before gently cupping her face in my hands.

"Avery, I'm not mad. I just want to understand, okay? I want to help. You can't hold back on me if we're going to move forward."

She nodded, her clear blue eyes fixed on my face. I wrapped my arms around her, holding her to my chest as I breathed her in. Slowly, I felt her body relax against mine, our heartbeats synching and slowing together.

"I didn't want to make things more complicated than they already were," she admitted into my shirt.

I smoothed my hand down her back, suddenly grateful that the truck's windows were tinted and that twilight was fast approaching. I couldn't care less if people saw us sitting like this, but I didn't want Avery to be uncomfortable. And I needed to hold her right now, to reassure her that whatever Elise said or insinuated wasn't important, only where we went from here.

"Whatever matters to you matters to me."

"Okay." She took a deep breath and slid off of my lap, back into her seat. "But can we eat? Because I'm hungry."

I watched her buckle her seatbelt as I started the truck. "Twenty minutes to Whataburger. We can talk on the way."

Avery directed me down the streets and when we finally pulled onto the highway, I rested a hand on her bare thigh and squeezed. She put both of her small hands over mine and leaned her head back against the seat, seeming much more comfortable than she had at Lucky's. I glanced over at her for a split second and she smiled at me.

"I love you," I told her. This wasn't when I'd planned on saying it for the first time — the first time that I would remember — but it would have to do. Avery needed to know, and I wanted to say it. I'd already waited too long.

I looked over at her again and saw her eyes were shining in the low light, her previously hesitant smile dialed up about a thousand notches. "I love you, too."

She squeezed my fingers again. "And I'm so sorry about earlier, about Elise. She's always been that way, insincere and catty. I can't believe she went out of her way to say all those things, though. That was a new low for her."

"I don't care about Elise. I care about you. Tell me about grad school." I really wanted to ask her about J.D., but I'd start with the more pleasant of the two issues.

I felt Avery tense up again under my hand, so I slowly rubbed circles onto her leg with my thumb, feeling that familiar stirring in my blood whenever I touched her. I didn't want her to be stressed anymore. She'd been through so much. We both had. I wanted to take a little of her burden, ease it if I could.

"I applied for grad school at NYU last year, for the

creative writing program at Tisch," she began. "It was the only application I sent in, and I was basing all of my plans on moving as soon as I got my acceptance. My degree is in English with an Advertising minor," she reminded me.

I nodded but kept silent, encouraging her to continue. New York would work for me. I could probably join a FDNY fire house, or finally take Lucas up on his offer to join the security firm. Or maybe even something else… something I knew I wanted but hadn't given myself the luxury of considering until now.

"But then," Avery paused. "Then you came into my life and New York sort of felt like running away. I knew I wanted grad school, but I wanted you too, and I wasn't sure how to make the two coincide."

"Avery, I would never ask you to choose between me and your education." I couldn't imagine myself giving her an ultimatum. *Had I?* She'd obviously been fine with me going back for another season in the Hotshots, wouldn't I extend her the same flexibility, the same encouragement?

"Of course you wouldn't." She slid a little closer to me. "I wish you remembered this," she said wistfully. "You don't, right? Not at all?"

I shook my head slowly. I wished I did too. "I'm sorry."

"Well, it's awkward, but I guess I'll have to tell you for like, the thousandth time how amazing you are." I heard the grin in her voice.

"What?"

"You sent in my other applications, the ones I'd finished but couldn't afford to submit. University of Washington, Berkeley, and UCLA. You said you wanted me to have options, and wherever I ended up, we'd go together."

A feeling of incredible relief washed over me when she confirmed that I'd supported her. My instinct was right. "And you got in?"

"Yes," she admitted shyly. "Everywhere except Berkeley."

"That's amazing, Avery. I've probably said it before, but

I'm really proud of you. I know you've worked hard and you deserve it." She deserved the world and more, including a husband who had all parts of his memory fully functional, but I was working on it.

"It was kind of surreal," she said.

She wasn't volunteering the information, so I asked for it. "Where did you decide to accept?" I needed to know where we were moving.

"NYU."

"So we're New York-bound, then? When do we leave?" I wasn't entirely sure about grad school timelines.

"We aren't." Again, a short, clipped answer, but this one I wasn't expecting.

"What do you mean? Don't classes start soon?"

"I— I deferred. For a year." She gestured for me to exit at the next offramp. "I thought it was best."

My head spun as I pulled off the freeway onto a commercial street. I turned into the first driveway I saw, which happened to be the overcrowded parking lot for the burger place, and killed the engine.

"You deferred," I repeated, staring out the front windshield at the line of cars in the drive-thru. "Why?" I already knew. She'd put her life, her plans, on hold because of me.

"Fox, look at me," she said, twisting in her seat.

I turned, forcing myself to bring my eyes to hers even if I wasn't going to like what I saw there.

"None of this is your fault. You know you didn't cause the accident. The police report even said that you probably minimized the injuries with the way you cut the bike across the lanes at the last minute to avoid the oil tanker."

I'd read that report, pored over what it said and what it left out. My split-second decision to cut the lanes might've kept the tanker from exploding and killing everyone, she could be right about that. It was a calculated risk that had paid off until I couldn't control the skid, but it could've been a lot worse.

"I wish you'd told me before you decided."

"You'd only been conscious a few days. We didn't know what your recovery looked like, and that was more important than anything. I don't regret it," she insisted. "Grad school will always be there, and a year will go by in a flash."

"You've sacrificed too much for me."

"Impossible," she said, scooting closer. "You've given me and Annabelle everything."

But I hadn't, not by a long shot. I'd make this up to her. I'd start with the new bathroom, and build her a second story too, or a movie theatre with surround sound, a book of poetry written by hand, a million edited clips that showed her exactly how I felt, or a garden with a pool in the backyard and a fucking waterslide, whatever she wanted. It wouldn't be on the same level as grad school, but when that year was up I'd make sure we were on the first plane to New York City.

"What about your parents?" I asked suddenly. "Were they upset?"

Avery laughed. "Upset that their only child, grandchild, and favorite line cook slash son-in-law weren't moving two thousand miles away to live in the biggest, busiest city in the world where people actually lock their doors and nobody knows their neighbors? No, they weren't upset. They're happy to have us here for another year."

"What will you do?"

She looked up at me, confused. "What do you mean? I'll go back to work at the diner — I've been gone for over a month, but that's one of the perks of your folks being the owners. That, and I have an extra apron. Don't tell anyone."

I laughed once. "I'll take it to the grave."

"You can come back and cook too, if you want," Avery said hesitantly. "My dad would love it."

"And you?" I asked her.

"You know I'd love it too." She pinched me on the arm. "Although Joy doesn't always like us to work together because...

well. Anyway."

I raised an eyebrow at her. "What?"

"She caught us making out a few times."

"That doesn't surprise me at all." I felt a grin break out over my face. "Not at all." I was a walking hard-on when it came to this girl.

Avery's suggestion that I come back to work at the diner, combined with the emerging thoughts I had about what I wanted to do with myself — in Brancher, New York, or elsewhere — really started my mind working. For the first time in as long as I could remember, I wasn't tied to a career. Who was I if I wasn't a firefighter, a paramedic? I wasn't sure.

I put my arm around Avery, pulling her against me and kissing the top of her head. Tonight wasn't about me and my internal conflict. The mood had lifted, but there was still a large elephant lurking around the cab in the form of Annabelle's biological father. I wasn't going to bring it up. She would tell me when she was ready.

Avery's stomach growled and made her laugh. We'd been sitting in the parking lot long enough for the drive-thru line to decrease substantially, and I started the engine again and pulled into the queue.

"I'm going to check in with Heather really quick," she said, retrieving her phone from her purse. "We should be back in time to put Annabelle to bed."

I slowly inched the truck through the line, scanning the neon menu as we waited. From the snippets of their one-sided conversation, it seemed like everything was fine at home, and Avery ended the call just as we approached the loudspeaker.

Minutes later, we were both digging into our burgers and shakes.

"Is this extra good because I was starving? Or because I've eaten too many Lucky's burgers in my lifetime?" Avery asked.

"Not sure," I said around a mouthful of fries. "Probably both."

Three bites later, I'd downed my second burger and was turning back onto the freeway. Avery shook her head.

"The way you eat like that and still look," she gestured with her hand "like *that* is really annoying."

"Sorry." I reached over for handful of her fries, keeping my eyes on the road. "I'm a growing boy."

"If I ran forty miles a week and had my own bench press I could eat multiple burgers too," Avery said wistfully.

"You," I stole another fry, "look amazing no matter what. Next time I'm buying you two burgers. And I have a bench press?" I'd been meaning to ask her if there was a gym nearby, something more than the playground equipment, but maybe this solved my problem.

"For that sweet compliment, and the promise of an extra burger, you can have them all," she said, putting the cardboard sleeve of fries in my free hand. "And yes, you have a bench press. It's in your old apartment, upstairs at the diner. It's one of those machine things that takes up a lot of room — you bought it after you moved in but we couldn't keep it at the house."

The remodeling plan I had for Avery's tiny cottage was getting more complicated with every revelation. We had the lot size to make the property much more substantial than it currently was. But was it worth it, if we were going to New York in a year? For resale or rental purposes, probably not. I wasn't sure what the market was like in Brancher, but it wasn't exactly a metropolis. But for comfort value, anything that made Avery smile was worth it to me.

I polished off her fries in a matter of seconds, and we lapsed into an easy silence, underscored by a block of nineties Pearl Jam playing low on the truck's stereo. I didn't think Avery was going to bring up J.D. now that our more serious conversation had abated, but she surprised me by diving in right when we were about halfway home.

"I didn't know anything about the J.D. situation until a few weeks ago. Lucas told me in Seattle."

"What situation would that be?" I asked gently, reminding her that I was new to this topic.

"After we got married, you told me you'd like to adopt Annabelle officially, and I agreed, of course. You were going to look into it, find out the logistics and see about the paperwork."

I nodded and she continued. "Apparently, the easiest way was to get J.D. to relinquish his rights, so you tracked him down in Wyoming and he said yes. But then you got hurt and lost your memory, so Lucas postponed the meeting."

There was something more here, something that made it less cut and dry than Avery insinuated. "And then what?"

She sighed. "I don't know. Lucas didn't tell me all the details, aside from what I mentioned. But I think J.D. isn't being as cooperative as he was before, for whatever reason. Lucas told me he'd handle it for now, and that we'd talk to you about it soon. But then Elise opened her mouth and… I didn't want you to find out that way. I was so excited, so happy when you told me you wanted to adopt her, but now I'm afraid it's getting messy. And I don't like to be in the dark about this; I want to know what's going on."

She twisted her hands nervously in her lap until I reached over and stilled them with one of my own.

"Whatever is happening, we will handle it. I'll talk to Lucas, get it straightened out. And you'll know everything, I promise." Interesting. Things must be getting messy, as Avery put it, if Lucas was keeping details from her. "You are her mother and you make the final call on all of it. Non-negotiable."

Avery squeezed my hand. "Okay. I feel better now that we've gotten this all out into the open."

"Me too," I told her, but that was only half true. I wouldn't feel better until I spoke to Lucas and found out exactly what he was hiding.

Annabelle was in her pajamas when we got home, and I walked Heather to her car while Avery started the usual nighttime routine of teeth brushing and story time.

After Heather was safely on her way — "You know this is *Brancher*, right Fox? You're very sweet, but no one is going to attack me on the street in front of the house!" — I came back inside and leaned against the wall next to Annabelle's door, listening quietly for a moment while Avery read to her.

I couldn't stop thinking about J.D. and Lucas' evasiveness on the subject, and before I knew it I was backtracking down the hall, pulling my phone from my pocket and tapping Lucas' number on my speed dial. He answered on the second ring.

"Hey, little brother," he drawled. "How's the great state of Texas?"

"Tell me about J.D."

That should catch him off guard. Keeping me out of the loop on things a month ago was understandable, but everything had changed and now it was just fucking irritating. I couldn't wait to give him Heather's response to his seemingly innocent hello, either.

"Shit." Lucas blew out a breath. "Avery told you?"

"In a roundabout way, after she got ambushed by Chase's sister. What the hell, Lucas? Why haven't you mentioned the legal situation brewing between me and my wife's ex?"

"I didn't know how to bring it up, okay? I thought I was doing you a favor by handling it."

It was the truth, but I was still pissed. "I appreciate your effort, but the time to clue me in would've been before I had to hear it from the town rumor mill."

"Fair enough. So what do you know, and where can I fill in the blanks?"

"Avery told me about us contacting J.D. prior to the accident, and how afterward you postponed with him, but that apparently he wasn't as amicable as in the beginning. There's more to the story that you didn't tell her, and I want to know what the fuck it is."

Lucas sighed. "There's always more to the story."

"And?"

"And Avery doesn't know half of it. I'm going to tell you everything, then you get to decide what to tell her."

"All of it."

"You say that now…" Lucas trailed off. "He's a real slimy piece of shit, B."

"So, you found him, I called him up, and what? He said thank you very much and grabbed a pen? I don't believe it."

"That's because you're a realist, so you'd be right. The information I dug up on one James Dean Warren wasn't pretty. When Avery met him, he was a top seeded rodeo cowboy, but the mighty have fallen pretty far over the years. Multiple injuries, gambling debts, and a healthy appetite for booze and pain pills haven't helped."

"Great." I rubbed my forehead in agitation. No wonder Lucas hadn't shared all of this with Avery.

"He has a couple warrants out for other stuff, but no one ever tapped him for child support because Avery never filed, which kept him off the family court's radar entirely. So imagine his surprise when he found out about Annabelle — or his denial, I should say. He barely even remembered Avery's name."

This was getting better and better. "So it's true, he doesn't want his rights." That was a bright spot, at least. No-contest would be ideal here.

"He didn't know she existed, tried to deny she was his, and essentially backpedaled all over himself trying to deflect any blame, so no, I would say he's not ready to be anyone's daddy."

The idea of this guy trying to be Annabelle's father figure had my hackles up, but I took a deep breath and tried to focus on the big picture. "Then what?"

"Well, this is the part that was slightly confusing for to me," Lucas admitted. "You wanted to help him."

"I— what?"

"You told me that you were worried that it wasn't fair to completely remove J.D. from Annabelle's life as though he had never existed. What if someday she wanted to know her biological father? You didn't want to deny her that right, but at the same time, you didn't want J.D. to have any potentially detrimental ties to her. So you offered him a choice."

"What kind of choice?" I had a feeling I already knew.

"He was willing to sign over his rights to avoid any future responsibility to Annabelle. But you offered to help him clean up and get out of debt, on the condition that if Annabelle ever reached out to him, he'd respond to her — as long as he was sober."

"And how would I know if he'd keep up his end of the deal?" Unlikely, given what I'd just learned.

"You wouldn't, and you still don't, but you were willing to try, so that someday *if* Annabelle wanted to know him, she might have a chance."

I considered that for a second. Was it right for me to step in and take J.D. away from Annabelle before she was old enough to make a choice? My gut said she was better off without him, but my head told me that there would come a day when she would start asking questions, and I wanted to be prepared with answers.

"I don't think I like it, but I guess that's how it needs to be. For Annabelle," I paused. "So when did things start to get messy?"

"Pretty much immediately," Lucas said sardonically. "When I told J.D. we needed to postpone, while you were still in the coma, he was okay with it. He already had the plane ticket, and I told him I'd let him know when we could reschedule, that it would likely be within weeks, but—"

"But then I woke up and had no idea what was going on," I finished for him.

"Right. So I called him again, told him to put everything on hold for now, and he flipped."

"Did you tell him I was injured?"

"No, but he already knew. He still has friends in Texas, and you've experienced the power of small-town gossip. So he lost his shit, yelling about the money we owed him and how he was going to get a lawyer and take us to court. I didn't think much of it, but then today I checked the status on his plane ticket and saw that he rebooked his flight."

"He's coming here?" Suddenly the abstract of idea of J.D. being involved in Annabelle and Avery's life just got too real.

"Next week," Lucas admitted. "He maxed out the voucher I gave him, using it for a flight, a rental car, and a motel in San Angelo."

"San Angelo? That's like a hundred miles away."

"Rodeo buddies, I'm assuming. Better than him staying closer though, until we figure it out."

"And when were you planning on telling me, Lucas? Before or after it was possible for J.D. to just show up at my fucking door?" I paced the kitchen in annoyance.

"I booked a ticket to fly out this weekend. I was going to call you tomorrow, B. I promise. I'm in this with you. I'll help in whatever way I can."

"You'd better see if you can get on standby for an earlier flight. For multiple reasons. One, I need to know exactly what we're dealing with when it comes to the legalities of this, and we don't have much time. And two, I gave Heather your little message, and she's pissed."

Lucas exhaled loudly. "Shit."

I grinned into the phone. "See you soon."

I hung up and poured myself a glass of water, replaying the conversation with Lucas in my mind. J.D. was coming here in just a few days, which was actually good, if unexpected. I didn't want to draw this situation out — if he was willing to terminate his rights and needed my help to get clean and out of whatever hole he'd dug for himself, I'd do it. For Annabelle and for Avery. I'd give him the benefit of the doubt for now as a desperate man, but I'd be damned if I let his bad decisions touch the life I was trying to rebuild for myself and my girls.

The cool water felt good on my throat, and I pressed the glass against my forehead quickly before downing the rest of it. The night was still, the air thick and hot, and I mentally added the idea of central air conditioning to my ongoing construction list.

Avery had yet to exit Annabelle's room, which was unusual, so I kicked off my boots by the front door to walk more quietly down the hall and investigate. I paused at the door frame, smiling at the sight of Avery and Annabelle curled up together in Annabelle's twin bed, fast asleep.

"A big bed for a big girl," Avery kissed Annabelle on the forehead. "Do you like it?"

"I love it!" Annabelle clambered up onto the mattress and smiled at me. "I'm a big girl now, Fox!"

The memory hit me like a freight train, and I reached a hand to the wall to steady myself. A flash of me, my hair longer, my face relaxed, lying on the floor in this very room, my head pillowed on one of Annabelle's stuffed animals while Avery read us a story. I remembered that day.

Annabelle had been so excited about her new bed, she'd wanted us all to sleep in her room. And we had — me on the floor and Avery up next to her, until the middle of the night when I'd felt Avery curl into my side. By morning, all three of us had been on the floor, Annabelle snoring softly under my arm.

I scrambled to keep up with the images, trying to recall every detail, hoping there would be more where that came from. As quickly as it came, it was gone, but it didn't matter. It was a start. I crept over to the bed, debating whether to wake Avery, to bring her into our room and tell her what happened, but decided against it when I saw how peacefully she slept.

Tonight was supposed to be relaxing and it turned into a raging clusterfuck, but at least I felt rooted in the present. I'd even been given a tiny gift from the past, so overall I was going to call it a win. It was too hot for heavy blankets but I drew the sheet up further over Avery and Annabelle, covering them lightly. I pressed my lips to the top of Annabelle's blond head, and when I pulled away, Avery opened her eyes and looked at me.

"Hi," she whispered.

"Hey… I didn't mean to to wake you. Go back to sleep."

I ran my hand gently over her shoulder. Of course, I'd rather she was sleeping stretched out next to me and we were both naked, but I'd live. That day in the shower was only a taste of her but it had given me plenty of ideas.

She shook her head a tiny bit, her sleepy expression clearing. "No."

"No?"

Pushing the sheet back, she eased out from beside Annabelle and into my arms. "Take me to bed, Fox."

CHAPTER FOURTEEN

It took me a second to register Avery's whispered words, her wide eyes, the soft smile on her parted lips. But only a second, because then I had her in my arms, feeling the beating of her heart through my shirt — slightly accelerated — and the warmth of her body as I cradled her and carried her into our bedroom.

Once we were inside the door, I set her down gently on her feet, reluctant to let go but happy to have my hands free to touch her. She kept her head on my shoulder as my arms encircled her, my fingers lightly tracing a pattern on the small of her back.

"Avery."

There was so much I wanted to say, always so much to say, but I raised her chin with my fingers instead, looking deep into her eyes. Avery blinked as though she was somewhat disoriented, dark eyelashes against flushed cheeks. So much to say, but that would have to wait.

I brought my mouth to hers, gentle at first, the pressure just enough to make us both want more. She let me in, slowly, slowly, tasting her tongue as our intensity built but our movements stayed unhurried.

Tonight was ours, and I would show her that. This wasn't a fast fuck in the backseat of the truck or even that desperate, passionate afternoon in the shower, up against the wall with her body wrapped so tightly around mine that I could still feel her the next day. This was different, and we both knew it.

I broke our kiss briefly, skimming my lips up to her jaw and down her neck before I raised my head again. "Turn around."

Her bare feet swiveled slowly until her back was to me, and I saw goosebumps rise as I swept her hair to one side, leaving the sensitive nape of her neck exposed. The buttons I'd fastened earlier were quickly undone, and the warm night air caressed her skin when I gently tugged her dress down to pool on the floor. I wanted her naked, I needed her naked.

My hands went to her shoulders, kneading lightly, then my fingers pushed the straps of her bra down her arms before unsnapping it altogether. These were all just barriers, just things that kept me from her. I needed them gone.

I couldn't see her face, but I imagined it, the way she sometimes bit her lip, the way her eyes clouded when I touched her. I didn't want to turn her around, not yet, not when there was something so fucking hot about her not knowing where my hands would roam next. I slid my fingers over her torso, her ribs, listening to her breath come faster in anticipation.

I traced tiny circles onto Avery's skin, my calloused fingertips rough against her, watching in fascination as the goosebumps spread over her body again. She was so sensitive, my girl, so sensitive and responsive and ready for me. Slowly, I pulled her bra down until she was completely free, standing there in just her panties, but there was still too much between us. I released her for just a second so I could reach behind my back and pull my shirt over my head, desperate to feel her skin against mine.

No sooner had my shirt hit the floor than I had her in my arms again, unwilling to lose contact for more than the two seconds it took for me to get rid of anything that kept me from her. I held her firmly, and now it was my turn to have my breath catch as my palm skimmed up over her breasts, teasing her, my lips on her neck, her head falling back onto my shoulder.

I would take my time with her tonight, I wanted to, but when she reached up behind her and wrapped her arms around my neck to steady herself, arching her back and pressing into my touch, I almost lost it.

Avery's skin called to me, a siren's song I couldn't ignore. Her breathing grew more ragged as I wrapped an arm around her waist, teasing her full breasts with my other hand, my fingers flicking over her nipples. Between the heat of her body and the slow movement of my mouth as I alternated sucking and kissing the expanse of skin between her jaw and collarbone, I thought she would come apart in my arms right there. But not yet.

My hand at her waist moved down, down, slipping into her thin, lacy underwear. She bit back a cry, a small, soft sound escaping her lips, her fingers tightening around the back of my neck as I slowly explored her center.

I put my mouth to her ear. "I need to feel you." Now.

I had to let go again, had to get my fucking pants off and feel all of her against me, and the minute I did, I pulled her close again, lifting her body slightly to rub myself back and forth against her heat, never losing contact where she needed it most. I knew her this way, I'd never forgotten this.

Avery cried out as I rocked against her, and I wanted to taste the moan as it spilled from her lips. I turned her head gently, kissing her in time with my movements, supporting her weight as I worshipped her body with mine.

It wasn't enough, though, it would probably never be enough. I used one hand to strip the blankets back from our bed, and then we were there, her back to my chest still as I positioned myself and sank into her, so deep that she cried out again, so deep that I felt my eyes roll back in my head even as I steadied her hips against me. I pulled her back, and she pushed up to meet me over and over again, filling her as I whispered kisses along her spine and shoulder blades, her skin smooth, her wet heat so tight all around me.

I felt every stroke, every slide as we moved together, each one better than the last, building and building until my vision blurred and my muscles trembled with restraint. I'd never known what it was like to give someone all of myself like this, to carry their heartbeat, their pulse within my own, but I knew now. Avery would be a lifetime of firsts for me.

She tensed, her core gripping me as all of her nerve endings shattered and she went over the edge, pulling my arm across her chest, bringing me closer to push me even deeper inside her. I pressed in once more, my groan low in her ear as I let myself go along with her.

We lay like that for a while before she turned her head to kiss me, all sweet lips and sleepy, slow tongue. I breathed her in during the moments between, smoothing a hand down her body to where we were still joined together. I couldn't get enough, I never would, and she knew it. I felt myself getting hard again, and Avery clenched around me and started to move. I smiled against her mouth as I rocked my hips in time with hers. Wanting Avery was amazing, but her wanting me was even fucking better.

"I need more," she said.

Always. "Take whatever I have," I told her.

She shifted in my arms, sliding over me and resting her thigh on my hip so we were face to face, never stopping our slow, languid movement together that wasn't just sex — it was sealing a pact, promising something that my words could never say.

I moved with her, into her, all around her, my hands roaming her skin, dipping between her legs and over those gorgeous breasts and anywhere I could reach, gradually building again, unhurried, like we had all the time in the world, like she'd let me love her forever and even after that.

If I didn't get out of this bed I was going to reach for Avery again and, as much as I wanted to, at least one of us should get some sleep. In the heat of the moment I had enough clarity to know that this was different, that tonight would stay with me forever. Would Avery feel the same? Would she still feel my hands on her, still hear my voice in her ear, low and raspy as I whispered how much I loved her, how it felt when she touched me? I hoped so.

It was different, yes, more intense than anything I'd ever felt, but that didn't mean I wouldn't try to replicate it at every given opportunity. We could relive this all tomorrow, and the next night, and the one after that too, if I was lucky.

I slid out from under the sheets silently so I wouldn't wake her, intending to head to the living room to watch some reruns, but at the last second I grabbed my laptop and detoured into the kitchen.

My memory from earlier of the three of us in Annabelle's room still danced around the corners of my thoughts, and after I plugged in my laptop and set a pot of coffee to brew, I sat down to look through my archives.

It took me a few tries but I found what I needed, sandwiched between a teddy bear tea party and a recording of the truck's engine while I worked on a tuneup. I watched the unedited footage two times, then three, as ideas started to form in my head about what I wanted to do with it.

First, it needed a soundtrack, but that was easy enough. Annabelle had a stuffed giraffe with a music box inside that Avery played every night at bedtime, and after a few clicks through my options, I found a simple piano and violin version of the same lullaby that would work perfectly. With that set as the background, I started to work on molding the clip to fit my memory, so I could show Avery what would be impossible to fully explain to her.

After about a half hour of editing, I sat back with a satisfied grin to watch my final product. Sliding my headphones on, I pressed play.

A small bright spot appeared in the darkness, out of focus and far away, until the camera zoomed in so you could see that it was Annabelle's castle-shaped night light. The screen blurred again, and the simple piano lullaby swelled as the camera focused and panned over her little sleeping face, long eyelashes that were so like her mama's resting against her cheek, and a stuffed bunny wrapped tightly in her arms and tucked under her chin.

The camera went in for a close-up on the bunny's whiskered face, and when it zoomed out again, Annabelle and the bunny were asleep on the floor, curled up in a pile of blankets with me next to her and Avery sleeping on my other side. I held the camera directly over all of our heads as I looked from one of them to the other with a sleepy half grin on my face before the lullaby and the scene faded together.

That was it. That was my memory, just about as perfectly as I could replicate it. I hoped Avery would see that, see it through my eyes and realize just how glad I was to remember that night with her and Annabelle. Sure, it involved me sleeping on the floor in a pile of stuffed animals, but I had my girls with me, so that made it great.

I knew she'd remember this, Annabelle's first night in her big girl bed, which obviously hadn't gone as planned. But the real reason I'd made it was to show her that *I* remembered. Showing her was the best way to go about it; it was a way of bringing two parts of our past — that night and the concept of the videos — into the present. We needed that. We needed anything we could get that knit the two halves of our reality together.

I opened my email application and typed out a quick note to Avery with the video attached.

"I couldn't sleep… too happy. I remembered something last night, and I felt like the best way to tell you was to show you. It'll come back, Avery. I know it will. It's too important to be gone for good."

It was serious and probably too mushy, but fuck it. The video part was more important anyway. Dawn was breaking as I clicked 'send' and stuck a post-it on my tablet, sneaking back into our room to put it on the pillow next to Avery.

~

"Good morning, Mama! We're making breakfast!"

I turned at the sound of Annabelle's voice, my eyes finding Avery's immediately. She smiled at me, a knowing smile that recapped the fucking amazing way I'd felt deep inside her last night, mixed with bright-eyed happiness that let me know she'd watched the video.

"Good morning. You guys are up early!" She crossed the room to plant a kiss in Annabelle's curls.

"Good morning, Avery," I said, handing her a glass of orange juice.

She took it, and I let my fingers brush hers and linger. My lips twisted and brought my grin up a notch as I noted her reaction to my very intentional touch. I wanted to touch her all the time. It was a perk of marriage that I planned to fully exploit.

"Mama, sit down. We're having pancakes and eggs. I'm in charge of the pancakes."

I came to stand directly behind Annabelle, shaking my head and mouthing the word "no" lest Avery be concerned about the state of breakfast. She stifled a laugh.

"That's great, baby," Avery told her.

Annabelle hopped off the step stool and grabbed the bowl from the counter. "See? This is my special mix. It's going to be so yummy!"

The mix in question looked lumpy and suspiciously thick, but Avery nodded enthusiastically. "I can't wait."

"Okay chef, it's my turn. Only big people touch the stove, remember?" Annabelle nodded and held the mixing bowl out to me with both hands.

"Can I go watch cartoons?"

Avery kissed her again and agreed, and she scampered off,

clearly feeling as though her work here was done. I quickly cracked two eggs and whipped them into Annabelle's mix along with a little milk and butter, then started to ladle small circles onto the griddle pan.

After a few moments of silence, Avery spoke up. "I watched your clip."

I didn't look at her, but I felt an automatic smile spread over my face again. "And?"

She stood and crossed the kitchen to the stove. "You remembered us."

I flipped the pancakes before I turned to look at her. "Yes. Just a small flashback, but it was clear."

"Thank you for sharing it with me." I started to speak but she silenced me with a kiss. "Thank you for the video, for every effort you've made in the past couple weeks, and for your huge, huge heart."

When she said things like that to me, I never knew how to respond. Shouldn't I be the one thanking her for helping me find my way out of the dark, not once but twice? I set the spatula down and wrapped my arms around her waist, pulling her warm body close to me like it was a magnet. "Thank you for waiting."

I kissed her again and we stood like that for a second, caught up in each other, before the pancakes demanded my attention again.

"Everything smells delicious."

"I'm practicing. Need to get my job back."

"Your— job? You're coming back to The Kitchen?"

"If they'll have me."

Avery laughed and grabbed my face to press her lips against mine, heedless of the delicate timing with the pancakes. "I'll put in a good word for you."

"Hey now," I said, trying half-heartedly to break away. "My sous chef worked hard on this and she'll be upset if it gets ruined."

"Fine, fine."

She jumped up to sit on the counter, and I squeezed her

knee with a wink before I remembered the other thing I needed to discuss with her this morning.

"I talked to Lucas last night."

"Oh?" Her voice was cautious.

"He filled me in on the situation. You were right, things have gotten a little messy."

She searched my face quizzically. "Messy like how?"

"J.D. is a bit down on his luck these days, apparently. He's having a hard time paying his bills, finding work, et cetera. If you want me to go into detail I will, but overall he's not doing well. I offered to help him out."

"What?"

I turned the burner off and came to stand in front of her, taking both of her hands in mine. "Avery, I want to adopt Annabelle. There is no doubt in my mind about that."

"But you want her to have the chance to know her biological father someday, if she wants to."

I blinked. "Right. How did—?"

"You told me that once. It was important to you."

"It still is."

"Okay." Avery squeezed my hands. "I trust you, Fox. I want you to be Annabelle's daddy, and I know she does too."

"As far as I'm concerned, I already am," I said seriously.

That had clicked for me the minute Lucas confirmed our situation with J.D., sliding right into place like the rest of my feelings about my little family and, hopefully, my memories. It was getting easier and easier every day for me to tell Avery the truth about what I was thinking, which was inherently opposite of my usual interactions. I never lied, but I rarely volunteered information. *Not a talker*, my mother always said. That was Lucas.

"If you think it's important to help J.D., then that's what we should do. I don't think he needs to know Annabelle right now, but if she decides to contact him when she's older, I'd like it to be as pleasant as possible."

I nodded in agreement. "That's what I want too, Avery.

He'll either make the most of it or crash and burn again. It's up to him."

"When are you meeting him? Should I be there?"

"Lucas is coming in a few days, and we're expecting J.D. next week. I'm going to speak with the lawyer, get the details. I'll find out everything we need to know." And probably a few things we wish we didn't.

"I'll be happy when this is all settled."

"Me too," I told her. "Me too."

CHAPTER FIFTEEN

"Avery? Y'all home?" I heard a voice call from the back door.

"In here!" Avery answered as she put away the last of the breakfast dishes.

Annabelle ran out of the living room where we were playing Go Fish to greet Heather. "Auntie Heather! Is all of that for my birthday?"

I got up, heading into the kitchen to see if Heather needed any help unloading whatever she'd brought this time. If she kept delivering pastries regularly, I'd have to step up my weekly mileage. But when I saw the enormity of what Heather had created, I knew this wasn't an ordinary baking day.

Avery came in through the back door behind Heather, bringing in another load while Annabelle ran around excitedly, opening boxes to peer in at their contents. I glanced around uncertainly, wondering exactly what I'd just walked into.

There were ten pink bakery boxes of different types of cookies, a freshly iced, three-tiered strawberry cake on the counter, a styrofoam block dotted with two dozen cake pops on sticks, an aluminum platter overflowing with chocolate tarts, and three trays of scones in plastic storage containers. All of that would be fine — maybe — if more things weren't entering the kitchen in the arms of Avery and Heather.

I took another cake from Avery's hands — carrot, I think — and made room for it on the kitchen table while Heather set down four long boxes filled to the brim with fresh donuts. Avery ran back to snag the remaining grocery bags she'd set right outside the door, and when every dessert finally had a resting place, we all stared around the room for a second.

"Wow!" Annabelle cried.

"Um, Heather?" Avery ventured. "You know the party isn't for a few weeks, right?"

When Avery had mentioned she wanted to throw a fourth birthday party for Annabelle, with cake and pony rides at the ranch, I told her I'd help with whatever she needed. I'd be okay with giving Annabelle anything, including a life-sized pony cake if she had her heart set on it, but somehow I felt like everything spread out in our kitchen wasn't exactly what Avery had in mind.

"This is just my trial run, silly!" Heather laughed nervously, glancing at Avery as she fussed with the icing on the bigger of the two cakes. "For the actual day there will be much more. You said the theme was Candyland, right? Candyland means sweets!"

"Well, yes," Avery admitted. "But I thought I'd just use a little Kool-Aid in the ponies' hair and get a cupcake piñata."

I tried to hide my smirk, and for the first time since she'd blown in with a year's worth of baked goods, Heather looked over at me like she just noticed I was there. "Oh, hi, Fox."

"Hey," I said slowly, looking from her to Avery. Something was up with Heather, and from Avery's subtly pointed eye widening in my direction, I got the hint that maybe it was time for me and Annabelle to clear out of the kitchen.

"I'm just going to—" I gestured vaguely in the direction of the living room. "Bells, want to go finish our game?"

"And then later can we eat some of this?" Annabelle asked.

"Here," Avery said, shoving a box of cookies into my hands. "You guys can take these."

"We're having cookies before lunch?" Annabelle tugged on my arm excitedly.

"Looks like it," I told her, herding her out of the kitchen.

Once we were settled back in the living room, I realized I could still hear most of what Avery and Heather were saying. I didn't want to eavesdrop, but I figured it wasn't my fault if I accidentally overheard something that pertained to the situation with her and Lucas.

"Do you have any reds?" Annabelle asked. Her special deck of Go Fish cards was age-appropriate, which was good because yesterday when she was counting with Elmo I noticed she knew her numbers by heart but not necessarily by sight. We'd have to work on that.

I gave her two red cards and a cookie.

"Am I a cold bitch?" Heather asked from the kitchen.

I stopped my hand with my own cookie midway to my mouth.

"What?" Avery asked incredulously.

"Am I? Am I callous and bitchy?" Heather wanted to know.

"Why would you ask me that?" Avery said warily. "What happened?"

Heather sighed. "Nothing. I got into a fight with Lucas a few days ago."

I couldn't believe Lucas would say something like that to her. If so, it was really fucked up, and he and I probably needed to have a conversation about it.

"He said that to you?"

I guess Avery couldn't believe it either.

"Of course not."

Well, at least now I didn't have to kick his ass.

"Your turn, Fox!" Annabelle chirped at me.

I played my turn, one ear still tuned into the girls' voices.

"I don't understand," Avery was saying.

"Do you remember Brandon?"

This conversation was giving me whiplash.

"From high school? Cute, nice guy that you broke up with for no real reason? Sure."

"He's getting married." Something clattered into the sink.

"Married? Who told you that? And, um… why do you care?"

My thoughts exactly.

"Do you have any greens?" I asked Annabelle, and she shook her head.

"Go fish!"

"His mother saw my mother at the grocery store. He met a pre-law girl in college, they're getting married in a few months, and his mom wanted to know if I'd make the cake. Apparently it's hard to find a specialty baker in the bride's hometown, and his mom tried the vegan no-sugar cupcakes I'd made for Selma Arnold's baby shower and thought they were delightful." Heather laughed bitterly. "Delightful!"

"And…?"

"Fox! I asked you for blues!"

"Sorry, Annabelle." I handed her my only blue card. "Go again."

"Am I not receptive to love? Do I push people away when they try to get close to me?" Heather asked sadly.

"You mean that thing you warned me not to do with Fox?" Avery asked, and I stifled a laugh.

So Avery remembered what Heather had told her when we were first dating — she wasn't kidding about giving out relationship advice. Hell, she'd given me some just yesterday. But now they were discussing *her* relationship. What *had* Lucas said to her? Avery and I had been so wrapped up in everything between us that we hadn't noticed whatever was going on between Heather and Lucas until now.

"What bullshit excuse did I give you about Brandon? Too

tall? Somehow skipped the seemingly mandatory awkward phase? Always had that freshly showered smell?" Heather demanded.

"No. Something about how he couldn't eat your pastries."

"Oh." Heather said in a small voice. "And you didn't call me out for being a horribly superficial and insensitive person, not to mention a liar? You know I love a baking challenge."

"I know you well enough to be able to tell when you're grasping at straws, Heather. I figured it was part of your process," Avery said sympathetically. "Plus, I got the real story from him."

"So he told you about his early acceptance to Ole Miss, then? And how he asked me to come with him? And how I might or might not have freaked out and broken up with him because I had lots of feelings?"

"Pretty much."

Hmm. Heather wasn't that good at getting close to people, either. She and Lucas really had their work cut out for themselves, then.

"Fox? Can you hear me?" Annabelle waved her little hand in front of my face as she climbed into my lap. "Can I have another cookie?"

"I don't know," I said, tickling her ribs until she giggled. "Will it spoil your lunch?"

Annabelle scrunched up her face as she laughed. "Maybe!"

It was my turn to laugh. "At least you're honest," I said, handing her the biggest one from the box. I looked at our cards. "I think you won the game."

"It's because you weren't paying attention," she said seriously. "Mama says we should always pay attention and do our best."

"She's right. Want to play again?"

Annabelle considered for a second. "No. I'm going to go play with my dolls. Can I bring my cookie?"

"Sure, but bring this napkin, too," I said, snagging one off of the coffee table. I watched as she skipped down the hall to her room. I'd go check on her in a minute, maybe see if she wanted to head outside and help me wash the truck.

"I cried into a thousand gallons of ice cream for two weeks afterward, but I was too stubborn to admit I'd made a mistake. Turns out I'm terrible at taking my own advice," Heather was saying.

"Everyone has to be terrible at something," Avery told her. "I wish you would've told me all of this back then."

"I'm happy for him, really, despite the unfortunate timing in regards to my current personal life. He deserves someone who appreciates him and I'm glad he found her." She paused, and I heard her blowing her nose daintily. "I'm going to make them the best damn sugar-free cake in the whole state of Texas."

"Of course you will."

"And Lucas can take a hike."

"I'll be sure to tell him."

"On second thought, don't."

"I wasn't actually going to… but you know he'll be here in a few days, right?"

Heather laughed and sniffled at the same time. "I know. I'll figure it out. And go ahead, I know you've been dying to ask me the details."

"Well, of course."

"At the wedding… we really hit it off. After y'all left to go up to your room, we danced all night, talked, drank champagne. It was a great evening."

"It really was," Avery said wistfully.

Hearing Heather and Avery discuss our wedding day reminded me just how much I was missing. I'd watched the videos, the small moments I'd managed to capture, but it wasn't the same as remembering the whole day. I hoped that someday I would.

"Anyhow, we're both busy — my special event work is really taking off, and Lucas has been back and forth to London for that band, not to mention his work in Los Angeles and New York. We talked on the phone and on Skype… a lot. But until the hospital in Seattle, we'd only seen each other twice since the wedding."

This was news to me. Heather talked to Lucas all the time? And she'd seen him? When?

"When?"

Avery wanted to know too, obviously.

"He came out to Dallas when I did that big wedding on Valentine's Day."

"He did?"

That sneaky bastard. I wasn't sure if I wanted to shake his hand or punch him for making things even more complicated in my world.

"And also, remember that long weekend when I told you I was visiting my aunt in Austin? He flew me to Los Angeles, and we spent the whole time together."

"What about your aunt?"

"Oh, I went to see her first. But only for a day," Heather admitted.

Well, well, well. This was getting interesting. My brother had a secret girlfriend in the form of my wife's best friend. It suddenly occurred to me that non-amnesiac Fox might've known about this development, but then I decided that wasn't very likely. I probably would've told Avery immediately, and it was obvious that she had no idea.

"And then what?"

"A few weeks before Fox's accident, Lucas and I got into an argument because he gave me an ultimatum."

"Really?"

I agreed with Avery, that didn't sound like Lucas.

"Well, sort of. He said we either needed to move forward or put things on hold for a while. He was tired of the long distance — he wanted us to spend more time together."

"What did he suggest?"

"That I move to Los Angeles."

Avery's silence reflected exactly how I felt. I didn't expect that, but I had to hand it to Lucas for going after what he wanted.

"I really liked it there, Avery," Heather continued. "And seeing as I'm getting more into the specialty baking, Lucas thinks I could easily build up a clientele who would appreciate my style — he called it a mix of Crisco and consciousness."

Avery laughed. "Is Lucas your new agent?"

Heather laughed too, but more softly. "I really considered the move. You, Fox, and Annabelle were going to New York, and I'd be here by myself. We've been best friends since we were six, Avery. What was I going to do without you?"

"So, you'll be in LA and I'll be in New York?" Avery's voice was a mixture of sadness and disbelief.

Heather sniffled. "You know I don't take kindly to strong suggestion, and so when Lucas wouldn't shut up about me moving, about how great it would be, I told him to back off."

I could just imagine Heather telling Lucas to shut up already. It was good for him, this girl who kept him grounded. I'd pass Heather's advice on to him — try not to screw it up any more than you already have. I knew firsthand how fucking annoying Lucas could be when he didn't get his way.

"Back off like how?" Avery asked.

"Back off like break up," she admitted. "But then Fox was in the coma, and when I saw Lucas in Seattle I couldn't stick to it. I care about him so much, and I hated to see him hurting. It was an awful time for three of the most important people in my life."

"I appreciated your support more than you'll ever know. Annabelle and I are really lucky to have you. Fox, too. But where does that leave you and Lucas?"

"I don't know," Heather sighed. "We talked, but I still feel the same way. I loved being on the West Coast, but I'm just not sure it's for me. I don't want to move so far away from everyone I know."

Avery was silent for a few moments. "We have that place in Seattle," she said finally. "And we could visit, vacation. All of us together."

"It's a big step," Heather said. "I don't know if I'm ready."

"Don't count it out. Lucas cares about you a lot, it's obvious. Don't push him away."

"I know. I'm trying not to, but…"

"You're terrible at taking your own advice, I remember."

"Thanks for being my best friend and putting up with all my crap."

"Same, girl, same." Avery paused. "How long did it take you to make all of this stuff?"

"I might've had a small baking meltdown," Heather admitted.

I smiled to myself as I got up to go get Annabelle from her room. It was too nice outside to be cooped up in here. I was pretty sure I could count on Avery to fill me in on the important points of the rest of their conversation. The last thing I heard was Avery's laugh.

"You know I like to eat my feelings, Heather, but this is ridiculous."

CHAPTER SIXTEEN

I checked my GPS again to make sure I was heading in the right direction. The main streets of Brancher were starting to become familiar, but the outlying country roads were still a mystery.

Avery was working, Annabelle was in preschool, and I found myself with the morning off before Lucas flew in and I had to pick him up at the airport. A trip out to see Avery's parents and have a private conversation with them was long overdue. Once I was confident that the GPS was pointing me in the right direction, I sat back to enjoy the relatively short drive.

Texas was a big state with lots of different terrain, but around here it was mainly scrubby, horizontal pasture with miles of barbed wire fences along the roads to keep meandering cattle off the highway. There wasn't much around to provide shade, but here and there I saw a few sporadic oaks and juniper trees. Right now everything seemed dry, and I wondered vaguely about the local precipitation levels.

On the side of the road to my right I passed an old oak, its trunk split in half by what had to be a lightning strike and marred by fire, but the remaining branches surprisingly full of green leaves despite the overall charred appearance of the bark.

I tested the limits of the SUV, screaming down the highway in this rain. Get to the ranch and see her car, then you can turn around and she'll never know you came all this way on a nervous hunch, I told myself. But she wasn't answering her cell phone. The storm knocked out reception all over the county… and I had a bad feeling. My gut didn't like the odds.

In the darkness ahead I saw the tree, blazing fire as it raged along with the wind. A downed telephone pole blocked the road, its live power lines crackling in the sporadic rain. Fire plus electricity could equal a big problem.

My high beams reflected off the taillights of a stalled car, the back of a familiar figure visible halfway out of the rear door. I was out of the SUV practically before I'd put it in park, running toward them.

"Avery!" I called. "AVERY!"

When the flashback hit me I swerved over to the shoulder, letting the images come as I sat immobile in the driver's seat, trying to breathe deeply. I knew that tree, that busted, scarred old oak. This was the stretch of road where I'd found Avery and Annabelle caught in a storm, their car broken down and just feet away from fire.

I liked this memory a lot less than the one from last night, but I'd take it. After sitting there for another moment, I checked over my shoulder and pulled the truck back out onto the highway. Within a mile or so I was pulling into the ranch's long driveway, taking in the big, rambling house, the neatly tended paddock and barn, and flat pastures extending beyond.

When I got out of the truck a small pack of dogs ran up to greet me, wagging their tails and barking excitedly. I recognized the old black lab mix from a few photos on my laptop, and I reached down to rub his ears.

"Hey there, boss," I said. The dog's tail thumped the dirt next to my boots.

"Hey there yourself," a voice replied, and I jerked my head up in surprise to see Avery's dad leaning against the porch railing with a cup of coffee in his hand. He raised the mug in greeting.

"Everything all right?" he asked casually. "Didn't expect

you this morning."

"Sorry to bother you," I began, feeling awkward without the buffer of Avery.

"Nonsense, son. Come inside. I need a refill."

I followed him through the front door and back to the kitchen, taking in the comfortable furniture and decor filling the rooms as we passed by. I could see Avery growing up here, a spread that had been in her family for generations, even though I knew she and her parents had lived in a smaller place closer to town until about ten years ago. It felt like her — the way she'd decorated her own space reflected this place.

"Mr. Kent, I—"

"First off, you'll need to call me Jim. Nothing's changed." His back was to me as he pulled out another mug from the cabinet and filled them both with fresh coffee from the kettle. He turned, bringing the cups to the farm table that dominated the kitchen, and jerked his chin at an empty chair.

I sat. "Jim."

"What brings you out here, Fox?"

I looked him right in the eye. "I love your daughter, sir. And if that hasn't been incredibly apparent over the last few weeks, I apologize."

Jim sat back in his chair, studying me with an indescribable expression on his face. "Bullshit."

I'd been about to take a sip of my coffee, but I set the cup down uneasily. "Which part?"

He shook his head. "Letting a girl go for her own good, or trying to… I'd call that love, wouldn't you?"

Is that what I'd done? I tried to think back to the very beginning of my post-coma haze, the self isolation, the anger. I didn't want Avery or Annabelle anywhere near that, so I'd pushed them away. And when my brain fog cleared, when I'd managed to take my past and reconcile it, tried to finally put it away — I'd realized that I couldn't lose her, couldn't lose them. Loving Avery was a privilege that I finally felt I'd earned.

"I— yeah. Maybe."

"I'd also call it stupid, but you figured that out on your own."

I raised an eyebrow at him. "Fair enough."

"So, you're back in Brancher. What now?" Jim set his mug on the table.

"We have a year until Avery can go to grad school. I'm not happy she deferred, but it was her choice. I have a few ideas for some projects I'd like to do on the house, and then Avery mentioned me going back to work at The Kitchen." I wondered if he even wanted me there, or if that was just Avery's idea.

"But what are *your* plans? Yours?"

I opened my mouth and then closed it quickly. The truth was I'd been asking myself that question for the last few weeks, and I wasn't any closer to having an answer. I loved being a firefighter, but I felt like that was part of my past. And I knew I could work with Lucas in the security firm, but I wasn't sure that was for me either. There was only one other thing I'd ever considered, and I hadn't had time to think about it until recently.

"I don't know yet," I told him honestly.

He nodded. "You want to come back and cook for me, I'd be glad to have you. But I can't say it wouldn't be a shame for that to be your endgame."

A small flicker of confidence ignited in my chest. There was nothing wrong with Kent's Kitchen or being a cook, but that's not what he meant and I knew it.

"Thank you. It's only temporary. We'll be in New York next year."

Jim regarded me thoughtfully. "My Avery, she thinks this town defines her, but that's never been the case. You write your own definition, and the rest is just geography."

His words resonated with me. "I think Avery can be whatever she wants," I agreed. There was no doubt in my mind about that.

"Same goes for you, son." He tapped his own head. "A

roadblock don't matter none when you have four-wheel drive."

I debated telling him about the memory surges but instead just nodded. "Yeah. I'm working on it."

"That's all you can do."

"I appreciate you taking the time out of your morning for me. And for…" I trailed off before I said something too sentimental. "For the coffee."

Jim gave me a look that said he wasn't fooled, but silently drained his cup, setting it on the table with a clunk. "If that shoulder is healed up enough, I could use another body to unload some hay. Since you're here."

"Sure."

"Good. And Fox?" Jim called over his shoulder on his way out of the kitchen.

"Yes?"

"Glad you're back, son. Real glad." I heard the front door open and shut, and then I was alone in the house.

Jim and I were cut from the same cloth — too many words and we started to get uncomfortable. The little that he did say meant a lot because of that. I got up to follow him into the barn, the now-familiar flicker of warmth in my chest sparking up again at the idea that things were slowly going back to normal.

"You're late," Lucas said, languidly stirring his cocktail as he slumped on a stool at the airport bar.

I surveyed him skeptically. "Fifteen minutes. How are you drunk already?"

"I'm not *drunk*. But to answer your question, I achieved this level of intoxication by pre-gaming on the plane." He cracked a grin. "The flight attendant loved me."

"You're an idiot."

"An idiot with three mini bottles of vodka in his carry-on,"

Lucas insisted. "You smell like a cow."

"I helped Avery's dad out at the ranch for a minute. C'mon, let's get going," I said, picking up his bag. "Unless you want to hit on the bartender now to try and score more free booze."

"I'm offended that you would insinuate something like that," Lucas grumbled. "Like I'm just some man-whore. I have feelings. I want love, too."

"Very heartwarming. Try that line out on Heather. Let's go."

At the mention of Heather, Lucas downed his cocktail quickly and stood up, brushing his pants off before he grabbed his carry-on. I refrained from making a comment about his eager response in an effort to get us out of the airport before I got a parking ticket.

Once we were back on the highway heading toward Brancher, Lucas pulled a few files out of his carry-on and opened them on his lap.

"What are those?" I asked.

"One is everything I have on J.D.," he said, holding up the thicker of the two. "The other is paperwork from the lawyer. Did you set up the meeting with him?"

"Yes, it's first thing in the morning."

"Good. J.D. comes in on the afternoon flight. I want you to read all of this, familiarize yourself so you'll know what questions need answering."

I nodded, my eyes on the road. "Have you spoken with him? J.D.?"

"Yeah," Lucas chuckled. "He was slightly unnerved by the fact that I knew his itinerary, but then I reminded him that I'd paid for his ticket. He's getting a little weird, B. I think he was hoping to use the element of surprise on us when he got to Texas."

"After this week, we'll have his signature and he'll have his money and his admission date for rehab. I'm not going to worry about him again unless and until Annabelle asks."

"I hope it goes that smoothly," Lucas said doubtfully.

"It probably won't," I agreed. "I'm conditioning myself to be optimistic, though, for Avery. Do me a favor and try it."

I pulled into a parking space in front of the diner, and Lucas glanced in the visor's mirror before I shut the engine off.

"Heather won't be here this early. She has deliveries today. But you look beautiful."

"Eat me."

"Nasty talk for such a pretty boy."

We got out of the truck and Lucas all but shoved me through the front door of the diner. I was just about to retaliate with an elbow to his ribs when I caught sight of Joy coming around the counter to meet us.

"Now, now," she drawled. "You boys behave. Y'all better not break anything or you'll be washing dishes."

"Yes, ma'am," Lucas said.

I kissed Joy on the cheek. Since I'd been back she'd visited us twice, once to catch Avery up on all the diner happenings and another to shoo us out of the house for a couple hours while she and Annabelle planted flowers in the window boxes on the front porch. I liked her spunky attitude, occasionally foul mouth, and the way she saw through everyone's bullshit. She and Savannah Miller would probably be great friends if they lived closer to each other.

"Don't try to butter me up, Fox." Joy's voice was no-nonsense but her eyes glinted as she spoke. "I'm not putting you and Avery on more than three shifts a week together."

I nodded, a small smile on my face. "I know."

"Good." Satisfied, she pointed to the booth closest to the kitchen. "Sit. I'll get y'all some pie."

Lucas and I obediently sat, and I looked around for Avery, catching a glimpse of her in the kitchen. When she saw me, a smile lit up her face and I thought for the thousandth time how glad I was that I pulled my head out of my ass before I lost her.

She came out of the swinging door immediately, and despite Joy's orders I stood up to greet her. I kissed her briefly, my hands at her waist, wanting more but not willing to put on a show for the rest of the diner.

"Hi."

"Hey," she breathed. "I'm glad you're here."

Lucas cleared his throat, and she looked over at him and laughed. "I'm glad you're here too, Lucas."

"Please don't kiss him," I said.

"I think there's someone else Lucas would much rather kiss," Avery remarked innocently. Too innocently. We both looked over at Lucas, enjoying the undiluted discomfort on his face.

"Can we change the subject, please?" he pleaded.

I sat back down in the booth and slid over to make room for Avery.

"This is a small town, Luke. We don't have much else to talk about. I got you a copy of the town Gazette from Sunday, there's a full page on it in there."

Lucas looked horrified before he realized I was kidding, and then he just looked like he wanted to murder me.

Avery tried to hold back her laughter and failed miserably. "I think this is the only time I've ever seen you really uncomfortable," she told him. "It's kind of endearing."

"So glad that my private life can be a source of amusement for you two," he remarked dryly, kicking me under the table when I snickered.

She shrugged. "It's not private when it involves my best friend, sorry."

Lucas sighed. "Point taken. Any idea where she is, by the way? I tried to call before I left LAX, and again when I landed, but she's not answering."

"I'm sure she'll turn up soon," Avery reassured him.

My attention was temporarily taken by a couple ranchers sitting at the booth in front of us, animatedly talking to Joy while she shook her head.

"That is terrible," I heard her say. "And there are no other options?"

"No," the older of the two men said. "Everyone who can

go is already out looking."

Joy clucked her tongue. "Those poor boys, all alone. Their parents must be besides themselves."

Avery excused herself to go check on a table, and I held up a finger to Lucas when he started to speak, still trying to hear the conversation between Joy and the ranchers. It was rude to eavesdrop, but a strange prickling on the back of my neck wouldn't let me ignore it.

"It's wilderness out there for sure. If they ain't found soon it won't be good."

Lucas heard them now too, and he looked to me, waiting for my reaction.

I leaned out of the booth slightly to get their attention. "I'm sorry for interrupting, but what are you talking about?"

"Lost track of a couple young kids from around here, about forty-eight hours ago," the older man replied. "Boys drove out early in the morning for a day hike over at Big Bend. The parents were away and there was a miscommunication with the grandparents, so no one realized how long they'd been gone until yesterday."

"They've been out overnight?" My blood felt like it was moving slowly, sluggishly through my veins.

The temperatures in Big Bend could drop quickly in the evening after the sun went down. I remembered that from the weeks I'd spent there during my Hotshot training. Unprepared hikers, especially young kids, could run into numerous problems when trying to start a fire to keep warm. And that was just the tip of it. There were parts of that park that were definitely considered cougar country.

"Two nights at least." The rancher shook his head. "Got local search parties out now, but the counties were overwhelmed by the flash floods from the last storm and the soonest they can get the main SARs out is tomorrow."

"Their ages? The hikers?" Somehow, I already knew the answer.

"Two brothers. Fourteen and sixteen."

I exchanged a glance with Lucas. He took in my expression and shook his head. "I don't know if this is a good idea, Beckett. Honestly. You're still recovering."

"I'm fine." My body was healed, and my head was almost there.

"You could wait for the SARs, join a team," he protested.

"Another night out there might be their last, B. You know it."

Lucas gave me a hard look, but my gaze remained even, steady.

"I know there's no talking you out of this, so tell me what you need. I'll help you however I can." He pulled out his phone.

"Get the necessary information, tap in, and find out where their cell phones pinged last." Before I even finished speaking, he was scrolling and typing furiously.

"On it," he said.

"Can you find me a pilot?" I asked the rancher. "Preferably someone a little crazy."

"Henry," Avery blurted. She'd come up beside the booth to hear the last part of our conversation. I looked at her quizzically.

"Joy's Henry, her, um, man friend," she clarified.

I looked to Joy, and she nodded. "If you need him, I'll call him right away."

"I'm almost afraid to ask… But why would you want a crazy pilot?" the rancher asked.

"Because those are the ones who don't flinch when you tell them you're jumping out of their plane."

Avery's eyes grew wide, but to give Joy her credit, she just excused herself to go make her phone call. Lucas was still typing on his phone, probably doing something borderline illegal, but I didn't care. The GPS ping was the best chance for locating those kids.

"I'm going to need some phone numbers, or at least names," he said. "But I'm halfway there."

"Can you give me more information, or point me toward someone who can?" I asked the ranchers.

The older man nodded. "The family is all posted up at the ranger station, hoping that someone will have good news," he said. "You can call them there."

My brain was scrambling, trying to think of everything I needed before I could make my best attempt at locating the boys. Ideally I'd be working with another searcher or a team, but the only qualified person I knew was two hours away in Lubbock, which made him almost six hours away from Big Bend. That was too far.

If I was going to have half a chance at getting those kids out, I had to drop in before nightfall. They'd been gone too long already and with only enough supplies for a day hike and the injury potential… the sooner I found them, the better.

Joy hurried back to the booth. "Henry said to give him two hours. He'll meet you at the small airfield out past the north highway."

Avery hadn't said a word after she suggested Henry as a potential pilot. I stood, wrapping an arm around her waist, and felt a small amount of relief as she leaned into me.

"Can we talk?" I asked her. "Outside?"

She nodded, letting me draw her away from everyone.

I heard Lucas on the phone, likely calling the ranger station, and I knew that he'd take care of the GPS situation, giving me a little time with my wife before I had to pack up.

Avery held my hand as we walked out the back door of the diner, and once we were outside, I turned her in my arms.

"Tell me what you're thinking."

She took a deep breath. "I love you for selflessly wanting to help those kids. I wouldn't expect anything less. But I'm worried," she admitted.

"If you told me to stay, I would." And I would, no questions asked. I wanted to help, I felt that I needed to go, but Avery trumped it all.

"You know I'd never do that," Avery said seriously. "You

wouldn't go if you weren't sure. I trust your judgement more than anything. But I'm human, and I just got you back." Her voice trembled slightly.

"This is a routine rescue," I told her. "It's unusual because I'm not working with a team, but there's no fire. I'm just locating some lost hikers and helping them get out."

Avery rolled her eyes. "You're jumping out of a *plane*, Fox."

"It's the best way to get there without having to hike in and waste time. It's going to be fine," I said, bringing my hands up to hold her face. Those were famous last words, but I stood by them. I leaned in, my mouth on hers the best reassurance I could come up with.

CHAPTER SEVENTEEN

I wanted to keep kissing her, feeling her softness against me, the small sound she made when her breath caught, and the way her heart jackrabbited when I gently ran my fingers down the curve of her neck.

But I had less than two hours until I'd be in a plane headed to Big Bend, and there was still a lot to do, so I pulled her up for another kiss and then reluctantly released her. We went back to the booth where Lucas was still staring intently at the screen of his smartphone.

"Everything okay?" he asked, looking up briefly.

I looked to Avery, and she gave me just a small smile, but it reached all the way to her eyes now. How I got so lucky to have a girl always willing to bet on me, I'd never know. I squeezed her hand.

"Yeah."

"Cool. I talked to the ranger station, got the information from the parents. Cam and Dylan Owens, ages sixteen and fourteen respectively. I have recent pictures for reference, and I tapped into their phones' GPS. The pings aren't great, but they'll be better than nothing."

I frowned. "When was the last one?"

"About eighteen hours ago."

Eighteen hours might as well have been a week. Two scared boys could cover a lot of ground in that time, if they were both uninjured. Lucas held out his phone and I studied the screen. Two brown-haired, half-grown teenagers in fishing waders smiled out at me, one a little smaller than the other. They held a string of rainbow trout between them.

"They fish?" This could be a good thing. Fishing wasn't great in Big Bend's part of the Rio, but it was a potential food source at least.

"Pretty regularly, the parents said," Lucas confirmed.

I nodded. I'd take that as a positive sign. Now that this was set in motion, I needed to focus on the details — the most concerning of which was a parachute.

"Do I have any other stuff somewhere? A storage facility, maybe?" I asked Avery. If I knew myself at all, I wouldn't have moved out here with none of my gear.

"Upstairs," she said immediately. "You have an entire closet of things that wouldn't fit in the house, along with that bench press thing."

The universal gym. I'd forgotten all about it in the adoption preparations over the past few days. And a closet full of stuff? That sounded promising. "Can you show me?"

Avery looked to Joy. "Go on, darlin'. I got it handled here."

Lucas and I followed Avery out the back and up a wooden staircase to a small porch over the diner. She unlocked the front door, and I stepped inside my old apartment for the first time since I'd been back to Brancher.

She was right, the machine did take up a lot of room. I wanted to inspect it but that would have to wait for another time.

"Ring any bells?" Avery asked cheerfully. "You pretty much remodeled this entire place."

I turned in a circle, taking in the hardwood floors and

newer fixtures. It seemed like me, like choices I would make, and I immediately felt comfortable in the little flat. "No. But it's nice."

"It is," Avery agreed. "If you like huge gym machines as living room furniture."

Lucas reached out and grabbed one of the pull downs, testing its weight. "Convenient, really."

Avery laughed and slipped a key from her key ring, offering it to him. "I was going to suggest this anyway, but why don't you stay here instead of the motel? It's just sitting empty and it's closer, plus it has amenities." She gestured to the gym.

"Sounds good to me." He pocketed the key with a smile.

Avery pointed me in the direction of the bedroom. "The closet is in there."

The first thing I saw when I opened the sliding doors was a familiar box, one that I knew from when it used to sit in my closet in Seattle. Inside I found two parachute packs and two harnesses, which would need some inspection, but their discovery took a huge weight off of my mind.

There was also some Nomex gear — the heat resistant shirts and pants worn by wildland firefighters on the daily — a pair of my boots, and a Kevlar jump suit and helmet.

"This is your just-in-case stuff?" Lucas shook his head. "You're taking the boy scout thing to a new level here, B."

I ignored him and kept digging. Another waterproof tub held some basic camping equipment: a tent, small first aid kit, lantern, sleeping bag, canteens. Lucas pulled out a pair of handheld radios from a metal case, along with a GPS and a satellite phone.

"Wow," Avery said. "What else could you need?"

I surveyed the equipment spread out on the bedroom floor. "Knives, and probably a multi-tool. Flares and a decent flashlight. An airhorn, if I can find one. And bear mace."

"You're worried about bears?" Avery couldn't keep the alarm out of her voice.

I wanted to reassure her, but I also didn't want to lie, especially about something that could be an easy Google search.

"Not really. There aren't many in Big Bend."

"Mountain lions, though," Lucas said, and I shot him a glare.

It was true, cougars were my main concern when it came to the boys' physical safety, aside from a circumstantial broken arm or ankle. The big cats were predatory when they were hungry, they could drop down on you from a tree without a moment's warning, and they were largely nocturnal, which gave them an even bigger advantage.

"Where is the nearest camping store?" I asked Avery, changing the subject before she could think too much about Lucas' big mouth.

"Midland. I don't think you'll have time to get there and back," she said, checking her watch. "But the general store at the end of the block will have the tools and flashlights, and I'll call Heather to see if her dad has any bear mace or anything else that might be useful. He hunts every season with her uncle, so he probably has stuff like that lying around."

"I'll need to hit the grocery store too, fill out the first aid kit, get some non-perishables and water."

"Your pack is going to be really heavy," Avery commented.

The regular smoke jumper's gear usually totaled out at over one hundred pounds, so by comparison I was getting off light. I'd ditch the Kevlar and helmet after my jump if needed, and then I'd be down to my usual pack weight that I'd carried for years in the Hotshots — except no chainsaw, which also lightened my load.

"I'll get my laptop from downstairs and find a more detailed map of Big Bend," Lucas said. "I'm going with you, B. Not jumping," he amended when he saw the look on my face. "But you're going to need some ground support."

Lucas was right. I knew I could count on communication from the other searchers and the ranger station, but not having a team hindered me significantly when it came to scouting and covering ground.

"Take the truck," I told him. "Find a place to stay nearby.

Outside of the park will have better coverage, but you can tap into the radio network. I'll have the satellite phone also."

"I'm coming too," Avery announced.

I opened my mouth to protest, tell her it wasn't necessary.

"Save your breath, Fox. I'm coming." She stepped closer to me, wrapping her arms around my waist. "I'll help Lucas. You can't ask me to stay here and wait by the phone, not after… everything. Please don't ask me to do that."

Of course I couldn't ask her to do that. What was I thinking? Avery would back me up no matter what, support my plans even if they seemed crazy, as long as I didn't exclude her, shut her out. That was her deal breaker. I knew it now.

"I want you there. Please come."

She smiled at my unexpected words, at the way I gathered her close to me and tipped her chin up to look into her eyes. "If you insist."

"You guys hit the stores, and I'll figure out the logistics," Lucas said, interrupting our moment. "B, I'll call the lawyer, but we're going to have to call J.D. too. He's expecting a meeting the day after tomorrow, and even in the best case scenario, I don't see how we'll be ready."

Shit. I'd pushed J.D. to the back of my mind in the preparation to head to Big Bend. Lucas was right, even if we were back in enough time, we were skipping our meeting with the lawyer and wouldn't have our documents in order.

"You're right. We need to postpone."

I looked to Avery for confirmation, and she nodded.

"Or I can have the lawyer handle it all as your proxy," Lucas suggested. "When J.D. goes in for the signature, he can give him everything then and there — the check, the rehab paperwork. We don't actually need to see him."

I felt a small twinge of guilt at the idea of putting J.D. off again, for not dealing with him directly after all this, and tried to remember that he was only in this for the money and not the actual person involved, Annabelle. But that only solidified my decision —

it was about Annabelle, and I wasn't leaving it to anyone else to handle.

"No. I'm going to contact him myself."

Avery went to call Heather, Lucas left to go downstairs for his laptop, and I was left alone in the apartment as I packed, trying to decide the best way to approach J.D.

Lucas had handled everything with him since my amnesia, and that left me at a disadvantage because I had no idea what to expect when it came to J.D.'s usual personality or temperament. But I didn't have the luxury of time on my side to think too much, so I picked up my phone and dialed.

J.D. answered on the third ring, and I realized that he would recognize my number because we'd spoken before. "Well, well, well. The man himself."

"Hello, J.D. Nice to speak with you again." I wanted to keep this pleasant, especially as I had news I knew he wouldn't be happy about.

"Wish I could say the same, Fox, but I feel like I been jerked around by your cocky asshole of a brother long enough to dislike both of you now." J.D. coughed, and I held the phone away from my ear briefly.

"Sorry about that. There were circumstances extending beyond our control," I said evenly.

"I heard. Heard about your little accident, how you don't remember anything. Including Avery and that kid," he added snidely.

I bristled when he referred to Annabelle as "that kid" but ignored his remark.

"As it relates to you, I know plenty, and nothing has changed. Except the dates once again. I need more time. I'll cover the extra days at your motel."

"Are you kidding me, asswipe?" J.D. spluttered. "AGAIN? I've waited weeks for you to get your shit together and give me my money!"

The money you didn't earn and aren't actually entitled to for any reason, that you're likely to just piss away and not use for what I intended? That money? Now *he* was starting to make *me* angry.

"I understand your frustration," I said, my voice calmer than I felt. "Once again, beyond my control."

"I don't believe you! I think you rich boys are just fucking with me now, and I don't like it. I'm not gonna cooperate with shit unless you get me my money as soon as I get to Texas."

"You'll be relieved of your responsibility, don't worry." I hated referring to Annabelle like that, even in abstract, but I had to impersonalize it in order to keep my temper in check. "I'll hold up my end of the bargain, and you'll hold up yours."

"It better happen, Fox. I got things I gotta take care of. Don't make me come lookin' for you. I remember that little town. Should be pretty easy to ask a few questions, find out where to go, and we can have that face-to-face on my terms."

"Attempting to threaten me is no way to get what you're after," I said tersely. While part of me would love nothing more than to let J.D. throw the first punch, I didn't want him around Avery and Annabelle in his obviously volatile state.

"JUST GIVE ME MY MONEY!" He was yelling now, his breathing coming rapidly.

Well, that escalated quickly, I thought. There's no way I would've attempted to broach an agreement with J.D. if he'd been this aggressive when we first spoke. Either the hole he'd dug for himself had gotten substantially deeper after I promised him a little relief, or he was an incredible actor clearly missing his fucking calling.

"You'll have it as soon as possible — within in the week. I'll be in touch." I'd let the lawyer handle it from here, expedite everything while I was gone, I decided. J.D. was too much of a loose cannon to have around. The faster he left Texas, the better.

"I know where to find you, Fox! Don't forget that! I know where to find you and that girl—"

My finger flicked the *end* button before J.D. could finish his sentence. *Deep breath, deep breath,* I reminded myself. *Take a deep breath and put him out of your mind. It's getting handled.* I looked around the room for something I could hit, but felt the anger seep out of me quickly as I kept breathing evenly. The last thing I needed was a broken hand right before I went into Big Bend, and I needed to focus on my jump and finding those lost boys.

The door swung open and I spun around to see Avery come through, a few packs of crackers in her hands.

"I found these in the kitchen, you know, for the soup? I thought they'd be lightweight for you to take. Are you ready to go to the store? Heather's coming to meet us before you head to the airport. She found bear mace and some flares — her dad told her to take whatever you needed. I think she wants to see Lucas too." She paused, noting the look on my face. "What's wrong?"

I crossed the room to her, feeling the rest of my anger drain away, replacing itself with a nagging worry as I pulled her into my arms. "Nothing. Thank you for getting ahold of Heather."

Avery leaned back to look at me again. "I don't believe you."

Speak now or regret it later, when you're fifty miles into the wilderness. "I want you to bring Annabelle with you and Lucas."

She looked at me quizzically. "Why?"

"Because I don't trust J.D., and I don't want to worry about you two while I'm out in Big Bend. I'll feel better if you're both with Lucas." I'd promised her honesty and full disclosure, so here it was.

"You're worried about J.D.? What happened?"

"Nothing yet. And likely nothing ever. I'm being overly cautious, though, because I won't be around. You'll bring her?"

Avery nodded. "She'll love it. She'll think it's an adventure."

I leaned down, kissing her softly. "Good."

She brought her hands up to my face, pulling me to her and kissing me again, slowly, until I backed her up against the wall and hitched her up so her legs wrapped around my waist, letting my hands roam while she sucked my lower lip into her mouth. My body strained against hers, wanting to be closer.

"If only Henry gave us a little more time," she managed to whisper between kisses.

I calculated how long it could take to finish shopping and pack everyone up before I headed to the airport. "We've got ten minutes," I told her.

She ran her hands through my hair, grazing my scalp lightly with her nails. "I only need five."

I hunched over my tablet, focused intently on the map Lucas had synched just minutes ago.

"The local searchers started here, closest to where the boys entered the park," Lucas pointed. "They've worked about a twenty-five square mile area so far. What I don't understand is why they didn't follow the ping — it's all the way over here."

I looked to where he gestured. "Because it doesn't seem possible. There's no way they covered that ground in two days."

"I know, and the pings can be off depending on satellite positioning, but there were three different hits, all in that area, before they lost signal. It's too strong to ignore."

I stared at the map for a moment, processing everything Lucas just said. How did two kids get from—

"Wait. Wait a second. I need another map, a topographical." I tapped the screen quickly, searching. "Here. This is how. The river."

I thought of a million different scenarios, a fishing misstep, a fall down a mountainside, anything that would put them in that river with sections of whitewater and currents that would be hard for anyone to swim against. But the river was lower in areas now, so there were places of calm too. Places where brothers could help each other climb out of the water. Places to be found alive.

Lucas leaned in close. "Shit. The river. You're right. But what if they just lost a backpack and it floated down?"

"If they're closer to where they left their truck, the other search parties will find them. I'm going where no one's looked yet."

I hoisted my pack onto my shoulder. I'd strap in once I got into the plane. Henry waited just down the runway, checking his gauges and fuel level. Avery and Annabelle were sitting in the truck, packed and ready to head out to Big Bend as soon as I took off.

This last-minute strategy talk with Lucas was the final piece of the puzzle. I called Henry over to let him know the changes.

"Can you get me as close as possible to here?"

Avery was right about him, he didn't bat an eye when I told him my plans. I knew we'd met before, but I obviously didn't remember. Now I wished I had. Henry was as tough as nails and didn't hesitate a minute when I explained exactly why we were flying out over Big Bend. When we arrived at the airstrip he'd been a step ahead, already removing the plane's passenger door to allow me an easier exit.

Henry looked at the map closely. "If you're jumping, that's gonna be a shitty drop. You sure, kid?"

"Sure enough," I told him.

"We'll clear over this mountain and then go a little lower." He pointed to an area on the map. "Right there. You ain't got a spotter to test for wind, so we get one try."

I nodded. "I know."

"Let's go then. Burning daylight." Henry shook Lucas' hand, then waved to Avery and Annabelle as he walked back to the small plane.

"How's the hotel?" I asked Lucas. "Not too remote, right? Okay for Annabelle?"

"You have no faith in my choice of accommodations these

days. It's good, B. Really nice, actually. Don't worry about that. I'd feel like I was on a vacation if I wasn't tracking your ass through the wilderness twenty-four seven."

I smirked at him. "Fine. You have your handheld?"

"It's in the truck with the laptop. You have the GPS and the satellite phone?"

I patted my pack. "Here."

"Call in as soon as you drop down and get your bearings. I'll track you through the GPS with the interactive positioning system and we'll go from there."

"Good. Your security spy shit really comes in handy sometimes."

Lucas laughed, then turned serious. "And B—"

"I know. I'll be careful."

"I wasn't going to say that. I was going to say that I know you'll find them."

I didn't realize I needed that vote of confidence from my brother until he said it. "Thanks for being my backup, Luke."

"You jump out of the planes, I'll do the security spy shit," he said with a small grin. "Go say see you later to your girls so we can get on the road. Our drive is twice as long as your flight."

CHAPTER EIGHTEEN

We reached our cruising altitude quickly, and I watched Texas fly by though the cutout of the plane's missing door. The first half of our flight was over before I knew it, and then we were heading into Big Bend territory.

Henry wasn't a talker either, which was fine by me. My thoughts were consumed by the conversation I'd had with Avery just before takeoff.

"This is your last chance to ask me not to go," I told her, brushing her hair away from her face.

"The idea of you out there by yourself is unnerving," she said. "But the alternative is worse. I want you to find your redemption, Fox."

Her words threw me for a moment. "My what?"

Avery clasped my hand in both of hers. "You're the only person who thinks you didn't do enough that day in the forest. No one could've saved them, Fox. You know that, and yet you've never forgiven yourself. You'll find these boys and bring them home. I have no doubt about it. And if that is what will bring you some peace, I'm all for it."

I stared at her. "I'm not— that's not why..." I didn't know what to say.

Was she right? Avery knew the deepest regrets of my life. She'd been there when I woke up, frantic for Landry and that little girl we lost. She'd heard every guilty, gut-wrenching word I'd said over Landry's grave.

Avery kissed me softly. "For your head, and for your heart, Fox, you need to do this. Go find those kids. I know you won't come back until you do, and we'll be waiting for you."

"You all set?" Henry asked me through the headset.

I looked over at him before I responded.

"Yes."

Henry nodded. "Ten minutes."

I pulled out the satellite phone and dialed. "Lucas? Avery?"

"Yeah B, we're here. What's happening?" Lucas' voice crackled through the static.

"About ten minutes to jump," I said. "You ready?"

The wind noise from inside the plane made it incredibly hard to hear, but I wanted to make sure they were connected and ready to track.

"We're ready." Avery's voice was firm.

"Ten minutes," I repeated, then disconnected.

"Get your pack strapped, boy. Here we go."

It was immediately evident that I'd have to leave the parachute and Kevlar if I wanted to hike these acres, because I needed to drop weight if I was going to do any climbing. I'd hit hard on my jump, tucking and rolling like I'd done a hundred times, but Henry was right — there'd been no spotter, no decent place to touch down, and my body hated me for a few minutes right after I landed.

The static crackled as Lucas answered the call.

"I'm here."

"I see you on the screen, B. How was your landing?" Lucas asked.

"Not too bad, considering I haven't jumped in a while."

"Avery? Are you there?" I could just imagine her twisting her fingers together.

"Y— Yes, I'm here."

"I'm okay, I promise. Everything is fine. I love you."

"I love you, too."

"Lucas, I'm going to head east from here, to the river where we saw the first ping. I'll call again when I reach the water. Give me about two hours."

"We'll be here. I'll speak with the ranger station, fill you in when we talk again."

"Good. Two hours."

It was easy to move quickly through the ground where I knew the boys *wouldn't* be, and I reached the river faster than anticipated. Once I'd checked my GPS coordinates with that of the first ping, I stopped to scout around for a while, trying to find my next lead.

Landry was always the weather guy, but the guys on my Hotshot crew used to half-jokingly call me "the tracker" — I'd thought it was more of a cheap shot at the fact that I didn't like to talk much and usually preferred to observe. But then my skills were tested a few times during our search and rescue operations, and the nickname stuck. Maybe it was because I spent a good deal of time behind the lens, and with the advantage of instant replay I'd learned how to identify tendencies and characteristics. Or maybe I was just living up to my surname.

A flash of white against the dark, wet rocks caught my eye and I stepped into the river to investigate. It was fabric, torn and bloodied, like a T-shirt that someone had shredded and discarded. And wedged under another rock a few feet down, a knitted cap. Bingo.

I pulled the satellite phone out of my pack again to call Lucas and Avery.

"Fox, your positioning looks good. How are you, what's up?"

"I made good time. They were here at some point, which means we were right. Something had happened and they'd ended up in the river."

"How do you know?" Lucas asked.

"I found some things, a torn T-shirt — looks like they used part of it for temporary bandages."

"Bandages?" Avery repeated.

"There's some blood," I said. "Not much, but enough. Some of it might've washed away here on the river bank. It's dried up now but not that old."

"What's your plan?" Lucas asked.

"Call the ranger station, tell them my location. If the SARs are coming in tomorrow afternoon, this is the best lead we've got so far. I'll update every few hours. I'm going to move through the night."

A moving man was less of a target for mountain lions or any other predator in the wilderness. Plus, the boys were likely hunkered down somewhere for the night, which gave me the advantage in covering ground.

"Do you think they stayed close to the river?"

I paused for a moment, trying to merge all of my thoughts. "Yes. It would be the best way to reorient yourself if you were lost. But I don't think that's why. Maybe it was at first, but now I think there's more to it."

"They're injured."

"At least one. And the other is sticking by his brother."

This area wasn't as wooded as I'd grown used to, the terrain more rock and desert with pockets of trees, tall grass areas, and high jutting stone mountains creating lots of canyons and valleys. That meant places to hide, both for the boys and for anything that wanted to jump out at them.

The discovery of the bloody shirt was both good and bad, as far as I was concerned. On one hand, I knew I was on the right track. I'd known it before, I'd felt it as I hiked through the backcountry on my way to the river, but the shirt confirmed it.

On the other hand, it meant that at least one of the boys was injured, and there was no telling how badly. Fear was a motivator, it could bring you to move your legs and arms no matter how much your body tried to tell you to give up and lay down. Cam and Dylan Owens crawled out of that river, bloody and probably broken, but they hadn't stopped moving. Not there. Not yet.

"CAM! DYLAN!" I yelled every few minutes, sometimes blowing my airhorn as well. "CAM! CAN YOU HEAR ME? DYLAN!"

There were two different ways of searching — if you were trying to be covert, to find someone without letting them know they were being looked for, you were quiet. You moved quickly, silently, and left no trace that you'd ever been there. When you wanted to find them expediently, or make yourself easy to find, you were loud. You kicked rocks, you moved brush and trees and heaven and earth in hopes that they would hear you and alert you to their location.

I'd only done a minimal amount of the former but years and years of the latter. I hiked purposefully, using my GPS to stay as close to my original plan as possible and keep the river to my right. Twilight was setting in and I knew I'd be moving through the night, both to cover ground and to keep alert in case of a cougar or adventurous bear.

Every few minutes I paused my stride, listening for anything out of the ordinary. An injured, exhausted hiker might be too weak to yell loudly so stopping to listen was imperative.

I thought about Avery and Annabelle, at the hotel with Lucas. If I knew Avery at all, she was wringing her hands every time she thought no one would notice. I could hear the relief in her voice when I'd spoken with them right after my jump, and I was so glad that she understood me enough to know that I needed to be out here looking for the Owens brothers. I still wasn't sure if calling it my redemption was accurate, but it was something. A pull, a certainty. Maybe, if you wanted to be all flowery, a calling.

After I'd gone a couple miles, I stopped to call Avery and Lucas again, to see if they'd heard anything from the ranger station.

"Anything?" Lucas asked when he answered.

"Nothing since the shirt," I told him.

"You're coming up on the next ping, and then there's only one more after that, less than a mile away."

"I'm hugging the river. I think they're here somewhere."

"The rangers said that the SARs will be out tomorrow afternoon at the latest," Lucas said.

"They won't last that long, not without water. Hopefully they have some left, but they might've lost everything in the river. Did anyone decide to come from the other side?"

I was hoping that there was another search party available, one that could start past me so we could work toward each other, but at this point it didn't seem likely.

"We're working on it. They called a couple groups in, trying to redirect and mobilize down this way. Still, probably not until tomorrow. The county is tapped out with the flooding, they just don't have the manpower."

I understood that. Everyone was doing the best they could with what they had. That's why the Hotshots were called to go all over, because there was always a need.

"Where's Avery?"

"She took Annabelle on a little walk around the hotel grounds before bed. She'll be sorry she missed you."

Glancing at my watch, I calculated the time left until total darkness. There were three flashlights in my pack, but this terrain didn't lend itself well to night hikes. I'd have to head down to the river banks again if I wanted to keep moving.

"I'll call again in about four hours. Tell Avery I'm okay."

I took my time now that it was dark, stopping often, calling out and listening for any sound that was out of place in the wilderness. Sight wasn't on my side, so I had to rely on my other senses, the ones that told me to keep looking, and that gut instinct that the boys were out here somewhere.

In this part of the park, the valley was a little deeper and it was more wooded, with trees and tall grasses just yards off the riverbank. I turned to head down to where the water touched the rocky shore when I felt a prickle on the back of my neck. Turning around, I saw a gold flash in the trees, and then the glowing eyes of the big cat as they fixed themselves right on me.

I reached into my pack immediately, grabbing my big Mag-Lite and unsheathing the hunting knife I'd bought earlier today. Waving the flashlight over my head with one arm, I kept the knife close to my side with the other.

"Hey there, kitty," I said loudly, keeping eye contact with the mountain lion. I didn't move, just kept waving the flashlight as the cat continued to approach.

"Get on, now! GO!" I kicked a rock toward him, then another. The cougar stopped, his head low as he studied me. It wasn't until another well-placed kick sent a rock sailing right over his head that he turned his tail and ran away.

Shit. I slid my knife back into the sheath and clipped it at my hip for easy access but kept the flashlight in my hand. This wasn't my first mountain lion, but his boldness was a little unnerving. Typically when I encountered them in a wildfire situation, every living thing was running for its life and no animal was bothering with trying to attack anyone. This cougar was different.

The image of the torn, bloody shirt I'd found reappeared in my mind, and I dug through my pack again to find the bear mace, slipping it into my front pocket. Somehow, I didn't think this would be the last I saw of that cougar tonight.

Even though I'd watched him run away, I was unwilling to turn my back on where the mountain lion had disappeared, so I backed out of the small tree grove until I reached the water. The rock and sand shore stretched on past the low valley and I could see off in the distance, into what looked like a range of mid-size mountains, all cut through by the river.

I decided to take a zig-zag approach, walking along the riverbed and then hiking up into the hills to look out for a potential campfire. The night passed quickly — and twice more I saw the cougar, but at a distance, the only indication being a flash of gold-green eyes as I swiped the beam of my flashlight through the darkness. Every time I did, I headed back down to the riverbank where he wouldn't have the advantage over my head.

He was stalking me, waiting for a wrong move, but he'd be waiting awhile. I was too large for him to take down on his own, and I had a personal policy of never turning my back on anything that wanted to kill me.

The night ticked by and dawn approached, and I was up on the hill again, looking out for smoke or anything unusual as I called the boys. "CAM! DYLAN! Can you hear me?"

I waited a beat, listening intently in the slowly lifting darkness. That was when I heard it, faintly. An answering shout.

"Cam? Dylan?"

"HERE! WE'RE HERE!" I heard the shout again, so faint I thought maybe I imagined it. But it was definitely there.

"CAM? DYLAN? WHERE ARE YOU?"

"Down here!"

There was no easy way to get down the side of the boulder-studded mountain quickly, but I turned my boots sideways and half-jumped, half-slid until I reached the bottom of the valley. The river lapped at the shore just a few yards away, and I could see that there was plenty of rocky overhang nearby, both for shade and for protection.

"CAM? DYLAN?"

"Here!"

The voice was closer now, and as I ran through a patch of tall grass I heard it closer still. "Dylan! Cam!"

Footsteps pounded just ahead of me, and then a half-dressed, lanky boy crashed right into my chest. I grabbed him, holding him upright as he clung to me, babbling incoherently.

"Cam? My name is Fox. Are you okay?"

"Oh shit, oh man, thank you, we need help. My brother, he's hurt, he needs help, I can't—"

"Slow down, all right? Where's Dylan?" I gripped Cam's arms tightly, noting the cool temperature of his skin and the wild look in his eye. In the pre-dawn light I could barely make out his features, but I knew panic when I felt it. Cam was panicked.

"He's here, we're over here."

I followed him closely as he loped a few yards, tripping and scrambling over rocks and uneven terrain until we got to a sort of corner between the side of a mountain and the lee of a large stone. The mountain jutted over the top of the stone, creating a small, protected area.

"I put him here, but he's— he's still bleeding and he won't talk to me anymore and— "

Dylan Owens lay on a makeshift bed of a jacket and a balled-up undershirt, his face bruised and swollen, with dirty T-shirt bandages tied around his bare neck and shoulders. His skin was pale, and he was still. Too still.

I was on my knees in an instant, feeling around the blood-soaked fabric for a pulse on Dylan's neck. When I found it, thrumming faintly but steadily, I let out a relieved breath. "He's alive."

Cam sat down on the rocky ground, put his head in his hands, and started to cry. I let him be for a moment while I pulled what I needed out of my pack. Antiseptic, clean gauze, bandages, steri-strips — Dylan was bleeding and I had to stop it. I started to cut away the old, bloodied fabric, speaking calmly to Cam as I did so.

"What happened?"

Cam sucked in a breath, raising his head to look at me. "Mountain lion."

I nodded, not looking up from my work as I dressed Dylan's wounds. "When?"

"We— we stayed too long fishing at the river. It was getting dark, and I was afraid we'd get lost on the way back. So I told Dylan—" His voice broke, but he coughed and continued. "I told him that we should camp, hike out at dawn."

I waited, checking Dylan's pulse again as I worked my way through his lacerations. There were a few that were deep, consistent with markings from the big cat's teeth.

"But halfway through the night, we saw a cougar in the trees, and we got scared and tried to hike up the side to get out of the wooded area." Cam started to cry again, wiping at his face when he felt the tears.

"It's okay. Just breathe."

"He— he jumped on Dylan and knocked him down, and they rolled down the hill and into the river."

I could feel Cam's distress during the re-telling of their last couple days, his terrified voice hardly more than a whisper. I reached into my pack for a few more steri-strips and dug out a bottle of water and a granola bar, along with a clean T-shirt that I tossed his way.

"Here. Put this on, eat something. You must be starving."

Cam cracked the bottle of water open immediately, drinking half of it down in one gulp. "Thanks." He shrugged into the shirt, too big for him but better than nothing.

"What happened then?" I prompted him, spreading antiseptic cream over the more shallow of Dylan's scrapes. He shifted a bit and grimaced like he was in pain, but I took that as a good sign. At least he was semi-conscious, but his pulse wasn't as strong as I'd like, and I suspected hypothermia.

"I ran down after them, jumped into the water. The cougar let Dylan go, but he— he was crying and bleeding and I couldn't see because it was so dark, the current started to take us and I just tried to keep his head above water."

"How long did you drift?" I wanted to keep Cam talking, to lessen the chances of him going into shock, although he was probably already partway there.

I was fairly certain that Dylan's arm was broken, but I had no sling to stabilize it. Instead, I bound it to his chest with an elastic bandage, taking care around his other injuries. The poor kid really got the shit beat out of him between that lion and the river.

Cam shook his head. "I don't know. A long time. The river was white caps in a few places, and I lost all of our stuff because I was trying to hold on to Dylan. We were both wearing fishing life vests but Dylan's came off since it was all torn up."

"I found you because your cell phone pinged a few miles from here. There are lots of people looking for you, but not down this far."

"My phone was zipped into my jacket pocket. I still have it, but it won't turn on. I was hoping— if it dried out enough…" Cam's voice trailed off.

"How did you get out of the river?"

"There was a part up aways that got really shallow, and I dragged Dylan out. That's when I really saw all the blood. I tried to patch him up, get us somewhere safe to rest. He was so tired, he didn't want to walk and his ankle— I think his ankle is broken."

"I'll check it," I assured him.

"I tried to— I tried to get him—"

"You did great, Cam," I said gently. "You saved your brother's life."

Cam was still shaking, his entire body trembling from fatigue and fear. "But he's so— so cold, and he won't talk, and—" He paused and took a huge gulp of air. "Is he going to die? Is Dylan going to die?"

I looked him straight in the eye. "No, Cam. He's not going to die. We're not going to let him."

Cam nodded, wrapping both arms around himself tightly. "Okay. Okay, Fox. Tell me what you need me to do."

CHAPTER NINETEEN

Once Cam helped me build a stone-ringed fire and I'd wrapped two of my three emergency blankets around the boys, I walked down a few yards to try and call Lucas.

Cam was slowly eating soup from a can, a small amount of color returning to his face, and I felt a little better about Dylan's even breathing and the few sips of water I'd managed to get him to take. His condition was serious, but more serious than that was the challenge of how to get him out of here without injuring him further — or before infection and hypothermia really set in. The mountains presented a huge problem when it came to leveraging a helicopter, and I thought my only option would be to carry him out along the banks of the river in hopes that the terrain would flatten out and either a vehicle or a medevac could meet us.

The satellite phone registered two rings, then three, before Lucas answered. "Beckett? What happened?"

I glanced at my watch, noting that it was about five o'clock in the morning. I'd skipped the last call I was supposed to make.

"I found them, Lucas."

"Holy shit. I knew you would. Where? Are they hurt?"

"Cam is okay, a little shocky, but Dylan is hurt. A mountain lion took him down. That's how they fell into the river."

"Damn. How bad is it?"

"He's got some deep wounds and he's lost a lot of blood. Broken arm, maybe a broken ankle. Cam isn't sure if he passed out in the river or not, but I'm thinking potential concussion too, hypothermia. He's conscious now but he goes in and out. I've got him as stable as possible."

"Will he make it?" Lucas' voice was serious.

"Yeah, I think so, but he needs to get out of here. The question is, how? If you pull up my location on the topographical, you'll see that there's no way a helicopter is getting in here."

"I'm on it, B. I'll see what your options are."

I heard a rustling, and then Avery's voice in a whisper. "Lucas? What's going on?"

More rustling, then Avery again, her voice clear this time as she spoke directly into the phone. "Fox?"

"Hey, there she is," I said, keeping my voice light despite the heaviness of the night weighing on me. "I found the boys, and Lucas is going to figure out how to get us out of here."

"Are they okay? Are *you* okay?" Her voice cracked a tiny bit, but she recovered quickly.

"We will be. The younger one is hurt, but I'm going to do my best to bring him home as soon as possible."

I heard Lucas' voice in the background, and Avery said something quietly back to him.

"Lucas and I will figure out how to get you guys back here," she said firmly. "Don't worry."

The one thing I wasn't worried about was her, thanks to her and Annabelle's proximity to my brother and subsequent distance from Brancher and J.D. But if I had to make a list of other things I was currently concerned about, getting these kids out of here was pretty high on that list.

"Keep me posted. Can't wait to see you." *And wrap my arms around you for about a day and a half before I can consider letting go. Even then, it'll take someone on a fucking mission to pry us apart.* Being without Avery was not an option for me these days.

"The feeling is entirely mutual. Call us back in—" she mumbled something to Lucas "an hour and we'll have some answers. I love you, Fox. I knew you'd find Cam and Dylan. I knew it."

"I love you too, sweetheart. I'll see you soon."

I disconnected the call and walked back over to the fire, scanning the area briefly for anything out of place, including the cougar. I hadn't seen him in a while, but I was sure he was out there. Now that there were more people around, a fire, and a solid rock wall against our backs, I didn't think he'd try to come any closer, but I'd made a pile of perfect-sized throwing rocks, just in case.

"You call your brother 'sweetheart'?" Cam asked.

"How much did you hear?" I said warily. I didn't want Cam to worry about anything other than staying warm and putting food in his belly.

"Enough to think that if you do call him that, it's kinda weird."

I laughed once. If Cam was making jokes, he must be feeling better. "That was my wife. She's monitoring us with my brother, helping plan our fastest way out of here."

"You're married? Wow."

"Wow?" I raised an eyebrow at him.

"I just mean, you're like this mountain guy, I figured you lived out here and did nature stuff or whatever… I dunno. I guess I didn't really think about it. But that's cool. Married."

I leaned forward to adjust a log on the fire. "It is cool. She's great. And for the record, I'm not a 'mountain guy.' I'm a wilderness firefighter and search-and-rescue paramedic. At least, I used to be."

"Used to be?" Cam looked up from his soup.

"It's a long story." *One that doesn't have a definitive ending yet.* "What do you want to be after high school, Cam? It's not that far away."

He looked over at his brother, lying more comfortably now that I'd put a real blanket over him and cleaned him up. "Maybe I'd like to help people, too."

"I think you'd be good at it," I told him.

Lots of kids his age would've lost their shit out here in the wilderness after a cougar attack, not to mention an injured little brother. Cam had kept his cool until I found them, and then let himself have a human moment. The General would've been proud of him, human moment and all.

"Thanks. I still can't believe you're, like, a normal married guy. It's like… like the best of both worlds, right? You get to go out and do cool stuff, then come home and have a regular life."

Nothing about my life in the past year had been regular, but I understood what he was saying. I got to be a badass, jump out of planes, battle with fire, then put it aside and also be a stable husband and father figure, with a Honey-Do list and my beautiful wife curled up next to me at night. If those worlds fit together a little better, I might be inclined to keep doing both. Some people made it work — of course they did. I just wasn't sure if I could, and I wanted the home life more now.

"I've never really thought of it that way, but yeah, I guess. Do you want that? To get married someday, I mean?"

"Maybe when I'm your age. Like, a *long* time from now."

"C'mon Cam, I'm barely ten years older than you. Don't make me into an old man already. I've got a few good years left."

Cam cracked a small grin. "Do you have any kids, Fox?"

"I do," I said, picturing Annabelle's blond curls. "A little girl."

"How old is she?"

"Almost four."

I reached over to adjust Dylan's blanket, careful not to disturb his bound up arm, and a flash ripped through my vision. I saw myself reaching out to adjust another arm, but this one was in a proper sling, and it was much smaller. I closed my eyes tightly, shaking my head, but another image popped in, this one of Avery, standing in the doorway of a hospital room, her expression a mix of love and worry. Then the pages of a picture book, my arms wrapped around Annabelle as we lay there among the starched white sheets, tucked up with her little bandaged head resting on my chest.

Annabelle. Hurt. Concussion. When was that? I searched through my brain, trying to piece it together.

"Fox?" Cam called my name worriedly. "What's wrong?"

I shook my head again to clear it. "Nothing. I'm good."

"You had a weird look on your face, man."

"Sorry. Just thinking."

I got up and walked over to my pack to pull out more food, still thinking about Annabelle in the hospital. I was so fucking tired of this, so fed up with not being able to remember my world, my wife, my little girl. Shoving the pack aside, I leaned against the rock, looking up at the stars. I let my eyes slide out of focus, allowing my body to truly relax for the first time since I'd heard those ranchers discuss Cam and Dylan's plight.

"Fox! She's hurt!"

Avery's terrified voice pierced through my body. I put my hands on her, wanting to pull her to me, hold her and promise her that everything would be okay, that I would never let anything happen to Annabelle, but time was ticking and Annabelle needed help now.

Within seconds of beginning to climb the broken Ferris wheel, I knew it wouldn't hold me. I couldn't reach Annabelle this way without endangering her further. A quick glance over to Jim Kent confirmed that we needed another plan.

"Focus, Avery. You have to do it. You have to get her."

And she did. Avery climbed that fucking disaster of a ride on that terrible night, putting her paralyzing fear aside to reach her baby. Minutes later Annabelle fell through the air and into my arms, because Avery had the courage to trust me and let her go. Seconds after that, I caught Avery too, and it seemed like our nightmare was over or at least on its way into the light.

I wanted to rage, to burn it all down, to damn the person responsible for almost taking away the two most important things in my life, nearly just after I'd found them.

But it was Chase.

I remembered that now. It had been *Chase*, and that made it different. Chase, who had still been trying to wrap his mind around the night in the woods when everything changed for our crew. If I'd chosen the rehab path of the straight and narrow, Chase's course was the exact opposite. It didn't excuse his drunken, broken behavior, didn't change the fact that I'd wanted to rip him limb from limb after endangering what was mine — but I understood it. Especially now.

We sat silently in the truck, me flexing my hand as I watched his eye start to swell.

"You don't know," Dempsey insisted finally, breaking the air. "You don't know what it's like to be in my head."

"You're right, I don't know exactly *what it's like to be you." I sucked in a deep breath. "But I can guess. Always looking over your shoulder, always preparing for the worst. Always on edge and afraid. I'm not going to lie to you, man, I don't know if that ever goes away completely."*

"So I'm just fucked, then?"

I laughed once, bitterly. "No. You're alive, which means it isn't over yet. You didn't experience that valley fire alone. We were all there, and now some of us aren't. So do me a favor, do Landry a favor, and try to find your balance again.

"It's in there somewhere, and fear and joy and everything else is all a part of it — those are the highs and the lows that mean you're still alive, because if you didn't have that you'd have nothing to lose, and that's no way to live. And I want you to live, *Dempsey. Fucking* LIVE*."*

I'd told Chase that I wanted him to live, to crawl his way out of the dark and the self-punishment and the uncertainty of the future, and I'd meant it. He could do it and he had, on his way with a fresh start in Lubbock. I'd done it once and I did it again, not without missteps, but I was here.

"I'm sorry, Fox. I'm so fucking sorry."

"I know, Dempsey. I am, too."

We'd endured deaths, any amount too many. Annabelle lived, the other four kids that night in the Oka-Wen lived, and I'd be damned if I couldn't say the same about Cam and Dylan Owens.

I straightened up, removing my body from the cold rock I'd leaned against and walking back toward the fire. Looking out of the rocky mountain overhang, I thought I saw a movement in the trees, another flash of tawny gold fur, but the light was changing and I couldn't be sure. Either way, I knew I had to start planning our exit. We'd overstayed our welcome here by a while already.

"Cam," I stood over him and nudged him with my leg gently. "Wake up, buddy."

Cam jerked awake. "Sorry."

"I know you're exhausted, but we have to go, okay? Dylan needs us to get him out."

I wanted to let him sleep, let his young body and mind rest and heal themselves without worry, but there would be plenty of time for that when we got out of the park.

"I had a dream, I think," Cam said slowly. "Everything is kind of a blur, but Dylan was talking to me, telling me he was scared." He rubbed his eyes and drew a slow, trembling breath as he tried to stand up.

I grabbed his arm, helping him to his feet. "You've been through a lot in the last couple days. Everything will make sense again, I promise."

"I don't think it was just a dream," Cam agreed. "I knew I had to try and find help. He made me promise I wouldn't leave him. But then he stopped talking — I knew we were running out of time."

"You did the right thing, Cam. If you would've split up, you might not have found your way back to him."

"I couldn't leave him, Fox. He's my little brother." Cam looked over at Dylan, his face starting to crumple.

I put my arm around him, thinking of brothers — of all

types of brothers, bound by blood and bound by honor. I thought of Avery, of the one thing she wanted all those weeks ago that would make everything seem right.

"We all go together or no one goes at all. I promise."

"I need to move, Lucas. What did you figure out?"

Dylan's temperature was rising, but not in the way I wanted. The river water was the best and worst thing that could've happened to his wounds — the water flushed them out, but the bacteria content was unknown. Infection was just around the corner; despite packing the gashes and bites with antibiotic cream I saw the telltale red streaks, the inflammation and swelling.

"The medevac is ready to go. The closest they can get to you, though, is about two miles away as the crow flies."

"That's pretty good," I said, relieved. "I can carry him two miles."

I'd have to be careful of his neck, and try my best not to jostle him or disturb any of the temporary bandages, but I figured I could meet up with the medevac within an hour.

Lucas sighed. "It's not a straight shot. Fifteen miles down the river or two miles up — up the rocks, through a gap in the range and down to the low valley behind."

Shit. "You're kidding."

"Look around, B. You know the helicopter can't come close to those sheer mountains — it's windy and they're too tall to drop a basket safely. Either you walk out, down the banks to the southeast until the land flattens out, or you climb. I know it's shitty, but those are the choices."

I thought fast. With the right equipment, I could do this. "We're going up. Tell them to drop the basket anyway — but actually drop it, as close as they can, and let me know where it is. They can fill it with supplies, and I'll use it as a stretcher."

"Okay, hold on, let me write this down. What else do you need?"

"A couple climbing harnesses and ropes, a padded arm sling, a neck brace, an IV set-up with a few bags of saline, a full first-aid trauma kit. Throw in some more food too, anything that's not too heavy, and a couple gallons of water."

"Got it, got it," Lucas said. "Anything else?"

"If I think of anything, I'll call. But tell them to hurry. We're getting out of here today."

I hung up and turned to Cam. "Let's get ready."

The basket drop went more smoothly than I'd imagined, although I had to hike more than a mile out to where they were able to place it. I knew that dropping the litter basket and cutting the line was probably against protocol, but if I had to get Dylan up the side of a rock wall mountain, through the boulders, and down into a valley, I didn't see any other way.

I left Cam with the rest of the food and water, one of my knives, and the airhorn, just in case the cougar decided to make an appearance. It was fully daylight now, but the big cat had exhibited bold behavior and I wasn't taking any chances.

"Not too bad," I muttered to myself as I inspected the litter. They'd sent me everything I'd asked for in a nice, lightweight basket with the standard two all-terrain wheels that would enable me to use it as a sort of wheelbarrow-like push cart to accommodate the ground in the area.

The basket itself was a little banged up from hitting the rock walls on the way down, but it would work. I could make all of this work. When I got back to our makeshift camp, I had Cam unpack and organize everything inside the litter while I redressed Dylan's wounds.

After I unwrapped the biggest of the cougar scratches

covering his shoulder, I hissed out a breath.

"What?" Cam looked up from where he was opening a pack of beef jerky.

I didn't want to worry him, but if it were my brother, I'd want to know. And he was old enough and mature enough. He'd proven that over and over the last few days. "See this?" I pointed to Dylan's swollen skin.

Cam swallowed audibly. "Yeah?"

"That's infection. And potentially sepsis."

"It's bad." It wasn't a question.

"Yeah, Cam. It is."

"What do we do now, Fox?"

"We get the hell out of here and get Dylan some help."

Any hesitation I'd had about going up the mountain was immediately overshadowed by the worsening of Dylan's condition. I didn't have a choice. Fifteen miles out would take too long, and we didn't have that kind of time anymore. I'd promised Cam that we wouldn't let Dylan die, and I meant it. After we had everything packed up and Dylan was situated in the litter, I rigged a climbing harness on Cam.

"Here's what we're going to do," I told him. "I'm going up to secure our lines, and then I'm coming back down for you. We'll head up together, all the way to the top, and then I need you to stay there while I come back down for Dylan."

Cam nodded. "Okay."

"Once I secure Dylan's pulley, I'm going to climb up next to him, and you're going to be in charge of his ropes. I'll have a rope on him, too, but I need you to help me."

I didn't know if Cam had enough body weight to pull Dylan up the mountain on his own, but it was the only option. I couldn't take the chance of leveraging his basket up without a spot climber. The mountain was too jagged, with too many overhangs and snags that could hit the basket and damage it, or catch the line and potentially flip the litter over. Dylan would be continually jostled and knocked around, and I wanted to try and minimize that as much as possible.

We had about two hundred feet to scale, and I'd need every rope they packed into the litter basket in order to rig a system to get Cam, Dylan, and myself to the top. Another mountain, another climb — I tried not to focus on the parallels between this and my last rescue, but it was difficult.

This time I had no official team, and there was no fire. What I did have was a half-conscious young kid with life-threatening injuries and his brother, both of whom were depending on me. That part hadn't changed. And neither had my determination, because I owed it to these boys to be my very best for them. Anything less was unacceptable.

I called Lucas on the satellite phone. "We're going up."

"You're in a good spot," Lucas said through the static. "Right behind this mountain is a rocky pass between the main range, and then you have a clear shot down into the valley."

"I have the coordinates for the medevac pick-up in my GPS. Once we scale this mountain, you can send them out."

"They'll be there."

We disconnected and I walked back over to where Cam was sitting next to Dylan in the litter basket. "Ready?"

He nodded. "Yes."

I went up the rocky wall a little more slowly than I usually would, trying to judge the best path for an inexperienced climber and also the easiest trajectory for the litter basket. Once I was satisfied that Cam could make it, I quickly rigged the pulleys at the top of the ledge and rappelled back down to the boys waiting for me below.

"You've got this, Cam. I'll be right behind you."

Cam climbed like a pro, much to my relief, and I was heading back down to Dylan sooner than expected. I rigged his basket, double and triple checking the lines, then yelled to Cam to start pulling.

We'd made it about halfway up when the air suddenly stilled, and then a huge gust blew through the river valley between the two sides of the rock mountain. I grabbed onto Dylan's litter, screaming at Cam not to let go, while I tried to keep a grip on the slippery rocks with my other hand.

"CAM! HOLD ON!"

The wind kept coming, swirling around us, and in the middle of it all I felt time stand still as I heard the rope snap. *Not again. Not this again. What were the fucking odds?* The broken line slid by me in slow motion, and I reached a hand out to grab it, feeling the weight of the rope through my glove, a solid sign that this time would be different than the last. It had to be.

"FOX!" Cam yelled. "FOX, WHAT'S HAPPENING?"

I looped my hand quickly around the loose line, holding it as taut as possible. Dylan was slipping, I was losing my grip, every muscle in my arm straining so hard that I could see my veins through the skin. No, not like this. I wouldn't let him go. *Not like this.*

We'll be waiting for you. I heard Avery's whisper in my head. *You'll find those boys. I know you won't come back until you do.* My brain echoed the sentiment. *We all go together. No more death.*

The wind picked up again as I closed my eyes and focused everything I had on the rope in my grip. I heard Cam's voice calling above me, felt the phantom pain in my leg, saw a flash of blood-stained rocks, of thick, smoky skies, medevac chopper blades — of a rain-drenched highway, an overturned oil tanker, the screeching of brakes — of music swirling around an old truck's cab, of Avery laughing as the breeze whipped through her blond waves.

"Your hair is like sunshine."

With the very last bit of my strength, I pulled Dylan's rope up an inch, and then two, then five, every muscle tested to the maximum and on the verge, and snapped it into my carabiner. No one was fucking dying today.

"C'mon Cam!" I yelled up to him. "PULL!"

I steadied Dylan in the basket as Cam inched us up, pulling with all of his might. Once I'd untwisted my own lines, I anchored myself on the rock wall, using my hands and legs to give an extra boost on top of Cam's efforts.

I just had to reach the other end of the snapped rope — I had to get there. I looked up, saw the carabiner dangling in the wind. If I could get us there, I could lock Dylan in and climb the rest of the way up to help Cam. But until then, I was Dylan's lifeline — in more ways than one.

My arms burned with the strain of my own weight combined with Dylan's. "Just a little farther, Cam! You can do it," I called to him.

If I lost my footing, our only chance was Cam's rope. The pulley I'd rigged for myself wasn't enough to hold both of us. I knew what I'd do if it came to that — I had a knife in my hip sheath, ready to cut my line off if I had to. *We all go together or no one goes at all.* I'd promised him. *I promised him.*

"You promised," Avery sobbed.

I shook my head and refocused on the carabiner hanging on the rocks over my head. "Three more feet, Cam! PULL!"

"I'm trying!" His voice came down, scared but strong.

"You're doing great! PULL!"

I braced my legs against the rocks and reached one hand up as far as I could, stretching, stretching, until my fingers closed around the metal, and with a herculean effort, I fastened Dylan's other line in with a snap. Relief washed over me, temporarily soothing my stressed and strained muscles.

"Hold the line, Cam. I'm coming up now."

Quickly, I scaled the rest of the mountain, ignoring the nagging pain in my previously separated shoulder and the burn of my leg muscles. When I pulled myself over the top, the first thing I registered was Cam's face, heavy with concentration and fear as he held tight to Dylan's rope, his hands slightly dwarfed in his borrowed gloves.

I shrugged off my harness and came to stand next to him, putting a hand on his tense shoulder. "We've got him."

Together we pulled, steadily, inch by inch so as to keep the basket as even as possible. When the litter neared the top, I anchored the rope on a scrub tree while Cam and I pulled it over the ledge.

"Is he okay, Fox?"

I checked Dylan's brace and bandages, noting that his wounds looked about the same but no worse. When the line snapped he'd hit the rock wall pretty hard, but the metal frame of the basket had protected him from the worst of the impact.

"Yeah. He's good for now." I whipped out my satellite phone and called Lucas. "We're here, we made it up. Send the chopper," I said as soon as he answered.

"Okay, B. Okay, that's great." The relief in Lucas' voice was palpable. "The medevac will be right there. How was it?"

I glanced over at Cam, who'd sat down on the ground next to Dylan in the basket, one hand covering his brother's protectively as he watched him sleep. "Necessary."

Lucas paused, knowing my word had weight. "Get down to the valley, and they'll pick you guys up."

"I'll see you soon, Luke."

"Yeah, B. We'll be there."

Somehow over the next forty minutes I got Cam and Dylan over those rocks and down into the valley, sometimes wheeling Dylan in his litter, sometimes carrying him with Cam over the biggest of the boulders, scrambling and sweating and all the while pushing like we were almost out of time, because we were, because life is like that and you don't always know when it's going to end. In fact, you rarely ever do.

But the sight of the medevac hovering in for a landing as we half-ran, half-stumbled down the grassy hill was everything — it was Dylan's even, untroubled breathing, it was the light in Cam's eyes when he realized this ordeal was almost over and they'd won, it was the relief on the paramedic's face when he saw I'd brought him two very alive boys.

"He's stable," the first medic said to the other. "Strong pulse. Start a bag of antibiotics for the infection."

"You did it, man," he said to me. "I don't know how the

hell you managed it, but you did it."

I nodded, slumping back against the helicopter's metal wall while I watched the medics check out Dylan and Cam. My shoulder ached and my fingers felt raw inside my gloves, but I managed a genuine smile for Cam when he glanced over at me. "I had a good team."

When the medevac landed, medical staff rushed out to the helipad to transport the boys into the trauma center where they'd get thorough examinations and, in Dylan's case, checked in for at least a short hospital stay.

I waved away the wheelchair when the porter offered it to me, choosing instead to shoulder my gear and walk on my own two feet to the regular elevator that would take me down to the emergency room. This wasn't about me now, I knew I was fine, and I wanted everyone to focus their attention on Dylan and Cam and making sure they had everything they needed. But I'd get checked, because it was protocol, and I'd broken enough of that in the past twenty-four hours already.

When the elevator doors opened into the emergency room waiting area, the first thing I saw was Avery, sitting nervously on a chair with Lucas standing nearby and Annabelle hopping around in front of them.

I might've smiled for Cam, but my face broke into a grin for my wife, who looked up and immediately burst into tears. She tried to hide them from Annabelle by covering her mouth with her hand, but then she was up, running across the waiting area and into my arms.

"Don't cry, sunshine," I said to her, brushing her hair away from her face. "I'm here."

Her eyes widened in shock when I called her that, but she recovered quickly and then her grin was just as bright as mine, even through her tears. "You found them. I knew you would. I'm so proud of you."

"I found a few things out there," I admitted.

"Even better," she said.

You could call it whatever you wanted — redemption, salvation, clarity. Saving the Owens brothers didn't make up for losing Landry and the girl. It couldn't, it never would, and I didn't honestly expect it to. But it was a plan that went right, a corrected wrong, a family's world that suddenly began turning again on its normal axis. And for those reasons and about a hundred more, it was a good thing.

CHAPTER TWENTY

Avery's confused voice penetrated the edge of my exhausted fog. "My dad called me and left a voicemail."

"When?" Lucas asked.

"About two hours ago. We must've been packing to leave the hotel."

I stretched a little in the backseat of the truck, where the momentum of Lucas speeding down the highway toward home had lulled me into a long-overdue nap. My muscles were sore, that was to be expected, but other than that I'd gotten a clean bill of health from the emergency room crew. They, like the medevac paramedics, expressed disbelief that I'd chosen to go that way, straight up instead of out, but they understood. In the same situation, we all did the same thing — whatever it took.

"And?" Lucas didn't know how rare it was to get a phone call from Jim Kent.

"He doesn't just call," I interjected. "What did he say?"

Avery turned around. "To call him back. I'm sorry if I woke you." She ran concerned eyes over my face.

I was pretty sure I looked like shit. I might've found Dylan and Cam and gotten them out in less than a day, but it was a *long* day. We'd barely slept last night after getting home from the hospital, and it hadn't taken the edge off my exhaustion.

"Just resting my eyes." I smiled before I leaned forward, reaching into her hyper-prepared road-trip tote to hand Annabelle another book. "Are you going to call him?"

She pressed the button and held the phone to her ear, looking worried. "Hi, Daddy. We're on our way home now. What's up?"

There was a pause, and I registered the change in Avery's facial expression. Her eyes widened and her cheeks paled.

"Someone was in the house?"

Shit. No way. No fucking way. Two things happened simultaneously after Avery asked her father that question. One, I grabbed my iPad and plugged in Annabelle's special headphones, placing them gently over her ears, and two, Lucas swore out loud and stepped on the gas a little harder.

"Speaker phone," I requested. "Please."

Avery clicked the audio button and her hand trembled slightly as she placed the phone on the center console so we could all hear it.

"What happened?" she asked her father.

"We got a call from Mrs. Vancity next door, telling me that she thought y'all were supposed to be out of town, so she was concerned when she saw a man through the window of your kitchen last night."

A heartbeat, then two. All of the air felt like it had been sucked out of the cab. I glanced at Annabelle quickly, but she was engrossed in her movie and not paying attention to us. Good. Better. I didn't want her to know a single thing about this. I didn't want Avery to know, either, but it was too late for that. And besides, I'd promised her full disclosure.

"I was knee-deep in muck out, so it took me an hour or so to get over to your place, but I'm here now. Fox is with you?" her dad asked.

"Yes sir. Jim," I amended.

"Lucas is here too, Daddy."

"Good. You'll want to do your own check, but I can't see much out of place. The side window by the kitchen door is broken, glass everywhere, but I'm gonna clean that up before y'all come home with Annabelle."

"Nothing missing?" Lucas asked.

"I can't tell for sure, but I don't think so. Avery, you keep cash in this house?"

"No, not really. Maybe fifty or sixty dollars in my dresser, just in case."

I darted my eyes quickly to her. That wasn't enough. In this particular situation, it was a good thing because that meant less to steal, but on the regular… I wanted her to know she had access to more, should she ever need it.

"Did you check the bedrooms, Jim? The closet safe?" I asked. Avery would freak out if she knew how much cash I kept in there. I was fairly certain she'd put the key I'd given her on her keyring and then forgotten all about it.

"I did, and it all looks okay. A couple things knocked over here and there, but I think y'all got off lucky for a break-in."

There was plenty Jim wasn't saying, and all three of us in the car were thinking it. Who else would break into our tiny house, in a tiny town, on a safe street in a neighborhood where everyone knows each other?

Avery's dad cleared his throat. "I went next door and talked to Mrs. Vancity — from her description I don't think it's any surprise who came in here."

"J.D." I couldn't keep the annoyance out of my voice.

Avery looked surprised, but I wasn't, and Lucas didn't seem to be either. I felt like I'd kept her in the loop, but she didn't ask many questions and I didn't volunteer anything extra. Now I felt like I should have, because she was obviously unprepared for this, and the look on her face made my fists clench.

J.D. was testing me, but if he was looking for results he

was going about it all the wrong way. I knew he would surface, that he couldn't leave well enough alone until a meeting with me or the lawyer. I wasn't sure what he expected to prove by breaking and entering at my house, but it wouldn't bode well long-term for him in any legal situation. And it definitely would've been detrimental to his immediate health if I'd been home at the time.

Or if Avery and Annabelle had been home alone. My fists clenched again.

"Can't say as I disagree with you, Fox," her dad said.

"Thank you, Daddy, for checking on the house," Avery said in a small voice.

"No problem, chickie. I'm going to head over to the hardware store, pick up some wood to board this window. I'll see y'all when you get home."

"Give us about an hour, Mr. Kent." Lucas changed lanes smoothly, focusing all of his attention on the road.

Avery jabbed at the button to hang up the phone, looking so upset that I almost asked Lucas to pull over so I could take her in my arms. It wouldn't make it okay, it wouldn't fix anything, but it might take that look off her face.

"Avery."

She shook her head. "I'm such a fool."

I slid as close to her as my seatbelt would allow, turning her face toward me. "Look at me."

"You tried to tell me that this was a big deal, that J.D. was acting strangely, but I didn't listen. I didn't ask enough questions, and now he's here in Brancher and I don't know what's going on."

I was incredulous. Did she somehow think that this was her fault? "Not true. You listened to me, you agreed when I said that we should bring Annabelle out to Big Bend. I can't predict J.D.'s actions and neither can you, but I know when a man is unstable. We took every precaution."

"Then why do I feel sick, like I got socked in the stomach?"

"He broke into your house, Avery. It's a violation, it's okay to feel upset about it." Lucas tightened his hands on the steering wheel. "*I'm* upset about it."

"Mama?" Annabelle lifted the headphones from her ears. "Are we almost home?"

I slid back into my seat, releasing Avery's cheek. "Just a little bit longer, Bells."

"Will you read this to me, Fox?" Annabelle asked sweetly, offering me one of her storybooks.

"Is it the pirate one? That's my favorite."

I could make things normal for Annabelle. I would do the very best I could. There was plenty of time for life to show her firsthand how disappointing, frightening, and all-around messed up it could be. I'd keep it wonderful for her as long as possible. Forever, if I had my way.

Annabelle giggled, and as there was nothing I could do right this minute, and despite my anger and annoyance, I pushed everything aside and opened the book.

Heather was waiting in the driveway when we pulled up in the truck. I saw Jim Kent come out of the door to stand behind her, raising his hand in greeting as Lucas turned off the engine.

"What are you doing here?" Avery hopped out of the cab and gave Heather a huge hug.

"Your mom called me, told me what happened. I can't believe it. Are they sure it was J.D?" she said in a low voice as I came around the side of the truck with a drowsy Annabelle in my arms.

Avery shrugged one shoulder, darting a glance at Annabelle who blinked at us sleepily. I carefully transferred Annabelle over to her while Heather grabbed Avery's backpack and turned to head inside.

"We'll be right in." I gestured to the bags, but really I

wanted a minute to talk to Jim without watching what I said. I skimmed my lips over Avery's cheek, and she pressed her face against mine for a second like she needed to be closer.

I knew she was really rattled by all this J.D. shit, and my anger flared up again. He'd scared my wife, made her worry, disturbed our home, and violated our privacy. Over what? Money that would only put a few bandaids over his self-destructive tendencies? It was fucking unbelievable.

After the girls disappeared inside, Jim helped us as we unloaded the truck. "Got everything cleaned up," he said. "Fixed the window for now, too."

I nodded, hefting the duffle Avery packed for me out of the truck's bed. "Appreciate it."

"I know there's wheels turning here. Mind if I ask what you have planned?" Jim set Annabelle's little bag on the cement driveway.

"Find J.D.," I said.

"Security overhaul," Lucas replied at the same time.

Jim looked from me to him, his expression serious. "He had a lot of nerve coming here. Any idea what he's after?"

"I can only assume he was coming over to make a scene, and when we weren't home he decided to come in and look around."

I hated that I didn't know J.D. well enough to know what he was capable of. When I'd told Avery to bring Annabelle with us to Big Bend, I was erring on the side of caution. Now I was glad I had — my gut-check was still accurate, even after the accident. I was holding everything that mattered to me as close as possible.

"And now?" Jim asked.

"We make sure this, or anything remotely resembling it, never happens again," I said firmly.

Lucas shook his head. "Things have gotten complicated with the adoption situation, but we'll handle it."

Jim looked me right in the eye. "I know you will." He pulled his keys from his pocket. "I've got to head on to the diner.

You need anything from me, that's where I'll be."

After we shook hands in the driveway, Lucas followed me up the porch with our bags, where I opened the door carefully under the assumption that Annabelle might've fallen asleep. After crossing the threshold I could faintly hear Heather and Avery's hushed voices coming from the other room.

The house looked the same, nothing out of place, nothing amiss. Only Avery would know that for certain, but it was a relief to confirm that J.D. hadn't trashed the place. I felt my blood settle a bit, my adrenaline abating for the first time since we'd heard the news. I could fix this. I could make sure that Avery felt safe in our home no matter what.

Lucas and I had just set down the bags when I registered Heather's voice.

"How are you?" she asked Avery in a stage whisper.

"It's been a very dramatic forty-eight hours," Avery sighed softly.

"The boys are okay, though?"

"Yeah. Fox was amazing, like usual."

Lucas rolled his eyes at me as he silently toed his high-top sneakers off by the door.

"He and Lucas had a hunch that the Owens brothers were further away than anyone suspected, and he found them quick, considering. The younger one was hurt badly, but the doctors think he'll be fine."

"That man is like a beautiful, blond superhero."

Lucas smirked and socked me in the shoulder. I shot him a dirty look as I kicked off my boots. "Shut up," I mumbled, turning to head into the living room.

We heard Avery laugh quietly. "Pretty much." She paused. "And what about his brother?"

"His brother… is like that time I made hot chocolate with whole milk and melted fudge. I can't go back and I'm pissed that I know what it tastes like because now I want it all the time," Heather huffed.

Lucas stopped short and I took the opportunity to return his punch with a harder one of my own. It required everything in my power to keep a straight face as I kept walking into the living room. I would never let him hear the end of this. Heather calling me superhero man-candy was funny — comparing Lucas to a Starbucks wet dream was *hilarious.*

I led the way in, smiling when I saw Avery staring at Heather with wide eyes and Annabelle curled up fast asleep on the couch. Lucas was right behind me, his usual swagger somewhat stilted when he entered the room and locked eyes with Heather.

They'd been conspicuously avoiding each other since we got out of the truck, not even a glance between them, but after Heather's hot chocolate analogy the tension grew exponentially. Avery gave me the side-eye and raised her eyebrows in Lucas' direction, indicating the weird stare-down the two of them had going.

I wanted to laugh but kept my face poker-serious while I gave Avery a minute shrug as if to say *who knew?* She smiled, and I quickened my step to cross the room and sit on the floor in front of the couch, pulling her into my lap.

"Hey, sunshine. Your dad left, he had to get to the diner."

Avery nodded, her eyes brightening when I used her newly remembered nickname. It fit her — now I couldn't imagine how I'd ever forgotten it.

"Hi." She relaxed slightly, and I wrapped my arms loosely around her waist.

We all watched as Lucas decided to park his ass awkwardly in the small armchair instead of the couch. I hid my grin in Avery's hair, easy to do because all I wanted was to press my lips against the skin of her neck and move on from there. The remaining tension in her body was evident even as she leaned into me. If we were alone right now, I could make her forget all of the bullshit we had going on. We only needed five minutes but I wanted at least an hour.

Lucas cleared his throat. "So."

He had everyone's attention now except Heather, and obviously Annabelle, who was still fast asleep. Heather was pointedly examining a photo collage on the living room wall as though it was the most interesting thing she'd ever seen and not, in fact, a group of photos that she herself was featured in and that she'd probably looked at a thousand times.

"We need to talk about home security." I broke the tension.

Avery twisted around in my lap to look at me curiously. "Home security?" she asked.

"Fox, I know I told you the other day that these things don't happen in Brancher," Heather began. "And as far as I'm concerned, they still don't. But maybe you have a point, even though this was a specific incident."

"It doesn't matter," Lucas disagreed. "Until the J.D. situation is resolved and he's out of town, we need to take a few minor precautions."

"What kind of precautions?" Avery ignored the death glare that Heather shot Lucas when he dared to somewhat argue with her.

"Rekeying the locks, for one. Installing a few deadbolts. I'd like to put in better window locks as well, and maybe even a wireless alarm system," I said.

Any other day, Avery probably would've told me that all of that sounded excessive, that we were perfectly safe in the tiny Brancher bubble, but today had proven her wrong. She was nervous, on edge. I hated that J.D. had the power to make her uncomfortable. As much as I loved when she reached for me, wanting to be close, I never wanted it to be out of fear.

"Look, in all likelihood, J.D. was drunk when he came over here. I don't know if he meant to break in, or if he was just too belligerent to realize what he was doing, but the bottom line is that if he tries it again, I'd rather he were less successful." Lucas ran his hands through his hair. "And really, you people have an incredibly lax outlook on security."

To my surprise, Avery stifled a laugh at Lucas' frustrated expression. "Sorry," she said. "Everything is inappropriately amusing to me today."

I ran a hand down her back in what I hoped was a comforting manner. She'd been through a lot in the past forty-eight hours. Hell, in the past eight weeks. Avery was strong, but maybe it was all starting to get to her a little. Otherwise, she was adjusting incredibly well to her life being slightly nuts and somehow managing to find the humor in it. If I knew my girl, I'd bet on the latter.

"I have two conditions," she continued.

"Is that a yes?" I asked.

She narrowed her eyes at me good-naturedly. "One, I want the all-in-one alarm that monitors fire and carbon monoxide too. It makes sense that if we're going to do it, we might as well upgrade the existing detectors and everything else. Two, I don't want Annabelle to see you installing anything. I don't want to scare her."

"Done and done," I said, kissing Avery softly.

Lucas stood up. "We'll head into Midland. I should be able to find everything we need there."

"When Annabelle wakes up, maybe you could take her out for a while so we can get everything set up," I suggested. This condition of Avery's worked in my favor. It would definitely be better if she was gone while I drilled holes into the walls.

"C'mon over to my house," Heather said, speaking up for the first time since Lucas cut her off. "I'm trying out a new buttercream recipe."

"I have two conditions," I began, and Heather and Avery laughed. If we were going to play up the humorous side of this, I could do that. "One, that the buttercream makes its way onto a cake and that cake makes its way back home to me. And two," I pointed to Lucas, "either you apologize for whatever stupid shit you did, or Heather cuts you some slack. You guys can decide which way that one goes.

CHAPTER TWENTY-ONE

Thanks to one of Lucas' security contacts, we found someone willing to sell us everything we needed for the alarm without having to go through a typical commercial company. Lucas would connect us to his mainframe for monitoring and we'd be all set. It was better this way, because with Fox Protective Services I would have more control over the system, and I wasn't letting anyone else be the primary guard over what was mine.

"Make a left here," Lucas said, consulting his phone's GPS.

I pulled up in front of what looked to be a three-car garage facing the street. "This is it?"

Lucas' lip curled into a smirk. "What did you expect? A big sign saying 'Security Spy Shit' or something?"

"Just get out of the truck," I said, slamming the door before he could respond.

We walked up the side path next to the garages to a solid steel security gate. Lucas hit the buzzer and it swung open within seconds.

"You Fox?" The man speaking was probably in his early fifties, short, with dark, slicked-back hair, weathered skin, and a broad, muscular frame. He darted glances over the both of us, up and down quickly.

"Yes," we said in unison, and Lucas rolled his eyes.

"I'm Lucas Fox. Garrett?"

"Nice to meet you boys," Garrett said, shaking our hands. "You need to set up a new system?"

He opened the gate wider and ushered us in. From the street, I had no idea that the compound would be so large. Off to one side was another garage, with two auto bays and a hydraulic lift. Three black Humvees were parked there, fully upgraded and shining in the sun. Toward the back I saw a landscaped area, clearly more residential, with a modest brick house and flowerbeds lining the small path. Apparently Garrett liked to keep his work close to home.

"What are you lookin' for exactly?"

"I need some things for my house," I began. "Window and door sensors, an indoor motion detector. Maybe a couple cameras for outside, motion lights, and the best fire and CO2 monitoring system you have. If you have window locks and deadbolts I'll take some of those too, otherwise we can hit the hardware store on the way out of town."

"Y'all havin' some trouble?" Garrett asked, raising an eyebrow. "I have a team on standby if you need any help before you can get your guys in. They can patrol 'round the clock if need be."

Lucas shook his head. "We appreciate it, but for now we'll handle it in-house."

"Fair enough," Garrett nodded. "Offer stands. C'mon over here with me, pick out what you need. I have it all." He walked to the side of the street-facing garages and reached down to raise a rollup metal door. "Take your time."

"Holy shit," Lucas muttered.

If there was a zombie apocalypse, or an alien invasion, or any sort of Will-Smith-action-movie-come-to-life situation that I needed to be prepared for, I was getting in the truck and heading straight over to Garrett's Garage of Security Spy Shit.

Between the racks and racks of floodlights, wall-mounted spotlights, and fish-eye security cameras, Garrett had huge rolls of barbed wire, stacks of iron fencing, and tables full of all the gear you could imagine — alarm panels, binoculars, walkie talkies, keyed deadbolts, coded deadbolts, and other things I couldn't recognize but looked useful. A glass case to the left held all types of ear monitors, microphone wires, and headsets designed for stealth communication. On the far wall was a gun safe, and next to it a knife board full of wicked-looking blades. There was an assortment of Kevlar gear and hand weapons also — clubs, crowbars, brass knuckles, tasers… I think I even saw some nunchucks on display.

"I keep all of the sensors over there," Garrett said, jerking his chin toward a large open pantry-like closet to the right, where I could see shelves of storage bins. "Start with those and we'll fill in the rest."

Two hours later, we'd loaded up the truck and thanked Garrett for his help. Lucas handed him a wad of bills that he tried to refuse, but Lucas insisted.

"You did us a big favor," he said, laying the money on the counter next to a few tactical helmets. "We're paying for your time and equipment."

"Fine, but I owe you one. I know you got those kids out from Big Bend. My niece goes to school with the younger boy, she was real upset when he was missing. You run into any problems, I'm only a phone call away."

I shook Garrett's hand firmly. "I'll remember that."

Lucas and I were in the truck heading out to the highway when I finally asked the question I'd been wondering for the better part of the afternoon.

"Who the hell *is* that guy?" I wasn't sure if anything Garrett had in his garage by itself was necessarily illegal, but the sheer volume and combination had to be breaking at least a few laws.

"Private security, just like me," Lucas said nonchalantly.

"Nope. He's way cooler than you." I shook my head. "He's like a Texas version of Rambo."

"Garrett leads with a combination of muscle and stealth, whereas I prefer to be one step ahead and have cooler tech shit." Lucas shrugged. "We all have our methods."

"Your methods look like a garden party compared to his." I snorted at the annoyed expression on Lucas' face. "I'm just saying."

"My methods are fine. I have high-profile clients who prefer to be guarded by a guy in a suit versus a nunchuck-wielding ex-wrestler. It's less conspicuous that way."

I shrugged. "Whatever you say."

"Put on the suit, go on guard detail for a couple hours with the lead singer of the biggest band in the world who gets mobbed everywhere he goes, and then come talk to me about Garrett's barbed wire," Lucas huffed.

"I know, I know," I said placatingly. "Your jobs might both be security-based but they're different."

His words stuck with me for a second longer than anticipated, though, because he'd brought up the very thing I'd been thinking about lately. Did I want to take a job with Lucas' security firm? Would I like the work? I knew it could be stressful and even dangerous at times, but I was used to that. And depending on my role and the clients I managed, I would get to come home to Avery and Annabelle almost every night. That was motivation enough to think about a future with Fox Protective Services.

The other option, the one I'd been toying around with lately, seemed irresponsible now that I had a family to consider. I wasn't sure why — it wasn't money or worrying about taking care of my girls, because I was lucky enough to be able to fall back on the smart financial decisions I'd made. So what was it? What kept me from taking a chance and potentially turning a hobby into a career?

I thought about my resistance the rest of the way home,

still brooding a bit as Lucas and I prepped and started our installation.

"We should be hearing back from the lawyer soon," Lucas said as he replaced the somewhat flimsy deadbolt in the front door with an industrial steel one. "Are you sure you don't want to call the police about the break-in? I know there's not much evidence, but we can probably rustle up enough facts to send a uniform over to J.D.'s hotel and ask his whereabouts for the other night."

"No," I said shortly. "No cops. I don't want him to catch wind of it and spook before we get the legal shit all finished up. He could disappear very easily with the check I wrote him."

"True." Lucas stood back to admire his handiwork. "What's next?"

"Start on the windows," I pointed into the kitchen.

We worked in silence for a few minutes until Lucas' phone bleated through the air. He reached to grab it from the counter, silencing the ring as he did so.

"Lawyer," he mumbled, connecting the call quickly. "This is Lucas Fox."

I resumed my work, drilling a home for the alarm panel in the hallway. Hopefully, Avery wouldn't be too upset about a few more holes in the wall when she saw how unobtrusive this system actually was.

"You're kidding," Lucas said into the phone. I looked over at him, waiting for him to speak again and clarify. "I'll call you back." He jabbed the screen and turned to face me, his brows pulled together and his lip curled in irritation. "Guess who blew off the meeting with the lawyer?"

"This guy is determined to be a fucking pain in the ass, isn't he?" I dropped my drill onto the floor in disgust, rubbing the back of my neck as I started to pace the hallway. Why wouldn't he want to meet with the lawyer, get his money, and get the hell out of Brancher? *What's your endgame, J.D.?*

"It gets better. Apparently he only wants to deal with *you* now, and in person."

"What? Why?"

Lucas shook his head. "No idea. He called the lawyer, told him not to bother with any meeting because he was going straight to the source."

The source? Every time I wanted to give J.D. the benefit of the doubt, he did something stupid like break into my house or refer to me as "the source," which only confirmed that he didn't give two shits about Annabelle or what was best for her — his only interest was in the money I promised him. As far as I was concerned, our contract was null and void the minute he'd slammed his fist through my kitchen window.

"He wants to come find me? I'll make it really easy for him," I growled, pulling my phone from my pocket.

"What—"

I interrupted him when I heard the generic recorded message. "Disconnected. Figures." I tossed the phone onto the kitchen counter a little harder than necessary.

"I can tap in, but my guess is that he probably didn't pay his bill. We'll have to get ahold of him another way." Lucas finished fitting a sensor to the small window over the sink. "Let's keep moving with these," he said, walking into the living room.

I followed him, and within twenty minutes we had the entire interior of the house done, but still no concrete plan on how to find J.D. Lucas suggested a private investigator, but I was certain J.D. was still in town. Either I could wait for him to show himself, or I could flush him out.

Lucas stood below me as I climbed up the ladder to the roof with one hand, the other holding a motion-sensor floodlight. It would be dark in a couple hours, and I wanted to get the final touches on the security system in place before we spent our first night back here since the break-in. It would comfort Avery, and make me feel better in the process. Being fifteen feet or so in the air probably should've required more of my concentration, but I couldn't stop thinking about tracking J.D.

What would I do? If I were him, indignant on my own behalf, desperate, and looking to gain the upper hand on a guy I thought was giving me the runaround, what would I do?

I knew what *I* would do, but if I were J.D., it would be something completely different. J.D. needed an ally here, he needed someone to talk to, to give him information, to encourage his bravado. And he needed a bottle. If there was one thing that was consistent about J.D., it was that. There was a chance that he hit a liquor store and was drinking alone, but if I combined the two needs together… I had a pretty good idea of where to look for him.

"Want to get a beer later?" I called down to Lucas.

When Avery and Annabelle got home, I had everything cleaned up and the table set for dinner. I greeted them at the door, taking the round plastic storage container Avery carried that I knew contained Heather's buttercream cake. I'd met both of Avery's conditions today about our new home security, and so far Heather delivered on half of mine. I'd have to ask Lucas later if they'd managed to work anything out between them after he left to go back to the diner apartment.

"Hi, Fox!" Annabelle bounced up and down cheerfully. "Did you miss us? We were at Auntie Heather's, but we brought you a cake!"

"I'm glad you're home now," I told her, looking over to Avery and quickly catching her eye. "I always miss you when you're gone."

"I think my dolls missed me too," Annabelle said. "And probably my ponies! I'd better check." She ran off into her room and Avery laughed.

"The security system looks good," she said softly, running a finger over the lighted panel. "Did you find everything you needed?"

I nodded, pulling her closer to me. "It's all taken care of. I'll show you everything tomorrow."

I leaned down to kiss her, the blood heating in my veins as she opened her mouth and let me taste her tongue. I wasn't lying to Annabelle; I'd missed them both. But with Avery it was different than anyone else I'd ever been with. She was like a phantom limb — I could feel her even when she wasn't there.

She broke our kiss, smiling up at me. "Something smells good. You cooked?"

"I did. Just a roasted chicken, mashed potatoes, salad."

"Just a roasted chicken," she said, shaking her head. "No biggie."

"What?" I grinned at her, enjoying the exasperated expression on her face.

"I bet the mashed potatoes are from scratch, too."

I shrugged. "They're better that way."

"I am so lucky to have you. *We* are so lucky to have you," she amended, kissing me again. "No one except my mom has ever roasted me a chicken."

"I'm going to take that as a strange yet well-intentioned compliment," I told her. "Next week I'm making eggplant parmesan. I asked Joy to add fresh mozzarella to the weekly vendor order."

"Stop talking dirty to me in front of the child," Avery whispered with a smirk as Annabelle came running into the living room.

I haven't even started, sunshine. The overwhelming desire to get her alone hit me, and suddenly bedtime couldn't come soon enough. Damn me and my stupid ideas about going out with Lucas. Now all I could think about was promising to cook Avery whatever she wanted while I buried myself deep inside her — and the look on her face when she would finally come undone in my arms.

"Going to check on the chicken," I mumbled, escaping to the kitchen with my inappropriate thoughts. I heard Avery laughing as I left the room, and the grin on my face widened. I fucking loved that girl.

After we ate and I put my libido on ice for a minute, I sat down on the couch with Avery next to me while Annabelle put her dolls to bed. It was a nightly precursor to her own bedtime that she took very seriously, and we usually just left her to it.

"Will you be okay if I go out with Lucas for a little while?" I asked her. "I'll set the alarm before I go, and I'm monitoring everything on my phone. Lucas and I both are," I added. "We could be back in five minutes if anything happened."

"Fox." She rolled her eyes at me. "I'm not afraid to be alone in the house. Honestly."

"Are you sure?" The expression on her face when her dad told her someone had broken in was something I wouldn't forget any time soon.

"Yes. And also, I know you're not just going out for beers. This has something to do with J.D., otherwise you'd never leave. Tell me what's going on."

"He didn't show up to the meeting with the lawyer. Instead, he called and said that from now on, he only wanted to deal with me, in person."

If Avery wanted to know, I would tell her, but that didn't mean I would like it. If I could send J.D. on a one-way voyage to the farthest place on earth from wherever she was, I'd do it. I was beginning to think that my whole pipe dream of adopting Annabelle and somehow saving her father in the process was about to come crashing down around my ears. It was unacceptable. I hated failure.

"That's weird, right? Why would he say that?"

"The short answer is because he's pissed. The long one is that he wants to try to intimidate me, wants money, wants it now, and can't think logically with a whiskey-soaked brain and a short temper."

"He's been kicked in the head by bulls, and he wasn't the sharpest tool to begin with," Avery agreed.

I laughed in spite of my irritation. "Probably true."

"I was going through a rough time when we hooked up," she admitted. "Feeling sad about Chase, scared about my future… the people I met from the rodeo were the best distraction. They lived fast and had fun, but I felt like they were a family, too. They traveled together, looked out for each other. At first I thought J.D. was like that, but I found out I was wrong pretty quickly. I don't know who he really is."

I kissed the top of her head when she rested her cheek on my shoulder, wishing I could turn back time and take this all away from her. She might not have harbored any illusions about J.D., but the reality still had to sting, especially when it was shoved in her face again after all these years. "He's not even competing anymore. That's probably contributed to some of his downfall, the loss of community. But he can turn it around if he wants to, Avery. He just has to try."

"Maybe I should go with you to see him."

She looked up at me to gauge my reaction, but I very carefully kept my face neutral. Every cell in my body said *no, no, keep her far away, keep Annabelle away away away* but it wasn't my choice to make. I didn't control Avery. She'd listen to my opinion, but she had final say. You could bet your ass I'd be right there if she decided to meet with him, but I wouldn't make that decision for her.

"I think maybe it would put it in perspective for him, Fox. Humanize it a little. As of now he's only dealt with you in the abstract — You're the husband of a girl he got pregnant, and you want something from him. I don't know if seeing me, if hearing it from me would make a difference, but it might."

She had a point, but I didn't love it. "If that's what you want to do, I'll make it happen and support you. All I ask is that you let me try to find him, try to meet up with him one more time, to feel out why he changed his mind about getting this done with as soon as possible."

Avery nodded without a second thought. "Okay."

"Thank you." The amount of love and trust this girl had in me was staggering sometimes. I wished our plate was clean, with no mistakes or chips in it that would make me feel like I didn't deserve her unwavering loyalty. But we had time now. If there were lingering sharp edges, I'd smooth them with the gift of that time.

"Did Lucas say anything to you today about Heather?" Avery asked, completely changing the subject.

"No. But a few beers will loosen him up."

She laughed. "Make sure you're ready. It's kind of a big deal."

I knew that already from my eavesdropping, but I still wanted to hear it from Lucas. I raised an eyebrow at her. "I can't wait."

"Mama, Fox!" Annabelle called from her room. "I'm ready for bed!"

Twenty minutes later, I was walking down the driveway to my truck, slowly surveying the street on both sides of the house. Nothing looked out of place, but I still felt a persistent uneasiness about leaving Avery and Annabelle at home. I thought I'd taken every precaution before and I'd still been surprised. It wouldn't happen again. My eyes swept over the cars nearby until I found the one I wanted.

I nodded at the slick black Humvee parked down the block and got an answering flicker of headlights. Sometimes it was better to be safe than sorry.

CHAPTER TWENTY-TWO

Lucky's was fairly packed for a weeknight, the long wooden bar crowded with bodies and a chalkboard waiting list already in place for the pool tables. When there was only one real bar in a town, I supposed it was normal for it to see a lot of action.

I had a flash of another night, a little broken glass, a bemused older man calling me "Backdraft." *Lucky. And Chase. He was upset about me and Avery, but it was his pride and his fear — not really about her.* I searched for more pieces of the memory but found none. I'd have to ask Avery later.

I slid onto a bar stool next to Lucas and motioned to the bartender that I'd have what he was having — a beer and what looked suspiciously like a glass of scotch.

"This is nice and familiar," I said, gesturing to his choice in drinks. "What are we commiserating, besides the obvious?"

"Nothing," Lucas said quickly. "What did Avery think about the alarm system?"

"She hasn't seen all of the features yet and she made me promise to touch up the paint and patch where you accidentally drilled a hole into the living room wall, but other than that, she's cool with it."

Lucas laughed once. "Sorry. I got overzealous with the power tools."

My drinks arrived and I took a sip of my beer. I probably wouldn't touch the scotch tonight — Lucas looked like he needed it more than me, and at least one of us had to keep our head straight in case we actually ran into J.D. Lucas had taken one for the team last time, so it was my turn now. I owed him that, and so much more.

"Thank you," I began.

"For what? You're buying tonight."

"Whatever. That's not what I meant." I set the bottle down. "I wanted to thank you for everything you've done for me, and especially for Avery and Annabelle, since my motorcycle accident."

He gave me a half-shrug. "No worries, B. I was—"

"Shut up, Lucas. I wasn't finished."

"Sorry."

"You've done nothing but come through for me and my family, time and time again over these last couple months. Even when I was being an insufferable prick, you were there."

Lucas put his glass down and turned on his stool to face me. "I'm not gonna lie, B. You in that coma was the most fucked-up thing that's ever happened… to any of us. It scared the shit out of me. You've always been the strong one, nothing shakes you. Ever. I didn't realize how much we all counted on that."

I knew he was right, but it wasn't something I thought about too often. Until I had Avery and Annabelle in my life, the idea of someone counting on me in a personal way was too much. I needed to be free, free to walk into the burning woods and not look back. *Separate and do the job.* That was one of the General's favorites.

"I couldn't have made it through all of this without you. If I was the one that everyone counted on, you did a damn good job of taking over for me."

"You can go back to being that guy now," Lucas said with a smirk. "It's tiring as fuck and the pay is lousy."

"I think I've got it from here, Luke."

"I think you do, too."

We drank our beers in easy silence for few minutes until Lucas spoke again.

"I've really messed things up with Heather."

I snorted. "Of course you have. You're a jerk."

"Thanks for the vote of confidence." He slid his empty scotch glass away and signaled for another.

Okay, I'd bite. "What did you do?"

"I don't know. Scared her? Wanted stuff? Moved too fast? Didn't consider her feelings? All of the above, probably."

"Do you love her?"

Lucas choked on his drink. "What? There's this— I wanted— I mean, we just—"

"So, you love her." I spun my empty beer bottle in circles on the bar, incredibly enjoying the look on his face. "Have you told her?"

"No." He paused. "Should I?"

"No, by all means, keep it to yourself and prolong everyone's misery," I said wryly. "Yeah, I think you should tell her. It's the truth, right? Girls are big on that."

I thought of Avery, of how that was all she ever asked of me. Let her in, and tell the truth. Simple as that. It wasn't always that uncomplicated, but it was the core.

"Okay. You're right. I don't think it'll fix everything, but I want her to know."

"Good." I stood up. "Heart-to-heart officially over for a least a year."

Lucas laughed. "Done."

"I'm going to put our names on the list for a pool table," I said, and then I felt someone tap me on the shoulder.

Lucas stood up too, glancing behind me with an unreadable expression on his face. I turned around slowly.

"Hey Fox, Lucas." The taller of the two men standing in front of me offered his hand. "I know you probably don't remember me, man. I'm Derek, and this is Kyle." He gestured to the shorter, stockier guy next to him. "We're friends of Chase's. And of yours. Sort of."

I shook Derek's proffered hand with only a slight hesitation, then Kyle's. I vaguely remembered Avery saying something about Chase's friends, how things were awkward for a while but then smoothed over once Chase moved to Lubbock and got back on track.

Lucas greeted Derek and Kyle with an easy smile and quick handshakes, and I realized that they already knew each other, probably from time that Lucas had spent in Brancher prior to my accident.

"We just wanted to come over and say that we've heard what's been going on with J.D., and we're here if you need us. Avery's a nice girl, and Annabelle is a little sweetheart — he shouldn't be anywhere near them."

I nodded slowly, wondering exactly how much they knew. News traveled fast in a small town — they might even know things that I didn't, especially in relation to J.D.'s past or temperament.

"Chase asked us, you know, to keep an eye on things with the girls, just in case," Kyle spoke up.

"We really appreciate everything you did for Chase, getting him set up with people who could help him. He's doing much better. Now you might need it — help, I mean. We figure you're, um, a little incapacitated right now. So we're just doing our part until you get it back. You'll get it back, Fox. We know you will."

I was strangely touched by their gesture and the awkward sincerity behind it. "Thank you."

Derek nodded. "Least we can do. We'll keep an eye out for anything weird, ask some questions. Let you know what we hear."

Kyle's eyes focused over my shoulder, widening then narrowing quickly. "Speak of the devil. What's that washed-up little fuck doing here?"

I turned, knowing exactly who I'd see. "He's here for me."

The picture I'd glimpsed of J.D. in Lucas' file hadn't captured the hard miles he'd put on himself in the past few years, but I recognized him just the same. I stared across the bar, searching for a shred of Annabelle under the shaggy hair and tanned, weathered skin but finding none. Genetically she might've been his, but physically she was all Avery.

"At least this saves us from having to track him down," Lucas muttered by my ear.

Part of me thought the same, but another part was annoyed by the nerve he had. I'd half expected him to hole up somewhere, maybe even outside of Brancher especially after he broke into my house, but then I remembered who I was dealing with.

J.D.'s moral compass was not calibrated correctly these days, or maybe he'd just stopped consulting it. Either way, he fell into my lap tonight and I was determined to make the most of it.

I watched him make his way toward us to the bar, two other men flanking him as he pushed through the crowd. He hadn't seen me yet, or if he did, he didn't recognize me. I wasn't sure he even knew what I looked like. I'd have the element of surprise instead of the other way around.

"Glad he brought reinforcements," Derek said, cracking his knuckles. "We'll be over on the other side if you need us." He disappeared with Kyle into the crowd, and I turned to Lucas.

"Game time."

J.D. waited at the bar just a few feet from where we were standing. I tapped him on the shoulder and he whirled around. "What?"

"Hello, J.D."

"Fox?" He squinted at me.

"Nice to finally meet you in person. Wish I could've been there when you let yourself into our house the other night." I stared him straight in the eye, and he was the first to look away.

"What? I didn't do anything, I don't know what you're talking about," he said in a bored voice.

"Let me see your hand." I grabbed his wrist. "Where'd you get these cuts? Looks like you might've put your fist through something hard and sharp, like a window."

J.D. had the grace to look slightly panicked by my overly calm tone. I felt like it took everything I had not to lose my temper with him every time we interacted, and so my method of coping post-coma was "overly calm." Lucas said it was scary, and apparently J.D. agreed.

"No, no. I got into a fight," he insisted.

Yeah, with my window. "Oh?"

"That's what I said, okay?"

"Sure, J.D. Next question — why'd you blow off the meeting with the lawyer?"

"I don't trust lawyers! I don't trust anyone. I just want my money. You want me to go away, you want that kid, you'll give me my money." His voice took on a petulant sound, like a whining child.

"I'll adopt Annabelle with or without your consent." The "overly calm" thing was not working very well for me right now. "Why did you break into my house?"

"I told you, I didn't." The two men standing behind J.D. started to look restless as they drank their beers. I'm sure they wanted nothing more than to leave J.D. to whatever shit he'd gotten himself into this time, but they stuck around.

"Even if I believed you, which I don't, I'd still be less than inclined to keep our arrangement, because I think that even if you didn't do the actual forced entry, you know who did." I gestured at the two guys he was with. "Maybe one of them?"

They both shook their heads vehemently, then walked across the bar, denying any association with J.D. whatsoever.

Without his friends, J.D.'s bravado dropped a notch.

"Look, I barely remember that girl, and as far as I'm concerned that kid might not even be mine, you know what I mean?"

I bristled at his insinuation about Avery, that she would lie about Annabelle's paternity, but I didn't share it. If I let go of the strangled hold on my temper, there was no reining it back in.

"So why all the fanfare then? You could ask for a DNA test, or just take the way out I've been trying to give you. Why would you mess this up with refusals to contact our lawyer, not showing up to meetings… What's the point? What do you want?"

J.D. glanced around the bar uneasily, but he didn't speak.

"What do you want, J.D.?" I repeated the same words, but my voice had an extra edge to it this time.

"You know what I want." He took a long pull from his beer.

"I thought I did. Now I need you to tell me."

"Make it worth my while, and I'll disappear forever." *There it was.* "Say, double what we talked about before. Fifty grand."

"Not a chance." I crossed my arms over my chest. "You blew it already."

"What does that mean?" he asked suspiciously.

"It means that if you'd stick to our original plan, even now after everything, I'd still be willing to help you get your life back on track. If you show up at the lawyer's office tomorrow morning and sign the papers, you'll get your check and we can go our separate ways."

"And if I don't?" I couldn't tell if the gleam in J.D.'s eye was alcohol induced or just plain arrogance.

"If you don't, the deal's off. We'll go to court, it'll be ugly, and you'll definitely lose. And it would be in your best interest to clear out of Brancher ASAP."

J.D.'s eyes turned wild, and his face flamed into color. "You promised me! I need that money! You lying sack of shit — I knew it!"

"If I thought for one second that you cared about that little girl one-tenth as much as you care about this money, I'd more inclined to bargain with you, J.D. But you don't. So do yourself a favor — take what I'm offering, the original twenty-five thousand, and go before I force you to with a restraining order."

"Fuck you, Fox. You'll cough up more. I'm just gonna wait it out." He finished his beer and slammed it down on the bar.

"This is how I see it," I said, my voice low. I was much taller than J.D. but I was fairly certain his eyes widened at the thinly veiled anger in my voice and not the height difference. "You can either do as I ask and then disappear back into whatever barrel you crawled out of, or I can make it happen."

J.D. looked momentarily stunned, and then he looked at me and laughed nervously. "What are you gonna do? Who the fuck do you think you are? Mission Impossible?"

I heard Lucas snort behind me and I shook my head. "Unbelievable. What is it about this bar? Everyone is a comedian."

"What?" J.D. asked. "I don't even know you, man. And you don't know me."

"False. I *do* know you, James Dean Warren — cruel joke your parents played on you there by the way, a lot to live up to — born July 13th, 1989 in San Antonio. Five-eight, one hundred and sixty-five pounds. Your father is a truck driver and your mother is a night-shift motel clerk. You have one sister who lives in Dallas and works in a clothing store. You haven't been home to visit in over three years. At six, you broke your arm. At eighteen, your collarbone. In 2011, you were ranked third in the Texas circuit; in 2014, you ranked twenty-seventh."

"What the hell?" J.D.'s confusion only incited my rage.

"You currently have two warrants out for your arrest — one in Oklahoma for failing to make your DUI court appearance, and the other in Llano for skipping bail on a drunk and disorderly. You haven't paid taxes in four years, and you have two outstanding speeding tickets and an unpaid truck registration."

Dr. Woods would be proud of the short-term memory

retention I displayed in recalling a large chunk of J.D.'s file. I watched his face turn from red to white as my words sunk in.

"H— how do you know all that?" he stuttered.

I ignored his question and leaned in further. "Either cooperate or don't, and then we'll let the courts decide. But stay away from Avery and Annabelle or everything I just listed goes into a file and comes out as a big fat reason for an APB in every county from New Mexico to Mississippi. You'll spend enough time behind bars that the idea of a two-thousand-pound bull stepping directly on your face sounds like a fucking vacation."

I turned and walked out of the bar, my chest heaving with the restraint I'd exerted in not punching J.D. directly in the throat. Derek caught my eye on the way out and nodded briefly. If anything else happened, I knew I'd hear about it.

Outside with Lucas, I dragged in huge lungfuls of fresh air, trying to slow my racing mind that all but demanded I go back into the bar and slam J.D.'s head against the wall. *It wouldn't help anything,* I reminded myself. *It would only make things worse, and you're not that guy anyway.*

But I could be. I never wanted to be that guy more. I didn't back down from a fight, not ever, but I rarely started them. Letting your temper go until you couldn't restrain your body was a foreign concept to me. I liked to be in control. I needed it. If I had to use my fists to prove a point, I would. But I preferred calculated movements, like that night at the bar in Seattle. More control, more impact. Just like a fire.

"You good?" Lucas asked after a moment.

"Yeah," I said. "Let's get out of here."

"You can't save everybody, B," Lucas shook his head.

I acknowledged that. I'd learned it the hard way. But I still tried, because that's what I knew how to do.

CHAPTER TWENTY-THREE

I knew Avery could sense my frustration — it seeped out of my pores even as I gentled my hands to hold her later that night. I was agitated, my fists easily recalling the feeling of wanting to pound J.D.'s face into a wall, but I didn't say anything except the bare minimum — we would probably have to go to court for Annabelle's adoption.

But she knew, because Avery could read me without words. We were intimately familiar with each other's bodies; I loved every single hollow and smooth expanse of skin and gentle curve on that girl. That's how I could tell that she felt it, my anger and annoyance — and even my disappointment.

We've come so far in the last few months. We've come so far, Fox. She whispered it to me after she thought I was asleep. *This can't be a dead end.*

The legal part of the adoption was just a piece of paper as far as Avery was concerned. She considered me Annabelle's father, the only real one she'd ever had. Avery believed it and Annabelle believed it, though Avery also understood the need I had to make it official.

But we didn't discuss it further, weeks started to go by, and I tried to let myself settle, to forget about J.D. until the upcoming court dates and enjoy my family. If this was normal life, I'd take it.

I rolled a little pent-up tension out of my shoulders while I sat on our bed, tapping out an email on my tablet to finish up my latest round of memory exercises for Dr. Woods. Avery walked into the room with a basket of clean laundry in her arms and I looked up to see her smiling at me.

"That looks heavy." I got to my feet quickly, shoving the tablet aside, and took the basket from her hands as I kissed her cheek softly.

"Thanks." She started to fold the clothes and I grabbed a few shirts to hang. "What were you working on?" she asked, curiosity evident in her voice.

"Just some compensatory memory stuff," I said, crossing the room to the closet. "I have that meeting with the specialist in Odessa next week."

My memories were coming back slowly, but just pieces at a time. It was the other frustrating element of my life, the one I could do almost nothing about. I only got bits of every story, and Avery tried her best to fill in the blanks. Woods told me in the beginning that eighteen months post trauma would be about as good as things would ever get, and I'd be damned if I didn't have more of my puzzle put together before then. Hence, the memory exercises and the long-avoided specialist visit.

"I'm proud of you for making the appointment," Avery said softly. "I know you don't love it."

No, I didn't love the idea of more doctors, but I liked Woods and I knew he had my best interests at heart. If he wanted me to see the specialist, I'd go. I gave her a shrug and a half-smile. "Most of my recollections happen with a current-event trigger, like Woods predicted. If there was a surefire thing I could do to make it all come back, I'd be doing it every day."

Avery stopped folding and put a hand on me, her fingers slipping lightly over the suddenly tense muscles in my forearm.

"We're good, okay? Even if you never have another flash, we're solid. We're making new memories all the time."

It was more than what we were discussing on the surface, and once again Avery knew it. Breaking through the dark and feeling like myself again was something I continually worked at just as hard as I did when I exercised my body. There were days when the loss of Landry hit me like a landslide the minute I awoke, when I could hear my own voice in my head pleading with him not to give up, and Sloane's equally desperate attempts to resuscitate the little girl.

Maybe my recovery trajectory was more difficult due to experiencing everything twice, but I didn't know the difference. All I understood was that I needed to fight and keep moving forward, for Avery and Annabelle, but mostly for myself. Fire was a formidable enemy, but nothing compared to the war you can wage with yourself on the daily. I knew that now.

My eyes burned into hers with understanding, but my lips fell into a shit-eating grin as I shoved the laundry basket aside. "I can think of a couple memories I'd like to recreate with you right now if you're willing, Mrs. Fox." I reached for her. "Come here."

Avery let me lay her down and cover her body with mine as I trailed my mouth up her neck and across her jaw to her lips. My fingers slipped under her shirt, feeling her warm skin under my rough palms. Her hands slid around my lower back as I pressed her into the bed, letting her know exactly what she did to me.

"This is so much better than laundry," she murmured when we came up for air.

"It can get even better." Another nudge of my hips had her breath catching in her throat.

"Can I— can I get a raincheck? We need to get ready for work."

I was expecting it, but I jokingly groaned into her neck anyway, making her giggle. "Count on it." Our lips touched once, twice more before I rolled off of her and propped myself up on my elbow. "I have to stop touching you now."

She laughed again, and when I looked into her beautiful, open face I hated what I knew I had to say next.

My expression must've sobered some because she raised an eyebrow at me. "What?"

"I hate to ruin the mood, but I did just get an email about J.D."

Avery sat up, smoothing her shirt down where my hands had pushed it out of place. "What happened?"

"Nothing." I turned onto my back as she rose and reached for the laundry. "That's what makes it so frustrating. We know that he never used his return ticket back to Wyoming or exchanged it for another flight, so he has to be fairly close. But no one's seen him."

"What does the P.I. think?"

Lucas gave us a contact for a local private investigator, the best stealth guy he could find in our limited area, who would hopefully sniff out J.D.'s little hidey-hole and serve him with the papers our lawyer had drafted. So far, no luck.

I shrugged. "That he'll turn up eventually."

"But you don't think that's good enough," she said.

Not by a fucking mile. And I wanted to take matters into my own hands, but for now I'd wait. "Nope. Not when it comes to J.D. I'd rather have too much information than not enough."

My annoyance about the never-ending J.D. situation wouldn't abate as Avery and I got ready to head into the diner. I was working the mid shift also, but Avery was only on for the early lunch so she could pick up Annabelle from preschool. Joy was true to her word, only scheduling us about three shifts a week together, but it worked when we added juggling Annabelle's school schedule to the mix.

After a couple hours of non-stop burgers and fries, I finally had a lull in the rush and took that time to catch up on a few prep chores to make the mid shift easier. Avery came back into the kitchen to see me, her mouth twitching in amusement while she watched me arrange a cut fruit plate I planned to add to the daily specials. After I'd YouTubed the origami animals for Annabelle, I sort of fell down the rabbit hole of knife-skill videos, and apparently my wife found my strawberry rose garnishes hilarious.

"Careful now," Avery said with a smile. "Heather will subcontract you out for decorating duty."

I smirked at her, wanting to kiss that grin off her face. "I take the health-conscious section of our menu very seriously."

"I know you do," she laughed.

"What's up, sunshine? Want a quick sandwich before you go get Bells?"

"No." She came closer, kissing my cheek and lingering there. "Just wanted to say hi."

Her warmth called to me, and I dropped the strawberries I held. "I'm still thinking about our raincheck," I said in a low voice, leaning toward her.

"Oh really?" She slid her eyes up to meet mine.

"Yeah. I actually—"

"Avery!" Joy called from the pass-through. "Table eight is requesting you as their waitress." She gave me a quasi-stern look. "Stop distracting my servers during the lunch rush."

My lips twisted into a grin. "Sorry, Joy."

She grabbed the fruit plate as I set it in the window and tried to keep her face impassive, but I saw a hint of a smile. I knew Joy was happy for us, despite her constant harping for fooling around on diner time.

In a different situation I might've been embarrassed for being called out as a horny teenager, but it was true — and my wife was hot. The benefits would always outweigh the consequences.

Table eight turned out to be our neighbors, Mr. and Mrs. Vancity. After Avery served their garden quiches and fruit salad, they invited her to join them as the last few minutes of her shift ticked by. I saw the elderly woman waving at me from the table, beckoning me out, so I motioned to Joy that I was taking my break and untied my apron. I set an iced tea down in front of Avery and took a seat in the empty fourth chair.

"Mr. and Mrs. Vancity, nice to see you. Is the food okay?" I ran a discreet hand over the small of Avery's back. I couldn't stop touching her today.

"Delicious, like always, dear!" Mrs. Vancity smiled at me, and her husband nodded his agreement.

At my touch, Avery turned and offered a small smile in my direction. "Thanks for the iced tea."

I winked at her and turned to Mrs. Vancity. "I'm glad."

"Avery, your Mr. Fox has done such a nice job on those home improvements he's been working on," Mrs. Vancity said, patting my arm. "I just love how your house is so well-lit now. I told Mr. Vancity that we should see about putting up some more lights of our own."

Mr. Vancity grunted into his quiche. "Unnecessary."

The older man had a slightly prickly exterior, but I knew he'd do whatever his wife wanted. I could see us being similar to the Vancitys as we grew older — I already had the slightly prickly thing on lock. And the old man was a softy for my little girl too. Avery said Annabelle could always count on two full-size candy bars when she trick-or-treated at their house for Halloween — Mr. Vancity got a kick out of putting them into her plastic pumpkin personally.

"I'd be happy to help if you decide to hang any, sir," I said to Mr. Vancity, and we shared a small nod. Better to offer to assist than piss the old man off by inferring he couldn't do it. I'd seen him wield some long-handled hedge trimmers with a vengeance.

"That's so nice, dear. Thank you." Mrs. Vancity paused. "We're really going to miss you three around here next year. What will we do without our little Annabelle to keep us laughing?"

Avery told me the Vancitys didn't have any grandchildren and that their only son had moved to Washington, D.C. many years ago. They were such nice people, she said, so caring. Avery's grandparents had already passed, so she'd basically adopted them as surrogates. Mrs. Vancity had even crocheted the soft woven blanket that draped over the foot of Annabelle's bed, a gift she'd given Avery when she came home from the hospital with her baby.

"We're going to miss you too," Avery told Mrs. Vancity sincerely. "But we'll be back for visits all the time, I promise."

"I'm happy for you, dear. I really am. New York City sounds mighty exciting," Mrs. Vancity said, her eyes bright.

"I think it will be," Avery said slowly.

My eyes quickly jumped over to Avery as I registered the uncertainty in her words. Was she having doubts about New York? Why? I watched as she absentmindedly stirred the straw in her iced tea, trying to read her face.

Mrs. Vancity chattered on about the time they'd visited their son in D.C. a few years ago, but Avery and I were only half listening. There was something going on here. My mind ran through a thousand scenarios, ranging from nervousness about grad school to regret for deferring to preoccupation about the adoption. All of those were valid and to be expected, but this was more. Avery wasn't talking though, and I didn't want to ask her in front of our neighbors. I'd let it rest for now.

Noting the time, I said my goodbyes and made my way back into the kitchen for the second part of my shift, still thinking about what could be going on with Avery. A few minutes later, she got up as well, needing to head out to pick up Annabelle from school.

"It was really nice chatting with you, Mr. and Mrs. Vancity," I heard her say.

She blew me a kiss and I waved at her from the kitchen as I watched her head out into the rarely changing Texas sun. Something was up. I just wasn't sure what it was yet.

"I don't think I want to go to New York anymore," Avery blurted that night as we got ready for bed.

"What?" I must be hearing things. At the same time, I recognized that I'd sensed hesitation from her, earlier at the diner.

She turned down the covers and slid in, deliberately keeping her face hidden. "I just think maybe it's not the right move. It's so far away, and we don't know anyone… I'm not sure if it's the place for us."

"Avery." I sat down on her side of the bed. "What are you talking about?"

She finally looked at me. "I think I want to go to Seattle."

Nothing else could've been more unexpected than those words coming out of her beautiful mouth. "Seattle?"

"Yes. I think we should move to Seattle and live in the condo while I go to the University of Washington. You'd like that, wouldn't you? Being back in Seattle? You could see Sloane and McDaniels sometimes, maybe even join your old firehouse. Or Hotshot crew," she added softly. "If you wanted to."

No. No. She was doing this for me because she knew I wasn't sure about joining Fox Protective Services in New York. It was true, I hadn't yet decided, but there were plenty of things I could do in a huge city. If Avery was throwing away the idea of New York for me — well, I couldn't allow it.

"I don't want to," I said shortly.

"You don't? But I thought you loved Seattle and your condo." Her eyes searched mine.

"Avery, what is this all about? Why the sudden change of heart? New York has always been your dream, and you're so close to making it happen. Why now?"

"I think it makes sense. I don't know if New York is the place for me, for us. After your accident, I realized how much I needed my family and my community, not just for me, but for Annabelle too."

"I get that," I said slowly. "But what does that have to do with Seattle? We won't have family or community there. At least in

New York we'll have Lucas sometimes, and even my parents on occasion."

"It just doesn't feel right," she insisted. "Lucas spends most of his time on the West Coast these days, and there's a good chance Heather will be out in Los Angeles soon too. We could easily find time to visit them often, or have them come up to us."

She'd regret this. I knew she would. "I can't let you give anything else up for me, Avery. You've already deferred grad school for a year. If you think that this will make things better for me, I want you to put that thought out of your head right now. I've gotten enough special treatment. Next year is about *you*."

"I'm not giving anything up, Fox. I promise." She slid her hand into mine and looked at me earnestly. "Seattle is where we found each other again after I wasn't sure that we would. You made a home for us there when we needed it the most. I want to build on that, build on those memories. Seattle means something to me now. New York seems like a lifetime ago."

I rubbed my free hand over my eyes. "I just— give me a little time to think about this, okay? And you take some more time as well. We don't have to decide anything tonight."

Avery nodded, but she seemed disappointed. "All right."

There was no way that she really wanted this. Every single move she'd made in college was to get to this very point, and now she wanted to throw it all away. I couldn't believe it was a coincidence, that she'd suddenly had a change of heart and now wanted to move us back to a place where she knew I was inherently comfortable. I could do New York, happily even. I could live anywhere as long as I had her.

We'd let it settle for now, and I'd think about it like I'd said I would. Would I love to go back to Seattle? Yes, of course. But we'd decided on New York before I'd run my bike off the road and jeopardized our entire future. It was a decision we'd made together even if I didn't remember it, an anticipated, thoughtful move. I couldn't imagine my opinion changing — I wanted Avery to do something for herself now, above anyone else. She deserved it.

CHAPTER TWENTY-FOUR

"Avery?" I poked my head through the open barn door. "Are you in here?"

"We're coming out now," she called from the far stall. "Ready to see the prettiest ponies in Ector County?"

"Um, sure." I wasn't sure what that involved, but Avery had been in the barn for the better part of the morning after we'd finished setting up, so I knew it was probably elaborate.

"Ta-da!" Avery stepped out of the stall with a flourish, leading Tootsie and an irritated-looking Lobo behind her. "What do you think?"

I didn't know where to look first. Tootsie's palomino coat was stained a bright pink, and her blond mane sparkled with some kind of glitter in the sunny light of the open barn door. Avery had even braided her tail and tied it with a streamer of rainbow ribbons. Lobo was almost unrecognizable. Somehow she'd managed to stencil blue stars all over his gray dapple, and affixed to his bridle's browband was a big polka-dotted bow, giving him a sort of jaunty, off-kilter look as his ears twitched and flicked the bow around. His mane glittered too, and the same pattern polka-dot ribbon was tied at the top of his tail, which he swished a bit as I approached.

If the ponies looked like they'd stepped directly out of a rave, my wife fit right in with them. Avery was an explosion of color. Her long blond hair was extra wavy and wild today, decorated with a few pink and purple streaks, and her blue dress was covered with candy-shaped glitter cutouts, ending in a short, frilly rainbow skirt that rustled as she walked.

"You look—" I didn't know the right words. "Great. Colorful. Very Candyland."

"It's supposed to be a Rainbow Brite costume," Avery said, looking down at her multi-colored striped tights. "I could only find 'sexy' Rainbow Brite though, so it was kinda revealing. I had to sew in an extra ruffle to make it longer and find these leggings because the 'sexy' knee socks weren't cutting it, and then add the candy stuff for the party theme. I mean, seriously, it was so short it probably would've fit Annabelle. Sexy is fine and whatever, but I'd still like it to cover my ass." She glanced behind her to check. "So far so good."

"Don't get my hopes up." I grinned at her and she swatted at me.

"You're terrible."

"Just honest." I leaned forward and lightly brushed my lips against hers, and she smiled at me when I pulled away.

"I feel a little underdressed," I said. That wasn't an invitation for her to come at me with the glitter or anything, but I was a team player.

"You're perfect." She gestured to my T-shirt, jeans, and boots. "Just the way I like you. Plus you've been doing manual labor all morning, so the peppermint stick outfit I have for you would've gotten all sweaty."

"Peppermint stick?" I echoed. Shit. I glanced around, expecting to see it hanging somewhere.

Avery burst out laughing, clapping a hand over her mouth when Tootsie snorted at her in disapproval. "Sorry. You should've seen the look on your face."

I gave her a wry grin. "I could've pulled it off." I didn't *want* to, but I could've.

"I'm sure you would have. Don't the ponies look beautiful? Annabelle is going to love it."

"It's amazing, Avery. The whole thing. You've put a lot of work into this, and it's going to be a day Annabelle will definitely remember."

Avery's eyes brightened. "I hope so. I wasn't planning something so elaborate, but then when Heather had that crazy baking episode I sort of changed my mind."

"It all came together. Lobo looks kind of bummed, though."

"He's a good sport, aren't you, Lobo?" Avery rubbed his forehead softly as he snuffled into her skirt. "He'll be fine, just keep the apples coming. Plus, Annabelle is his favorite, so as soon as he sees her he'll be happy."

"Let me take them for you," I said, gathering both lead ropes into my hand.

Avery hesitated as she handed them over, and I felt the weight of everything we weren't saying. We'd launched ourselves into last-minute party details over the past couple days instead of talking. I didn't want our discussion about Seattle to mess with today. It was a big decision, but it would keep.

"No worries right now, sunshine. We're solid, remember? A disagreement doesn't change that. We'll shelve it and talk later, yeah? Let's have some fun today."

She nodded. "Okay."

"Go on. Make sure everything is the way you want it out there. Your dad is finishing up the last of the tables."

"How is the piñata?" she asked.

"It's a paper-mâché cupcake on steroids. Huge and heavy, but the tree will hold it."

"You're the best. Don't forget to bring Lobo's apples." Avery stood up on tiptoe to kiss my cheek. "Love you!" she called as she dashed out.

Tootsie nickered softly and nudged my stomach with her nose, so I gave her an apple from Lobo's bag.

"Good girl. Ready to see the kids?"

I caught Lobo's bow fluttering again and I turned my attention to him. "Lemme help you out, buddy."

Thirty seconds later I'd whipped the annoyance off of his head and attached it to his breast collar, where it sat like a gaudy bowtie, but at least it wouldn't irritate him anymore. "Much better." I fed him another apple, too. "Don't tell Avery I moved it."

He gave me an almost human-like sigh that was a cross between relief and resignation as he finished crunching his apple. "The things we do for the girls we love, right? Let's go."

Avery, her mother, and Heather had really transformed the ranch into a sugar-filled wonderland over the last day. Her dad and I had done a lot of the grunt work, but it was truly the girls' vision. Streamers, balloons, and glittered cardboard candy shapes dangled from every available tree and roofline, and brightly colored tablecloths draped the long tables set up in front of the porch where Heather displayed what looked to be an entire bakery's worth of cookies, sweets, cakes, and homemade candy.

The small front corral was decked out too, all ready for when Lobo and Tootsie would carry Annabelle's little guests around in all of their food-colored, glittered glory. Avery's mom had set up a few fun carnival games with prizes, Joy and Henry were in charge of the huge outdoor barbecue where they were grilling everything from ribs to corn, and Claire had a face-painting booth off to the side where she promised to make everyone Candyland-ready.

I understood Avery's need to make this party something special. The last time Annabelle went to a fair, it didn't end well. This would replace that memory for both of them. My recollection of that night was fragmented, but I was more than willing to put it behind me as well.

The guests were arriving as I walked the ponies up toward the house. Annabelle came down the porch, all smiles and squeals, looking so much like Avery in her rainbow tutu with her curls blowing in the breeze that I had to take a second and pull my GoPro out of my pocket to capture her reaction. I didn't want to miss a minute of this day.

"Mama! Fox! It's my Candyland!"

Lobo snapped right out of his funk as soon as we got to the ring because all the little kids made a huge fuss over him and Tootsie, patting their necks and giggling happiness into their whiskered muzzles.

"You old ham," I said, my voice low in his ear as I led the first of the preschoolers around on his back. I swear the pony was practically prancing, his discomfort over his makeover long forgotten. "Not so bad now, is it?"

We completed a few circles around the corral with the kids and then Jim Kent stepped up to me and held out his hand for Lobo's lead rope.

"Your brother is here. I'll take over so you can catch up with him — he's gettin' the cold shoulder from the sugary side of the party." Jim's lips quirked up into a smirk.

"He probably deserves it," I muttered, but I surrendered the rope and vaulted the fence quickly, scanning the small crowd for Lucas.

I spotted him over by the barbecue, talking to Henry, and headed in that direction. Avery caught my eye as she skipped past me with a few of the children in tow, jerking her head slightly to where Heather seemed to be viciously stirring the chocolate fountain. She shrugged and I stifled a groan. I was glad to see my brother, but I really didn't have time for this shit today.

"Glad you could make it, Luke."

"I wouldn't miss the kid's birthday, B. What kind of uncle would I be then?"

"The kind that would owe her a really kick-ass present, probably."

"I've got it covered." He smirked at me. "Be prepared for me to be the favorite indefinitely."

My eyes narrowed. "You asked Mom."

My parents couldn't be here, but they'd sent a gift of their own — an illustrated, collector's edition of the first Harry Potter book, signed by both the author and the artist, courtesy of my mother's gallery connections. I wasn't sure who was more excited about it, Avery or Annabelle.

"Of course I asked Mom. What the hell do I know about four-year-old girls?"

I smacked him on the back. "What the hell do you know about girls, period?"

Lucas' expression turned sour and he shoved his hands into his pockets. "Not too fucking much, apparently."

"She's right over there," I said, jerking my thumb over my shoulder to where Heather was obsessively organizing her dessert table. "What are you waiting for?"

"She probably doesn't want to see me."

"What? You left it that badly again? C'mon Lucas, get it together."

He gave me a dirty look. "What do you think I've been trying to do?"

The formerly superior feeling I'd had when I got the opportunity to bust Lucas on his piss-poor relationship skills wasn't as satisfying as it used to be. I hadn't heard anything about Lucas and Heather's situation since Lucas had to leave Brancher last month after our trip to Big Bend. Neither had Avery, but we'd suspected. Heather wasn't talking yet, and Avery insisted on waiting for her to volunteer the information. I wasn't that patient.

"Go over there. Try not to be a dick." I raised an eyebrow at him at the irony of the conversation. We'd said almost the exact same things to each other a few months ago when I was drowning in my own bullshit and in danger of losing Avery — except this time I was the one pulling no punches.

Lucas flipped me a slyly casual fuck-you as he walked away, but I just grinned at him. They'd figure it out. And if they didn't… there was always tomorrow. And the good chance that I wouldn't have to witness it.

"Okay, Annabelle, make a wish!"

Over the past few hours I'd played ring toss, eaten my weight in baked goods and barbecue, and jogged about a thousand laps leading one technicolor pony or another. Now we were cutting Annabelle's cake, a huge pink icing concoction so heavy that it took both me and Lucas to bring it to the table.

I watched Annabelle get ready to blow out her candles through the screen of my GoPro as all of her guests sang "Happy Birthday" in their various voices — some high-pitched and sweet, and in the case of my brother and Avery's dad, baritone and serious. Twilight was setting in, the glow from the little flames reflecting in Annabelle's eyes as she made her wish and took a deep breath, and in my head I was already editing the footage I'd shot of today.

While the parents of Annabelle's friends led their children — or in some sugar-crashed cases, carried them — to their cars, Avery waved goodbye and thanked them for coming as we started to break the party down.

"We did good today, Fox." Avery dropped down onto one of the picnic benches and started to scoop up an armful of paper cake plates to drop them into the trash. "Amazing what a little food coloring and glitter paint can do, right?"

"Annabelle had a great time," I told her. "Did you?"

"Yes," Avery said simply. "Almost everyone I love is right here."

I looked around at our family and friends helping to clean up our little girl's birthday party, laughing and talking in the fast-approaching darkness. Avery's mom sat with an exhausted Annabelle in her lap, slowly rocking her in the porch swing, while Avery's dad fed Tootsie and Lobo handfuls of hay as he unsaddled them and brushed out their coats in the small corral. Lucas and Heather had their heads together over by the dessert table, and I caught Heather smiling at him as they packed up the remaining cupcakes. It looked like they'd made up, and that was a fucking relief — at least I wouldn't have to hear him whine about her for a while.

It was so clear, suddenly, what Avery had been talking about the other day when she'd tried to get me to think about Seattle. New York just didn't feel right anymore. It didn't feel like us. We were Seattle and Texas and somewhere in between. Like it or not, things weren't the same as they were a few months ago. We'd all felt it, and I'd thought it was my fault, but now I realized that it wasn't just about me.

Dreams could change just as easily as plans. Hadn't my own, over the past few years? Hell, the past few days? Why couldn't Avery's? And how could I be so self-centered to think that she would throw away what she wanted, what she'd worked for, on a whim? She wasn't allowed to change her mind? I was an asshole.

But I was an asshole who wanted to go back to Washington.

CHAPTER TWENTY-FIVE

I spent all day making sure that everything was perfect. My package arrived from Los Angeles exactly when Lucas told me to expect it, and I was all set. Now it was my turn to initiate the serious conversation.

"Please, sit here." I pulled out a chair for Avery and held it.

After she was sitting, I grabbed another and perched next to her, taking her hands into mine.

"Fox? Is something wrong?" She bit her lip nervously.

"No, no. Not at all."

She let out a tiny sigh of relief, and I felt like a jerk for being so unintentionally dramatic.

"I just wanted to have a moment alone with you before we pick Annabelle up from school, to tell you I've done nothing but think about our conversation the other day."

We'd spent a few days dodging the continuation of this topic while I brooded and thought and brooded some more. Annabelle's birthday party bought me a little time too, along with a few other realizations. Avery probably never expected me to voluntarily bring up Seattle again, but I was about to be full of surprises today.

"Okay," she said slowly.

"I want you to know you can count on me, not just to be here, but to take care of you and Annabelle, no matter what."

She smiled, and I wanted to kiss her.

"I know that, silly."

I took a deep breath. "Good."

"Can you just tell me what this is all about? I'm still nervous like you're about to drop something big on me."

"I've been thinking about Seattle, and how you told me you want to go back, and I think it's a great idea."

"You do?" she asked hopefully. "You're not just saying that?"

"No." My voice was firm. "At first, I was a little taken aback, thinking that maybe you were changing your mind for the wrong reasons, but I see exactly where you're coming from now. We could build a great future there, on our terms."

It took me more time than I wanted to admit, but I think my initial reaction to Avery's suggestion was so negative because I liked the idea too much. She was right, Seattle had brought us back to each other, gave us that foothold to move on to Texas so I could remember as much as possible of our life together here. I would always be glad we came back, because I needed to experience life in our little house in this little town — and I was in the right place at the right time to help Cam and Dylan Owens. When we'd first come back, my recovery was still so uncertain, but now — like Avery said, we were solid. If she wanted to go to the West Coast, I was game. New York would always be there.

"I'm so happy that you feel that way," she said, squeezing my hands. "I'm going to contact the admissions officer today."

"Before you do that, there's another piece to this that I want to discuss with you."

"What is it?"

"I've been doing a lot of thinking, but what I've realized is that I've actually just been doing a lot of limiting. My entire life, I've known exactly what I wanted to do. I had my future planned out, and I stayed the course. I always knew what my next move would be, because that was the solid, dependable way to go." I thought about what Lucas said that night at Lucky's. "That's who I am."

Avery nodded, and I continued.

"But now, after the accident and the coma — after almost losing you and Annabelle to my downward spiral of uncertainty — I realized that it's okay to want to change my life, that it's not irresponsible to have goals that don't necessarily coincide with what I thought I'd always be doing."

"So… you want to change careers?" Avery asked. "I think that's great, Fox. You can do anything you want, you have so many skills."

"I think I want to go back to school," I admitted, feeling a huge leap of faith at saying the words out loud. "Maybe focus on cinematography, documentary filmmaking. There are stories out there that need to be told, Avery. I don't know if I'm the one to tell them, but I want to try."

Avery's eyes filled with tears. "As far as I'm concerned, you already are a filmmaker, Fox. And I'd love for the world to see what you can do."

Her words slid into my heart, chipping away the doubt, letting the tiny seed of an idea I'd planted there start to take hold. "That means a lot to me," I told her. "You've been my main inspiration since the day we met. I might not remember all of the clips I made for you, but watching them now shows me that's true."

"Stop it," she said, wiping her eyes with a half-laugh, half-sob. "I'm a mess already. You sure do talk a lot more now post-coma. It's wonderfully unsettling."

I grinned at her. "Gotta keep you on your toes, sunshine." I slid my tablet closer to her on the table. "Seeing as you're already crying, now is probably the best time to show you this."

The clip was already queued up, and I watched her take a deep breath as I pressed play. Watching her watch the screen was the best, guiltiest pleasure I could imagine, because through her eyes I saw everything, every emotion, no matter how small.

Music started softly, her favorite Ed Sheeran song, and the acoustic guitar rang with the familiar notes as Ed started to sing about keeping memories close. I saw her smile, and then the tears flowed again as clips of me and her flashed across the screen. I'd compiled everything I could find from the first time I'd filmed her to the sneaky footage I'd captured over the past couple weeks. There we were, our whole journey, laughing, kissing, goofing around. It was all there, all of our memories — the best ones, the ones I couldn't remember, and the ones I was starting to. This was the longest clip I'd ever made, and not the most heavily edited, but it showed our complicated story best with its simplicity.

When the song faded out, I released her hands and knelt in front of her.

Avery smiled at me through the remainder of her tears. "That was so beautiful, Fox. Thank you."

"One of the things I wish I could remember most is when I proposed," I said, my voice heavy with regret. "Maybe I will someday."

"Well, you did propose twice, so the odds are pretty good," Avery said, her smile still watery.

I couldn't stop grinning at her — I loved that smart mouth, our constant banter, and the fact that she could laugh and cry at the same time. Life was never boring with this girl. "Here's hoping. But since right now I can't, this will have to be a place-holder memory." I pulled a tiny jewelry box from my pocket and opened it, revealing a delicate, diamond studded band.

"When I bought your rings, the girl told me they were stacking bands, and that meant that along with the engagement ring, there were all different types and diamond cuts of bands that you could get to layer together. She said it was perfect for birthday gifts, anniversaries, what have you. I know this because she told me again when I called the jeweler the other day."

Avery shook her head. "It's beautiful."

"I don't remember giving you the first ones, Avery, but I

promise I'll never forget giving you this. We're building new memories on top of old ones, so it's all layers. The foundation is there, and now everything else is gravy."

I slid the ring onto her finger, liking how the bands stacked themselves, meshing their patterns together into a solid piece with her engagement ring as the focal point.

"You're already my wife, but I never take that for granted, not for one minute of any day. I love you. Thank you for keeping the faith in me, faith in us."

She was doing that thing again where she laughed while she cried. "If your movies are half as beautiful as your words, I don't think I'll be able to handle it." Avery stuck her hand out to admire the ring. "I can't believe you did this. I love it."

"The diamonds are only perks, right?" I teased her.

"Fox, I want *you*, however you are, wherever you are, forever. Anything outside of the skin you're in is a perk. The skin itself is actually a really hot perk," she admitted. "But you're so much more than that. I love you."

I swept her up into my arms, my mouth on hers as I pressed her as close to my body as she could get. It still wasn't enough. She knew it too, because she understood me even when I couldn't find my words.

Within seconds we were naked, naked in the kitchen in the goddamn middle of the day with only a couple sheer curtains protecting us from the Vancitys' view, but I didn't care. I needed her skin all over me, and when I sat her down onto my lap, filling her, watching her eyes cloud and her body tense, I knew that no matter what happened or where, if it was Seattle, or New York, or fucking Antartica, as long as I had this girl with me we'd be okay.

I gripped her hips with my fingers, urging her to ride me as her arms wound around my neck and her tongue found its way into my mouth again.

"You feel so fucking good," I told her. "So good."

I bent my head to lick at her breasts, running my hands up from her hips to cup them as her pace increased, her breath coming in short pants and gasps.

"Fox— Fox," she moaned my name, and if it was possible I felt myself grow even harder inside of her. "Don't stop," she cried.

"I can't," I assured her, drawing a ragged breath against her neck. "I wouldn't."

My hips were moving against hers, and I felt the climax building at the base of my spine, forcing me to concentrate and give her what she needed before I exploded. I attached my lips to her breast again, holding her to me while my other hand gently stroked her where our bodies were joined.

We were both at the edge, gripping each other tightly as the last bits of our restraint fell away, and then we were lost — or found, depending on how you looked at it.

CHAPTER TWENTY-SIX

"You okay if I take off, Fox?" Claire leaned against the counter, a hopeful look on her face.

"I don't know," I teased her. "Where are you going in such a hurry?"

"FO-OX!" she whined. "Please?"

"I'm kidding. Go ahead. Is Travis picking you up? I can walk you to your car." I started to untie my apron.

"He's here, don't worry. See you tomorrow!"

She ran outside and I saw her hop into a waiting truck, heard the squeal as that little shit Travis peeled away from the curb. It made me feel approximately one hundred years old to think of Claire's boyfriend that way, but he really was a shit. I liked him, though, in spite of it. He reminded me of a younger Lucas.

I went back to scrubbing the range, trying my best to get the remnants of tonight's chili special off of the stovetop. My head jerked up again when I heard a knock on the diner's glass front door. I'd already turned the lights out over the tables, but I could make out a familiar man's form standing there waving at me.

Derek. A strangely uncomfortable feeling crawled up my chest. *What did he want?* I liked Derek, but he wasn't a casual visitor.

Something was up.

In seconds I'd jogged over to the door and opened it. It was still unlocked from Claire's exit, but I appreciated Derek's discretion in knocking. Sneaking up on me in a roomful of kitchen knives wasn't the best idea.

"Hey, Fox. Got a second?"

I held the door open for him. "C'mon in. The kitchen is dismantled already but I have coffee if you're interested."

"Thanks, I'm good." He paused, then followed suit as I slid onto a counter barstool. "I have news about J.D."

"Almost-midnight-worthy news?" I felt adrenaline start to thrum through my veins, wondering what Derek had to say that couldn't wait until morning.

"It's been brewing, but tonight it came to a head."

I nodded. "Go on."

"I've been hearing things, mainly coming from those assholes he hangs out with, the ones from that night at Lucky's. Apparently he talked a big game these past weeks, saying he was just biding his time and gonna hose you, really take you to the cleaners and get your money. I didn't pay much attention to their gossip until they said something that made me think."

"What?"

"He said your house had a floodlight out, on the left side of the roof."

My house… J.D… Avery and Annabelle. When was he there? When? And why? "He was at my house?"

"I don't know, Fox. All I know is that he was talking shit about some fancy security system you'd put in, some crap about how you thought you were high society in Brancher now, but that even with all your dough you couldn't get floodlights that worked."

J.D. had been to my house since the break-in. Not inside it, because I would know, but he'd been near. Or someone in his proxy. He was right, I did have a floodlight out — it got damaged by a falling branch and I'd made the trip out to Garrett's to replace it yesterday. They were fully functioning now, but the fact that he knew meant he was entirely too close to home in a literal sense.

"So he's been here the whole time. He never left." Why the fuck couldn't the P.I. find him, then? I needed to talk to Lucas immediately.

"Sounds like it," Derek agreed. "There's a little more."

"What?" This wasn't enough? J.D. borderline stalking my family?

"They said J.D. was running out of time with his bookies. And that they knew you were working tonight."

Those two sentences by themselves were fairly innocuous, but in context they made my blood boil. Whatever J.D. was plotting wouldn't work. If he thought he could go to my house and intimidate Avery, he severely underestimated her, me, and the power of Fox Protective Services with an assist by Rambo Garrett. And if he thought threats would get him anywhere when dealing directly with me — well, his memory loss rivaled mine in that case.

Desperate men were often dangerous. They could be frantic and that made them careless. When they were careless, they stood to lose even more, and the desperate cycle continued. I could not allow that to happen anymore.

"Thanks, Derek. I appreciate you looking out for us, for coming to tell me all of this."

He stood up. "J.D. is a piece of work, but I've known him for a long time, since he and my brother used to ride broncs together in the amateur lineups. I never thought he'd fall down as hard as he has. His thing with Avery — well, we all knew it wouldn't last, and then he took off to another circuit. The rodeo kept him sane, and now without it… he's nothing but trouble."

"Tell me about it." I flicked the main lights off again and grabbed my keys. The stove was clean enough for tonight — everything Derek had just revealed meant I needed to get home as soon as possible.

"They were still in the bar when I left, but there's no telling about J.D. I haven't seen his face since you have."

We walked out to our trucks together, the main streets of

Brancher still and quiet at this time of night. Part of me didn't think J.D. would attempt anything without backup, but another part of me knew not to put anything past him.

Desperate men had few limits. They were desperate to protect what they had, desperate to find a way out of where they'd ended up. On a purely basic level I understood that. I'd been there. I'd been desperate, but I'd never been careless. And I wouldn't start now.

I was in the truck ignoring the side street speed limits when I called Lucas. He was on the West Coast, two hours behind Texas, so I knew he'd still be awake and likely working.

"What's up, B?"

"I need you to check the house log. I've checked it myself but make sure. Has anything tripped the alarm in the past few weeks? Anything? No matter how minor?"

"Of course not. You'd get a notification, and I'd call you myself on top of that. You're good."

"I'm *not* good, Lucas. J.D. is around, and he's been on my street. Recently."

"What?"

"I don't have time to explain it, but Derek said J.D.'s bookie deadline is almost up, and he's looking for a way to get his money. He's been casing my house."

"Shit. Why'd didn't the P.I. turn up anything?" Lucas swore.

"I don't know, but that's a problem for another day. Derek said J.D.'s little friends knew I was working tonight, so I'm headed home now in case he tries to bother Avery at the house."

"I've got the cameras on my screen now, B. Everything looks fine."

"I don't want to scare Avery, but I'm tired of this bullshit. If J.D. wants to have it out with me tonight, I'm game. An attempted B&E on his record will only help my adoption case."

"Let's hope it doesn't come to that, okay?"

I pulled into the driveway and threw the truck into park.

"I'm home now. Keep me posted on anything you see."

Using my remote, I deactivated the alarm silently so as not to wake Avery and Annabelle when I came inside. After I'd shut the door securely behind me, I reactivated everything, including the cameras I knew Lucas would personally monitor until I told him otherwise.

I kicked my boots off and crept silently down the hallway, stopping first to check on Annabelle in her room. She was sleeping soundly, her baby doll under the blanket next to her. I felt my heart rate slow down close to normal for the first time since I'd let Derek into the diner. Kissing her forehead softly, I dimmed her nightlight a little bit more before heading across the hall to where Avery slept in our bedroom.

As much as I wanted to take off my clothes and climb into bed next to her, I felt like I needed to be ready at a moment's notice in case J.D. showed up, so I settled for stretching out on top of the comforter and pulling her onto my chest.

She curled into my side automatically with a little sigh. "Hey," she said sleepily. "You're home early."

"I missed you," I said. It was true but only half of the story. With any luck the rest could wait for tomorrow, for daylight and clear thinking.

"Me too," she said, pressing a kiss to my neck, right above the collar of my T-shirt. "You smell like cornbread."

"Chili night, remember?" I laughed softly.

"Yum."

We lay like that in silence for a while, just enjoying being close, but as the minutes ticked by I knew I wouldn't be able to keep my hands off her.

I turned her head, one hand on her cheek as the other wrapped more firmly around her back. She pressed her body against me as I slid my lips across hers, more urgently than I meant to but I couldn't help it. She always felt like she was slipping away from me, like I needed to hold on as tightly as I possibly could lest I lose her.

It had almost happened once, and I knew I wouldn't survive it. Maybe physically, but mentally I'd be off my anchor, drifting, without a purpose or even a center of gravity. I'd keep her safe, keep her and Annabelle next to me until I took my last breath.

I was kissing her, reveling in her softness, the way she breathed me in and let me take what I needed, when I heard the sirens. They started faintly then grew in volume, speeding off toward the main streets of town.

Something was wrong.

Avery felt it too, her body tensed and she slid off of me slowly. "Was that a fire truck?"

I was already up, out of the bed, sprinting toward the hallway to get my boots. I heard Avery go into Annabelle's room, gathering her and all of her blankets in her arms and then turning to run toward me as I stood by the front door.

"We're coming, too," she said.

If Avery hadn't already gotten Annabelle, I would've picked her up myself. There's no way I was leaving them here, alarm or no alarm, not tonight. I took Annabelle from her and we left the house quickly, running out to the truck and jumping inside. Avery peeled Annabelle's blankets back so I could buckle her in, and then we were speeding down the street, Avery's hand clutched firmly in my free one.

It could be anything, I told myself. *A bar brawl, a heart attack. It doesn't even have to be on the main street. Maybe you were mistaken about where the truck was headed.* First responders were first responders, and I knew better than anyone that a fire truck didn't always mean fire.

The second Avery's cell phone rang, it shattered all of my delusions. "Where is Fox?" I heard her father yell through the phone. "Was he inside? Oh, Christ. Dear God. Did he come home yet?"

I'd never heard Jim Kent's voice hold fear until now. Avery's hands shook as she fumbled with the phone. "He's here, Daddy. He's with me. We're on our way. We heard the sirens. Where are you? What happened?"

I turned a corner, and the scene in front of us answered the question before Avery's father could. Kent's Kitchen was engulfed in flames, licking high into the sky, the front plate-glass windows blown out, shards of glass littering the sidewalk. The fragments glistened in the fire's light, reflecting eerily like a moat of lava surrounding the burning building.

Avery cried out, putting her fist to her mouth in shock. She dropped the phone as I stopped the truck and opened the door. "Where are you going? Please, Fox, don't get too close!"

The fire truck had their hose running, water blasting, the crew doing the best they could with an old building that was doomed from the second it sparked into flame. I heard Avery behind me, pleading, but the fire drew me in. Like it always would.

I didn't know if J.D. had made it out or if he'd been trapped inside, but he was behind this. I knew he was. He didn't realize the irony of the situation, he couldn't possibly, but I did.

Fighting fire with fire still meant that everything burned.

EPILOGUE

AVERY

Fox told me once that there was beauty in devastation, you just had to look closely to find it.

He could be right, but I don't know yet. There's still too much smoke to see clearly.

STAY TUNED FOR

BOOK THREE

OF

THE HEY SUNSHINE TRILOGY

COMING

FALL/WINTER 2016

PLAYLIST

"Wonderland" - Taylor Swift
"The Pretender" - Foo Fighters
"Amnesia" - Justin Timberlake
"Like I'm Gonna Lose You" - Meghan Trainor & John Legend
"Heartbeat" - The Fray
"Come Back to Me" - David Cook
"Don't You Remember" - Adele
"If It Kills Me" - Jason Mraz
"Strong" - One Direction
"Try" - P!nk
"She is Love" - Parachute
"Shake it Out" - Florence + The Machine
"Through the Dark" - One Direction
"Falling Slowly" - Lee DeWyze & Crystal Bowersox
"Breath" - Pearl Jam
"Goodnight My Love (Pleasant Dreams)" - Fred Mollin
"Stars" - Grace Potter & The Nocturnals
"Catch Fire" - 5 Seconds of Summer
"Running" - James Bay
"Long Way Down" - One Direction
"Photograph" - Ed Sheeran

ACKNOWLEDGMENTS

Writing my second book was even more surreal, humbling, and enjoyable than the first, and definitely carried the same wealth of gratitude if not more. Just saying thank you to the following people isn't enough, but it's a start.

My husband and my daughter, who now understand what it's really like to live in the same house with a girl who is always on a deadline. Thank you for gracefully accepting the laptop that is now permanently attached to my fingers. I love you both so much and value my time with you more than I ever realized.

My mom, who continues to support me in my writing dreams. Thank you for always encouraging me to move forward with my goals and believing that I can not only achieve but surpass them.

Jenny, not just my editor but also forever friend, who willingly signed on for another round of craziness with me - WE DID IT, YO. Now let's do it again! I'll buy the snacks.

My Instagram girls, who embraced *Hey Sunshine* with an incredible amount of enthusiasm and passion for which I'll always be grateful. Thank you so much for including me and my work on your beautiful feeds, and for loving Avery and Fox just as much as I do.

My friends and family, who are wonderful, lovely people and the best support system a girl could have. Thank you for buying the book, the excited messages, and the heart emojis. Special shoutout to Jessica and Ben for always being just a text away - love you both.

ACKNOWLEDGMENTS

SPW, who tirelessly and patiently gave me a wealth of scientific information that I proceeded to ignore. Thank you for looking the other way while I completely disregarded how things actually work. You're the best - miss your face.

Nazarea Andrews, who kindly and cheerfully answers every single ridiculous question I have, and InkSlinger PR, for giving me the boost I was missing to get my books out into the world. Thank you for appreciating my work and letting me be a small part of your wonderful family of authors.

Sarah from Okay Creations, who once again made my vision come to life with another amazing cover. My books would not be the same without your talent. Thank you.

And to my readers, especially those of you who read and loved *Hey Sunshine* first, none of this would be possible without you. Thank you so much for taking a chance on an unknown author. I hope you enjoyed reading *Night Fox* as much as I enjoyed writing it. Stay tuned for the last installment of the *Hey Sunshine* trilogy — along with something new — in 2016!

ABOUT THE AUTHOR

Tia is a Southern California hairstylist, a former English Lit major, and blogger-turned-author. She was the voice behind the now-retired personal site Clever Girl Goes Blog, and her work has been featured on numerous forums including Open Salon and Hooray Collective. She believes in eyeliner as a defense mechanism, equal rights, and Marc Jacobs. Her favorite things include One Direction, story time, and the overzealous use of punctuation. When not writing and reading, she binge-watches only the best (subjective) TV shows. She lives in San Diego with her husband, daughter, and tiny dog. Stay updated on her upcoming projects by visiting her website at tiawritesbooks.com.

Made in the USA
Middletown, DE
12 June 2016